BROTHER'S ⚖ JUSTICE ⚖

BROTHER'S JUSTICE

By

Lineus Berry

Published by Line Berry INC.

ACKNOWLEDGEMENTS

The author wishes to thank the people who provided support and encouragement with this effort. Particularly my special friend who shared the frustrations and set-backs along the way. Her fortitude helped bring the whole process to completion.

Many thanks to my Viet Nam veteran friends especially Sammy for his inputs that contributed to some of the harsh realisms in the story.

Also a special thanks to my sister Judy wherever she is and a sincere hope this meets with her approval.

CONTENTS

PREFACE

The wrongs dished out by the harsh realities of life should have to answer to the justice of a perfect world. The problem is they seldom do. We seem to watch from the gallery as spectators to witness bad things and say to ourselves "that's a shame". Usually then we just move on to something else. Only those who actually live it and continue to live with it, know what a shame it really is. As children we are taught to "forgive those who trespass against us". As adults we realize just how difficult that prayer is to implement. In addition to forgiving, it seems there is a basic human need for things to be set straight in this world and for justice to be served. When justice doesn't arrive there is a void in the universe. This effort is an attempt to fill a minuscule part of that void. For one small moment through the illusion of fiction, it will give the victims of the world a chance to do a "high five" and let out a resounding "yes".

The story is set in the turbulent late 1960's to the early 1970's and is a fictional account of how thing might have played out at the time. The cast includes the entire cross section of American society from the best to the worst. Any similarity between these characters and real persons is completely coincidental.

CHAPTER 1

THE HOSPITAL

"Where's the I C U?" Chris asked anxiously, approaching the reception desk in the hospital lobby.

"Third floor, east wing, it's clearly marked. Use the elevators to your left," answers the receptionist without looking up.

The night flight from Nashville to St Louis seemed to take forever. His mood was a combination of anxiety and anger. He rented a car at the airport instead of having someone pick him up. The reports from his brother John about a possible threat to the kids prompted him to tell everyone to stay put and watch their backs. The butterflies in his stomach echoed some feelings that brought back his days in Southeast Asia and the resulting rush put him totally on edge. He was prepared for bad news. The last status report on his sister Jody's condition was a phone contact before leaving Nashville. At last report she was critical and in surgery fighting for her life. There was no way to shake the sobering thought his oldest sister might be dead from an attack on the street by a madman.

The trek down the long bright hall to the ICU in the early morning hours seemed surreal. He kept shaking his head, telling himself this wasn't really happening but the smells in his nostrils and the sounds in his ears say "yes it is". Entering the reception area of the ICU, he couldn't help but notice the uniformed cop seated where the hall split. *That's a good sign at least she is still alive.*

"I'm looking for Soles," he said to the nurse at the counter.

"Are you family?" she asked.

"Yea, her brother. Can I go in?"

"Unit three. She is heavily sedated and her husband is with her but go ahead."

As he cautiously pushed the door open the darkness of the room seemed to engulf him. The lights and sounds of the life support

1

equipment gave the place a strange aura and as he stepped forward his body involuntarily hesitated. The slow rhythm of the heart monitor beeping beckoned but the human response was telling him to run from the whole scene. On the bed covered by a tight sheet lay a lifeless body with the head completely bandaged. Only the face from the eyes to the chin was exposed. In the dim light it rather resembled a mummy wearing a death mask. The directed night lighting only illuminated a small area at the head of the bed and it gave the face a slight glow. In the opposite corner of the room on the other side of the bed sat a dark figure outstretched on a recliner chair with their feet up and eyes closed.

Chris walked over to the lighted area of the bed, looked down and could not believe his eyes. A year in Vietnam of viewing bloody bodies and personally witnessing the carnage of war didn't prepare him for this. He was appalled at the condition of her face. It was completely unrecognizable and resembled a swollen red and blue balloon with a thin strip of white tape across the center. Her nostrils were packed on the inside with dressing so the nose was recognizable but the rest of the tissues were so swollen there were no features. It was just a puffy mound with two narrow slits were the eyes should be. On each eyelid were small cuts that were sutured with tiny stitches. The darkness of the bruising around the eyes and the massive swollen lips were unreal. To think this was his sister involuntarily brought swelling to his throat and water to his eyes. He choked back the emotions. *How could this happen to such a kind and gentle soul. To think she could just go off to work and end up in this condition is beyond comprehension.* As the body in the chair stirred he realized it was Tom her husband.

"Is John still with the kids?" he asked.

"Yea, I talked to him couple hours ago," Tom replied.

"Did he find my shot gun?"

2

"Yea," was the reply.

"O K I'm going to the house to check in with him. Guess you'll finish the night here? I will probably sleep over there if any sleep is in the cards tonight. Do you have any type of firearm at the house?" he asked.

"No, but there is a gun shop up on Olive near the house. I could go over there in the morning. Thing is though, I don't really know much about guns or how to use one," Tom replied.

"Don't worry. I'll show you how to use it. Even if you can't hit anything with it, a firearm beats the hell out of your bare hands if something comes up. Here, take this and stop and get two handguns as early as possible tomorrow. Thirty-eight or larger caliber, preferably larger. See if you can find a Colt 45 automatic military issue for me. I can actually hit something with it. I carried one in the bush. Of course don't forget the ammo," he said peeling off two one hundred dollar bills.

"Oh and by the way, try to get out of the gun store without signing anything; we want these as cold and untraceable as possible. Buy them from the owner and pay cash. Maybe slip the guy an extra twenty to forget any paperwork," he said.

Leaving the hospital at four in the morning, he could feel an odd pressure in his chest that was foreign to him. He never felt it before and as he drove along the deserted streets, headed for his sister's place, the pressure finally manifested itself. Tears began to roll down his face and he broke out crying. The pent-up emotion of thinking his sister was dead combined with the relief of finding out she wasn't could not be restrained. He did a year in Viet Nam and bagged bodies of kids in his platoon that were killed time after time, but he never reacted like this. It was the sibling issue with his big sister as when they were kids playing house she was always the mother. Another thing was possibly some guilt that he could not

3

protect her from the world. After all, he was the one who recommended last winter she accept the job offer and get out in the world.

The house appeared dark and locked up tight but as he pulled up to the front porch the light came on and the door cracked. It was obvious his brother was watching the street and realized the strange car pulling in the driveway was a rental. John stepped out on the porch and the stress was visible in his face. It was obvious he was relieved. Now there was someone to back him up. After the assault the police warned the family. The suspect was definitely a prominent member of the Black Nation and one of their techniques to protect their members was to intimidate their enemies. The comment by the police to watch the children did not have to be repeated. These kids were the only grandchildren in the family and the whole bunch felt the kinship.

"Kids O K?" he asked getting out of the car.

"Yes, they're all in one bed in the front room. I tell you I've been as nervous as a whore in church all night. Every car that's passed has brought up goose pimples. I've been watching the street and the cops have gone by several times and needless to say that's helped some. It has been a long day and a longer night, that's for sure. You stopped at the hospital I assume. What did you think?"

"I have to say I have never seen anything like it even when I was overseas. This son-of-a-bitch pounded on her long after she was down and unconscious. I think he was enjoying punishing her. The same way a little kid beats up on a helpless rag doll. The only thing here is this bastard knew she was no doll. No way to know what this animal is capable of doing plus the word is he's wired to some pretty bad people. He definitely left her for dead but by now with the television news and all, he knows she isn't. The problem is we have no idea whether he will run off or stay around to try and silence her.

4

I gave Tom some cash and he is going to pick-up some ordinance first thing in the morning. Where's the old shot gun?"

"Behind the door," John replied.

"You should have seen the blood at the art store. Looked like someone butchered hogs on the front sidewalk. She staggered out the front door and collapsed. I was at work when I got the call and I went to the store first by mistake. Funny, the sidewalk café next door was full when it happened and nobody noticed a thing until she stumbled outside. Of course you know the son-of-bitch raped her, but the really serious wound is the four-inch diameter hole at the top of her skull. The face will heal but brain damage is the question now. The pig busted the skull into pieces with a claw hammer that was there in the store. Can you imagine what it would take to pound someone's head with a hammer until it was moosh? God damn, who is this guy? said John.

"I'll tell you who he is. He is a piece of the world that people like us can't even imagine," answered Chris.

"The incredible thing is he walked out the back door completely unnoticed. The police are sure they know who did it, black ex-con, on parole, worked up the street and stopped in all the time, some kind of artist. We are supposed to get a briefing tomorrow morning from the cops on what they know and recommend," John replied.

"Personally, I don't give a damn what the police recommend. I learned something a year or so ago in Asia. What I learned was this; recommendations don't count for much in life and death situations. The key is being the one who walks away alive and in all cases, I've witnessed; the one that walks away alive is the one who acts first. There is no reasoning with a mad dog. You just simply shoot him. Ain't that complicated brother. The problem with this mad dog is going to be finding the son-of-a-bitch."

As morning broke neither brother slept at all. Between the coffee and the tension, they were both running on pure adrenaline waiting for the day to yield some answers. There was some relief when Tom called with a positive report from the doctors. Jody made it through the night and her vitals looked good. There was still the question of residual brain damage but the doctors planned to pull the drugs and expected her to wake up around noon. There was a police public statement scheduled at the hospital for ten in the morning. Both brothers wanted to be at the bedside when she awakened but they also wanted to attend the conference. The police department offered to send over someone to watch the kids for the day. Everything was setup for them to make the conference and be at the bedside.

On the way to the hospital they drove past the crime scene and noticed the art store closed and the mess cleaned up. Out of curiosity, they drove around to the alley to view the rear entrance to the place. It was difficult to believe that such a violent assault could take place in a public spot at five o'clock on a Friday with people all around. Even more difficult to believe was the assailant could just stroll out the back door and disappear completely unnoticed. They both figured someone must have helped him escape.

The small hospital conference room on the ground floor was where the meeting with County P D was scheduled. It was crowded when they entered and the air in the room smelled a bit stuffy from the August humidity combined with the human bodies. Standing at the rear were the local news reporters from the T V stations and the newspapers. The table seemed to be too big for the room but at least there were enough chairs for the family. As the police lieutenant introduced himself, it was obvious that the amount of information they were going to release would be limited.

"I'm Lieutenant Buzz Westburg from the Saint Louis County Police Department and we want to first of all express our regrets that this has happened in our jurisdiction. We are very happy to hear of the improvements in Mrs. Soles' condition and we thank God she is off the critical list. The good news is we do have a prime suspect. The suspect is a thirty-three-year-old negro named Allen Braburn. He was paroled from Jeff City three months ago while serving two life sentences for three crimes. His convictions were for two rapes and one armed robbery. He worked a few blocks from the crime scene and was last seen at his job just before the assault. He is an artist himself and frequented the store regularly. We have every jurisdiction in the county looking for him right now and if he is on the street, we will find him. Now I'll take questions."

"Do you have any witnesses that can put your prime suspect at the scene of the crime?" asked a reporter at the back of the room.

"No, but we expect to be able to talk to the victim later today. Hopefully, she will I D him herself. Also the fact that he is a parolee and he has disappeared makes us even more confident that he is our perp," the Lieutenant replied.

"I guess you know his family says he is innocent. His mother claims he called her and said he was being framed because he's black and on parole," said the reporter.

"Then he should come in and clear his name," replied the cop.

"He has some support from the Black Nation's church down on Grand Avenue. I assume you are aware of that fact. They are saying this is just another case of pin it on a black man. They are saying he is the victim here and the real perpetrator is long gone. They're implying you are just after this man because he is an important person in the Black Nation. How does County P D respond to that accusation?" asked the reporter.

"Total crap, that's how I respond to it," answered the Lieutenant.

Listening to the excuses of the people in the press immediately telegraphed to Chris that their sympathies were going to be with the ex-con and that this was going to take on a racial tone. As the press bantered back and forth with the Lieutenant, Chris could feel the anger rising up in his craw. The weariness of a sleepless night combined with the vision of his sister with her head crushed; plus the overwhelming circumstantial evidence that this man was the assailant, started a low boil in his guts. He couldn't restrain himself and to his regret he blew and voiced it publicly to the crowd.

"You can all make any excuses for this guy you want but my sister didn't deserve this and take it from me I'm gonna'' drop this pig as soon as I can find him," Chris blurted out.

Immediately the demeanor of the policeman changed and Chris realized popping off was a mistake. He could feel the focus of the police zero in on him and that was last thing the family needed at this point.

"Shoulda' kept my mouth shut. That was a mistake. We're not going to learn anything here. There's too much press. We need a one-on-one with this cop. Let's get to hell out of here. I cannot listen to these news people without speaking up and shooting my mouth off. They are starting in with the race thing," Chris whispered in his brother's ear.

The stir down the hall at Jody's door in the I C U indicated to the brothers the patient was conscious. It was the first rush of relief either felt since the assault. Their pace quickened as they approached the room just as Tom broke through the door looking relieved.

"Doctors have been doing some motor skills and memory tests on her and things are all perfect so far. They are about finished. You might want to wait until they finish because it is rather crowded in there. I was just going to get some coffee myself. There's a visitor's lounge down the hall with free coffee. Why don't you join me and let them finish?" he said.

As they drew coffees and sank in three lounge chairs the fatigue of last twenty-four hours of being totally stressed was obvious on all three faces.

"Did you stop on Olive and get the hardware?" Chris asked Tom.

"Yea, they are in boxes in the car under the driver's seat. One is a thirty-eight special six-shot revolver and the other is the forty-five automatic you wanted. Got out with them clean. No names no papers no nothing. The old boy just stuffed the cash in his front pocket and walked away smiling," said Tom.

"Good, I'll get them on my way out. Give me your keys and I'll leave it unlocked with the keys under the mat. You can keep the thirty-eight at your house and I'll take the automatic. Do not take the gun with you in the car if you can avoid it. It would not be good if they stopped you and found a gun in your car with this stuff happening. The police are sneaky they might just stop you to see if you have something. They don't want you armed any more than the criminals," he replied.

"How are you going to get the forty-five home on a plane?" John asked.

"Wrap the box in birthday paper and carry it on. I've done it before to smuggle stuff for work. Put it in the hang up coat closet at the front of the plane on the shelf and take your seat with a smile. Works every time. Stewardess just thinks you are a wonderful father bringing your little girl something from your trip," he replied smiling.

"My flight back is in the morning. When we get to the house I will show you and Tom how to handle the thirty-eight. It's pretty simple really. You guys might want to find a private spot and take it out to fire it a few times just to get used to it."

On the flight home, Chris leaned his seat back and let down for the first time in a couple days. He closed his eyes to the vision of his sister lying there helpless and nearly beaten to death. The scene was indelibly burnt in his mind. The tears when she opened her eyes and saw both her brothers standing there were almost too much for his emotions. As usual, he was able to get a laugh out of her even though it was not a very big one. The swollen face and battered head were a testimony to her strength. *She just needs time to heal now.* The whole thing brought a slight smile. *If you want to kill one of our family, you better bring help.*

*   *   *   *

Little Vipol awoke to another day with the gnawing in his empty gut still there from the night before. The difficulty of life on the streets in a jungle village in the South American country of Guyana never took a break. Once again he faced the struggle to survive another day. Sleeping in his little nook under a building with his cat just off an alley in town, supplied what little peace his days offered. At least last night he escaped the horror of it all for a while as he dreamt of playing soccer with other kids. This was only a dream since his life was never normal and there was not any soccer or even schools where he lived. He was of mixed race and neither the African nor the Asian community accepted him. His mother was from India and she died when he was very little. All he knew was she fell from a helicopter out at sea and disappeared. The Guyanese Defense Force guards informed him of her death when they delivered him to the orphanage. His father was an African military man who hurt his mother. She despised him and never spoke of him or mentioned his name.

When he entered the orphanage he was alone at four years old to fend for himself. The life there was nothing but cruelty and work even for the very young. Although it was an Indian home, the fact he was half-African caused his total rejection and persecution. Finally, at eight he ran off into the jungle out of pure desperation. There he found a way to survive as he was good with fishing and could always make a few coins by selling his catch to the locals. The ways of the river came naturally to him and he settled in a mining village deep in the jungle on the Rhamshu River. The mining community minded their own business and he found a place to live where no one would bother him. His natural abilities provided him with a way to survive. He could pilot the riverboats and keep the old ratty outboard motors running. For that, he was allowed to ride along on ferrying runs with the old black captain who owned the small boat ferry service that served the mines. Fishing along the way he would usually return with a catch to sell. He was proud of himself for having built a life on his own. His mechanical abilities and independence made him feel good when he fixed a motor or sold a fish. Unlike at the orphanage, he always woke up happy these days and today was no different. He was free. Gone was the fear of being disciplined just for the sake of entertainment by some sadistic orphanage staff member.

The village did not offer much but the prosperity of the local white Bauxite miners delivered a message, even to a kid. It was clear to Vipol rising to their money level was the solution to his problems. In few years, he would be big enough to work the machinery and he would get a real job. Then his troubles would be over. He knew someday he was going to have plenty of money. He didn't know exactly how he would get it yet, but he just knew down deep the day was coming. As he skipped off to the dock for a day of fishing, he sang to himself. There was one song in his life stuck in his head. The memory of his mother singing it when he was very small made his heart swell. He blocked out the part of the memory where the cruel GDF sergeant they lived with yelled for her to shut up. Only her sweet voice echoed in his ears. As he reached the pier the old black boatman yelled out excitedly.

"Hey boy, bale the big boat out. We going all the way to the coast today to pick up some tools for the mine. You too. That motor kind of sick. Probably will need you."

"I'll get the wrenches," Vipol said turning and heading for the dock shed.

This was good news. It was his first chance to go all the way to the ocean. He wanted to learn the trip and see the coast to maybe qualify to take the boat there alone soon and be paid for it. As he bailed out the floor of the cargo skiff, he was happy and excited. There was a double benefit to this trip. In addition to the travel, the fishing was better closer to the coast. It seemed the piranha backed off when the water started to get a little salty. He should bring home a bigger catch that would bring a few extra coins.

CHAPTER 2

THE DISCHARGE

The sound of firing a thousand yards out started the juices flowing and tripped the instantaneous frozen state where the neck hair stands up. *The combat trackers have made contact behind the village. Those are shotgun reports.* One thing you learn quickly in the bush is standing still can get you killed so the paralyses pass quickly. Captain Black is screaming at the top of his lungs for Bravo Company to close-up the gap and no one is paying any attention to him.

The first thing you learn in the Nam is the best place to be when it hits the fan is in the bush. *This scene says, in no uncertain terms, it could hit the fan. Any first week grunt can see from the signs this bunch is at least battalion strength and they are regulars so they'll likely stand and fight.*

"Get your ass up there Sergeant Linn and get some men between here and the village. If they come back this way they'll cut us in half," rings out from behind.

"It looks like they're bugging out but the Captain thinks it could be a diversion," yells Jenkins.

Lieutenant Jenkins, another great flattop asshole straight from the ROTC world. Green as a gourd fresh off the boat. Our last fearless leader tripped a betty and iced himself. Gung-ho buys you nothing in this place. Our biggest problem is Jenkins is the kind of guy who can get you a body bag of your own. He hasn't been around long enough to know this ain't a movie. Shopping for a medal and won't mind risking our asses to get one. NVA regulars, unlike the VC, are aggressive. This bunch seems to be fresh from the north,

13

looking for a fight. They probably just crossed over from Cambodia last night all rested and ammoed up.

As the platoon forms up to move out Linn barks orders to the squad leaders.

"Sammy, you take the rest of the platoon and head through the rice paddies straight for the village, I'm going to take two guys and flank it to see what we're walking into. Green, Cotton come with me and stay in the cover," he shouts.

When one hangs it out in a combat situation he wants the best soldiers in the group with him. These two are birddogs at heart. They can smell dinks. They are the odd couple though with Cotton a city black from Seattle and Green a basic Alabama redneck. The contradiction is these two on the streets back home would tear each other's hearts out. In Viet Nam, they mirror each other's thoughts, laugh at each other's racial slurs, and make it a point to keep each other alive.

"Let's go into the village at the far end and ease through, stay behind the hoochs, keep your shit wired they're still in there," says Cotton.

As the three work their way up to the village and enter an open courtyard there is some activity and noise a couple hoochs up.

You might know we couldn't luck out and walk back out of here without a fight. Being a short timer all I want is to mark off one more day without any action. Sure as hell don't want to catch one now, just forty days out of my ride home.

Entering the village, he indicates hand signals from there on so he motions Cotton and Green to flank him. Then flashes hand signals to indicate he is going straight down the courtyard. Cotton suddenly fires two rounds for effect on the left to flush anything he can and throws up three fingers. There are three bogeys running for the bush about twenty yards away. Moving through, one hooch at a

14

time, he ducks into an open door for cover and stands still waiting for motion outside.

Can't stay in here with the stink. What is it with this country the whole fuckin' place smells like rot? Hits you when you step off the transport and doesn't leave till you land in the states or get tagged and bagged, whichever comes first.

One side step out the door, two figures disappear into the bush on the left and there stands the third with his back half turned. Obviously, he wasn't expecting company. The instant fight or flight response flashes from him and as he attempts to rotate there is a look on his face of surrender, kind of a half-smile and peaceful. He knows he's caught and accepts it. The whole thing happens in slow motion and before the dink can even get his weapon up three quick rounds peel off. The second shot kills him. Right through the heart.

"Damn this one ain't very old. I never had a shot. Looks like we flushed the rest of them," says Green as he walks up.

"Yea bet he's not sixteen," Chris replies

As the adrenaline rush dissipates the whole event flashes back in slow motion for some reason. He can picture the round entering the kid's heart and the gentle smile is a haunt. *I could have let him run.*

"His helmet is brand new. He ain't been in the field long," says Green.

"No, likely his first action. What a waste. At least it wasn't me," he replies as the Nam mentality comes through.

Funny, out of all the action he has seen this is the first time it hit him that he murdered someone and he feels a ting of guilt.

"Where's Cotton, did he go after them?" he asks.

"No, answers Green. You know the spook he won't surface till he sees the blood".

The surreal scene of standing over a man he just killed laughing at a joke suddenly rings through.

"Get Cotton and let's get to hell out of here before jarhead shows up".

"Excuse me Sergeant Linn we are beginning our descent you'll have to put up the tray table", says the flight attendant shaking everyone awake.

The drone of the engines at the rear of the plane was enough to induce sleep. As he opens his eyes he realizes he has obviously been dreaming. The whole thing at the village is starting to reoccur and getting disturbing. This was the fourth time for this same dream. The little boy's accepting smile and look of surrender are as clear as glass. He is wishing now he'd let the kid run.

The long ride from Pleuku to Fort Lewis on the ratty old seven twenty-seven was about to end and most of the passengers slept through the trip. These boys were just like him. Sleep was a luxury for them the last year. It was actually easier to sleep in the bush than in the base camps as the old country boy instincts of survival comforted there. The early part of his tour convinced him he'd never make this trip so the feelings of the moment were somewhat neutral. This was a day that wasn't meant to happen and there was no forethought or celebration boarding the plane. Everyone on board seemed reluctant to celebrate yet as if this wasn't really happening. The kid sitting next to him stared straight ahead the whole trip it seemed. The bug out eyeball long distance stare meant the kid obviously was still up. There were leach marks on his neck and it appeared he was fresh out of the field. Chris guessed probably less than forty-eight hours.

As he thought about it, he realized there is going to be a major adjustment. This last year he was always the old guy in the group.

At twenty-five he was light years older than what the draft supplied. That's why he earned the stripes early.

The kid hasn't spoken a word for thirteen hours and seems to be shaking a little. He should have had some attention before they put him on the transport. Typical Army they shuffled him off to let someone else have the problem. All I need is to have to deal with a head case coming unglued in this cramped space. Damn I need to forget it; my days as platoon sergeant are coming to an end in about an hour.

Worrying about his men will be a hard habit to break after so many days in the field with a bunch of kids to try to keep alive. The truth was he never lost a single one he didn't feel personally responsible.

Some lifer staff sergeant is on the intercom telling everyone what to expect when the plane lands. As Chris listens he just shakes his head in disgust. *It is hard to understand why they waste their time with instructions. In the Army, you just go where they point. No one is listening.* The sound of the old landing gear coming down breaks the silence. The realization hits him. Living through one simple touch down means his war is over, and he has survived. As he looks around, its back to reality and the prewar world. With the Sergeant still barking as they exit the plane he can't help but notice the old planes upholstery. It looked fifties vintage. *Some contractor obviously bought this old heap out of the scrap pile to milk a fortune out of the war as a contract carrier for the military.*

"Shake down time gentlemen when you hit the pavement turn to your right and follow the white line single file. If you are packing anything you shouldn't you will regret it big time," yells the top noncom from the front of the plane.

As they trek single file to the debriefing building in the falling darkness about twenty-five yards away at the chain-link fence are screaming antiwar demonstrators with their baby killer placards and their enthusiasm as a welcoming committee.

Seems like the dumb asses wouldn't waste their time on this bunch. We are finished with it. Do they not realize our war is over? Then again maybe it isn't as the dream on the plane would suggest. Scary thing is out of all the action over the last year the NVA kid seems to be the only one producing any negative feelings. Guess it was the cold bloodedness of it as the kid was not a real big threat.

The comedy of the scene with the peaceniks yelling plays out as ridiculous and brings a slight smile.

Do they honestly think they can rile these boys? Their protesting is mostly driven by hype and the need to belong. Fatigue jacket fashions and a bandana around their heads make them authentic in their own world. While they have been laying around high and tapping the free love well each night the boys in this line were living in a world without any type of love. The bandana in the bush was not a fashion statement it was a survival garment. It offset sweat obscured vision. The bandana hit the trash when packing to leave and was left behind with good riddance. All it represented was the five hundred gallons of sweat produced while trudging around in hell trying to save our world for this bunch. Funniest thing, these people don't have any idea who they are they are trying to piss off. Half the boys in this line are fresh out of the field and would cut their livers out and eat them if told to do so by one of these noncoms.

The inside of the old debriefing building was typical army. White clapboard barracks design and two-story frame construction with posts down the center and a high gloss hardwood floor. It was likely built during World War II and kept in service to satisfy the standard military mentality to never give anything up.

Completely empty tables lined the walls of the large room and everything smelled of fresh paint with not a chair in site. Stepping inside out of the darkness, the bright fluorescent lights drew a squint. The floor was marked with white lines perpendicular to the tables like little parking spots.

"Pick a spot and unload your bags gentlemen, then step back and shuck down to your skivvy's," barked the duty officer.

Three noncoms entered the room and methodically started through the possessions on the tables one person at a time. Obviously they are looking for dope as they already searched everyone for weapons on the other end. They confiscated a nickel plated 45 he snagged off of a dead chopper pilot, much to his regret.

The oldest and the shortest of the three noncoms shouts out, "If there is something you are trying to hide cough it up, it will go easier on you."

Don't think they would detain anyone for a little pot they must be looking for heroin.

As he scanned his pile he realized the only thing with any potential to be dope was a tin of standard issue tooth powder.

"Ok sergeant empty the can", the top says as he walks past.

"You have to be kidding, can't you just taste it", he replied.

"I don't like the taste of it so god-damn-it dump it out."

If we were still in country, I would tell this guy to kiss my ass. They knew better than to get military over there. Soldiers in the field really didn't care if they were called for an infraction. When a man spends the days with their life on the line he develops an attitude about stupid military protocol. In country the brass wouldn't act on small infractions because they needed us in the field, not in the brig and we knew it.

As he dumped the tin out on the table before the can was even empty the sergeant says, "O k, get dressed, clean up the mess and move on".

One last bitter pill and I'm outta here. Through that door on the other end of this building is the real world. I will have to leave the uniform on for travel but that door is the end of the military for me.

*   *   *   *

"Keep the change Mac and thanks. Don't pull in the driveway it's the end of the road for me. My car is right here. I can walk up," he says as he hands the driver the fare over the seat.

The ride from Lambert field was shorter than he remembered. The St Louis suburbs seemed to have shrunk since he'd left. As the cab taillights faded into the darkness there was no way not to reflect on where this trip ended. There he stood alone on a dark street with his duffel bag at his feet. *For Christ sakes, right back where I started, my sister's driveway.*

He dropped his car here on the way out a year ago and now was back to pick it up completely unannounced. The whole thing seemed unreal now as if it never happened. It was a full circle to Asia and back with not a scratch. The army hitch was over and the reality was finally starting to hit home. Things looked the same but he knew down deep one thing wasn't, and that was him. The whole experience had taken a toll.

The small frame house up the short lane seemed dark. The cool February night air soothed his lungs and smelled good. He hefted his duffel bag and started up the asphalt drive. It appeared everyone was settled-in for the evening. The place was decent looking and it felt of someone's family home. It was a feeling left behind a year ago. For the first time in months, the butterflies in his stomach were gone and he noticed his ears weren't ringing. As he walked he suddenly realized his guts stirred since the day he shipped out. His stomach was suddenly completely calm. There was the realization he was really home. It seemed he was finally letting down. *Is this for real or am I dreaming? Those three scotches on the plane from Sea-Tac might be part of it.*

The cool crisp air was a godsend and the realization the stink of Southeast Asia is not in his nostrils was finally registering.

His sister's kids will be excited to have company especially their uncle the army guy. *Hope I have some change to pass out. Never thought to bring the kids gifts.* The doorbell gave a bit of a start and things began to stir on the inside. Jody appeared through the curtain in her red robe. It is obvious she is getting ready for bed. In all her glory she is still as well kept and attractive as ever. She never went out of the house without looking like she just stepped out of a catalogue. She always prided herself on her looks especially her resemblance to Elizabeth Taylor and must still with her hair dyed jet black. For twenty-nine years old with four children she still looks good and he had to admit if he ran into her on the street as a stranger he would ask her out.

"Is this America?" he blurts out as the door opens.

"Oh dear god is it really you?" she replies.

"Well hell, aren't you going to ask your little brother in or am I past the curfew, it's only eight o'clock?"

"When did you get back?" she asked as he dropped his duffle bag in the corner of the foyer.

"Yesterday, I caught a flight out of Sea-Tac this afternoon. Where are the kids?"

"Just went to bed. I'll have to get them up. They will have a fit. Sit down I'll make some coffee and get Tom," she replied.

As Tom enters he telegraphs the feeling he's not very glad to have company. The unannounced visit might have interrupted a planned romantic evening with momma as it seems kind of early for the kids to be in bed.

I should have called ahead but what to hell.

"How was your trip?" Tom asked.

"Long," he replied.

"Why didn't you let anyone know you were coming? We could have picked you up at the airport," Tom grumbled.

"I only received word twelve hours before the transport departed. Took some humping to get my act together and get my sign-out orders. We were out in the field when the word came through. I barely got cleared and on the flight," he answered.

The truth was he bypassed the phones at the airport because he didn't want anyone expecting him, as he wasn't sure where he was headed. On the flight back Chris considered a sentimental journey from Fort Lewis up to Seattle to see his ex. He didn't know what that might entail so he decided against it. With his state of mind, he figured he wasn't ready for a confrontation with her.

Tom's questions didn't really fit the conversation and immediately stirred some suspicions about his real motive. Tom was always a little sour with all of Jody's family for some reason. He gave off a slight aura of distain at family functions. It was possible he resented the mental one up-man-ship of his in-laws. Whatever the case, he never tried to hide his feelings. He was always a hard person to interpret as he was always employed with a good job and seemed to work but was habitually short of money. Jody bitched about it but never bothered to take control of the checkbook so the turmoil went on and on for years. As a young couple, there were some rocky years at the beginning but the kids apparently settled it down. They were married too young as she got pregnant at nineteen years old and her oldest boy was a little premature as the family used to say. The problem seemed to be Jody was naïve from just plain old lack of experience in life. Her upbringing left her inexperienced with men and sex. She judged her relationships with her husband by her father daughter memories and couldn't seem to make hard decisions. In addition, she never really was out in the work world so she lacked the cynicism and moxie required to judge or deal with people.

"Is my trunk with the clothes still in the back of my car?" he said pulling up to the table. "I can't wait to shed this uniform. Speaking of my car, how is it? Has anyone started it since I left? Bet the dust cover is off and the kids have been using it for a playhouse all year."

"Your precious car is just like you left it and the trunk is in the store room but leave the uniform on till the boys see you. You're not planning on going out are you? What are your plans anyway?" she asked.

"No, I'm in for the night. I need to get some sleep. I'll probably head up tomorrow and see Mom for a day or so then hit the road for a little time off to do some thinking. Needless to say, I haven't done a lot of long range planning over the last year. Gotta' figure out what's next. Probably drive out to the coast, do some skiing on the way and then California for a beach fix and some scuba. I've got a little money so I don't really have to do anything till my head clears," he answers.

Jody was the one sibling out of four who always seemed to have a hard time with the world. Everyone always attributed it to the fact she was the oldest. School years for her were filled with never really being in the click of the popular girls. There were bouts of hysteria over meaningless episodes like her prom dress not fitting perfectly or her boyfriend sitting with somebody else at the movie. Stupid stuff like the school dance where her hair wouldn't lay a certain way seemed to cause her more than normal misery. Their mother couldn't deal with it and continually agonized over Jody's happiness. The rest of the family just laughed it off. His sister Mary Alice got the brunt of Jody's wrath as she shared a room with her as kids. She was only two years younger. She was close to the loop of peers that caused Jody's misery and was the opposite of her older sister. Her natural beauty with the dark complexion and personality to match lined the beaus up at the door and caused a little jealousy.

It was comforting to be in an actual home for the first time in a year. The smell of fresh coffee and the background aroma of a supper baking from earlier in the evening tripped some endorphins he'd lost. He wondered on the way back if things would ever be normal again and for the first time he was thinking maybe they would. The buzz of the kids broke his thoughts and the feel of physical contact with little bodies hanging on and tugging got his attention.

"Where's your gun Uncle Chris?" blurts out from the six-year-old.

"They don't let you take your gun home son. They give it to the next new guy that joins up," he replies.

"Here's some money for each of you. I'll give it to your mom to keep but you get to spend it," he said as he hands Jody a twenty.

As the kid's enthusiasm fizzles and they head back to bed Jody settles down at the large round dining table with her coffee cup and lights a cigarette. With the smoke rising through the glare of the hanging light fixture, he senses there is some tension in the background. Tom has disappeared into the bedroom. *Hope to hell I haven't walked into some kind of mess between these two.* The fatigue is starting to overwhelm him and he's not in the mood for a conversation about their marriage problems. Ever since her first months of marriage she always unloaded on him for some reason. He was only fifteen at the time and she would talk to him about her sex life. He guessed it was because he was the closest person she knew with an honest male opinion. The truth was, most of the time, he didn't even know what she was talking about.

"I hate to say this but can you loan me a little money? she mumbles.

"What is it, same old shit? When are you going to get a grip on his money issues? God damn, this household is half yours including the money part. Tell him you are taking over the paycheck and actually do it this time."

"I can't deal with him bulling up but the bills are all due and I'm going to have to use that twenty you gave the kids to pay the light bill tomorrow or we will be in the dark. I got the shut off notice last week," she says.

"How long have I been bailing you guys out with money? Seems to me it started when I first went to work in Seattle. Maybe getting tossed in the street with his kids might get his attention. Are you sure this guy is not chasing women or gambling because it doesn't make sense with the money he makes to constantly be two months behind on your bills. I remember before you were married when he lived down here alone he used to go across the river and bet on the harness races. He sure as hell isn't drinking it up but there has to be something here you don't know about. You are going to have to grow up and deal with it eventually. I've only got a couple hundred on me. I can let you have most of that if you promise not to tell him you've got it," he said with his aggravation surfacing.

"I've decided to go to work this summer now that the kids are getting bigger. Little Cindy next door will babysit pretty cheap so I can justify it. In fact, it might do me and everyone some good mentally to get away from the house a little not to mention the money. The Crists down the street have mentioned my working at their gallery over in Ladue and it sounds pretty cushy. Neat little art store on one of the new strip malls. Even has a sidewalk café next door. They mostly sell original art works some of it very expensive. I'd be my own boss and mostly deal one on one with high-end clients and the pay would include some commission plus a salary. There would be no pressure to sell or listen to people complain. The Crists make it sound too good to be true. Thinking I'm going to try it when school is out and see how it goes," she says.

"That's probably a good decision. Do you good to get into the real world and out from under Tom's influence. To be honest with you I'm not sure your marriage is going to last. Take some advice from someone who has experienced it. Spouses are sometimes not what they appear. You saw mine walk out one day for no apparent reason. Learn to take care of yourself. Yea, this job is good news in my opinion. Go for it. Now where do I sleep? I've had it for the day."

"Kids are down already so it will have to be the couch or the floor. Sorry we can't do better on this short notice," she replies.

"Couch is fine. Those scotches I drank on the plane should anesthetize me a little. Hell, two days ago I was sleeping on the ground with a bunch of filthy grunts. Should be able to doze off on a sofa and don't worry if you hear me up during the night. I usually don't sleep too sound. It was a very unhealthy thing to do where I just came from."

"Here's a blanket and pillow," she replies.

"I'm going to plug in that battery charger in the garage before I go down so that car will start in the morning. I'll probably leave before you all get up. If I wake up and can't go back to sleep, which I will, I'll probably get on the road and head for moms. You tell the kids good-bye for me and spend that twenty-dollar bill on them. Don't use it for the utilities. Here is another hundred and fifty. Don't tell Tom you have it. Hell buy yourself some clothes for that new job."

As he got up to enter the garage he turned and asked, "Where can I put that old rabbit gun that dad bought me when I was a kid. I have it in the floor of the car and I'm afraid to carry it around with me. Some nosey cop could take it away from me if I got stopped."

"Let me put it in my bedroom closet so the kids won't know it's here," she replied.

CHAPTER 3

THE RELEASE

The hall down to the administrative conference room was well lit, unlike most places in the prison. An inmate learned early on to look as far ahead as possible when walking down a corridor. At any moment he could get a surprise especially alone in a hall. Questions were rolling over in his mind.

What in the hell do they suddenly want with me today? The white motherfuckers are probably going to cancel the art classes again. These prison people seem to enjoy taking the only thing a man has left. White man's world has no place for a black man's art especially non-Christian black men. Hell, the classes finally got moved to the library for a place to work and we got some real paints and now it looks like it's back to the cells. They are probably going to blame it on the messing behind the bookshelves by Rag and his punk. The truth is they can't stand the fact that the black prisoners are not in their cages like good little niggers.

As Allen approached the door to the review room he hesitated and looked through the glass before entering. He felt his guts churn with hatred as he witnessed the scene.

There they sit all high and mighty just like that white judge that put me in this place. Looks like Warden Donnet is fixing to hand it down. Donnet is always just waiting for the chance to stick it to the first black inmate that comes along. With these prison people a black man can feel the pleasure they get watching him squirm. This motherfucker has always hated me. All black inmates know once they get a man in the Wall, they've got him, particularly a black lifer. The only salvation for blacks is the Nation. Joining the Nation gives a black man some protection. Without it, black in here means

29

good as dead. During the riot back in fifty-two, the Nation kept the blacks in their cellblock and out of the yard. They were right when they said the black inmates would fall first if they fire on the yard. The blacks sat it out inside A-block thanks to the Nation and when they opened up on the yard it was a total white show. That advice saved a lot of black inmates as everyone was up for the riot and wanted to participate. It definitely was an attention getter when the killing started, but the food did improve.

"Have a seat Mister Braburn," the warden grunts.

"Your number is 10 247, is that right?" he asks in a monotone scanning the file in front of him.

" Nothing here for the last few years but a couple of arguments in the shop. Guess you came up in the world with your art con. Might even call it a white-collar job with being a teacher and holding classes and all. Got you out of the shop though. Didn't it?"

Warden Donnet's demeanor changed as he looked up to make eye contact with Braburn.

"Well get one thing straight, I don't swallow it. Making a painting and winning an art contest might cut some ice in a high school class but it does not convert people like you to altar boys. Those old women artists that you are working on the outside have not spent the last sixteen years watching you as I have. They do not have a clue who they are dealing with and they don't know a black widow is a harmless insect right up until it bites you. Yea insect, Braburn that's where you fit in this world in my opinion," said the warden shaking slightly.

"The first ten years of this file I am holding is the part your friends need to read. That is the parts about the assaults and the rapes. Did you tell them about the time you raped and stabbed the little white boy and lied your way out of it with help from the Nation's threats. Lucky for you that kid lived through it so he could be threatened and then lie for you. Like I said, don't start believing your own stuff because we both know this art stuff is a pure ass con by a lifetime con. All I can say is this bleeding heart judge that these old women have swayed is making a mistake but you're sure the winner. Called you in here to tell you you're transferring from The Wall to minimum security at Renick. Won't say you are no longer my problem because I believe you will be back. It's just a matter of time."

As the warden signed the papers the stress in his face reflected a belief he was taking the first steps to unleashing a rabid dog. By contrast, the look of amazement on Braburn's face was a stare of disbelief. *Who would have thought that those old white women could take it to this level? That one old preacher's wife from Clayton is the front to get to the judge using religion. Religion works every time; I should have thought of it sooner. Time at Renick is the first step to parole. Hell, depending on the crowding at Renick, I could be completely out in six months. Taking up painting was to try to stay sane. In the beginning there wasn't even any paints only rusty water and ketchup. Winning the contest in St Louis got the whole thing classified as a rehabilitative activity by prison standards and that started the ball rolling. It is hard to believe it led to today.*

"Sign right here Braburn. Do you have anything to say?" the warden asked.

Braburn looked off in the distance as if a thought suddenly crossed his mind. He was speechless and trying to process it all.

"What year is it?" he asked

"1968, you've been our guest for almost fifteen years and I'll bet you'll be back in fifteen days," answered the warden.

"Just how soon do I leave this hell hole that's all I want to know?"

"Right now, go get your stuff. They are holding the bus for you. I want your ass out of here"

The feeling walking back up to the cellblock was surreal. The emotional swing of expecting to be punished and instead getting the ultimate reward defied description. He noticed the hall looked entirely different walking in this direction. It was now the first corridor to the way out of the nastiest prison in the country. A hole that was built before electricity and running water and its only claim to fame is the nickname "The bloodiest 46 acres in America". Sixteen years of living with the smell of rot and death was coming to an end. Half of everything that ever happened in this place was unspeakable and that was exactly the way it was dealt with. To stay alive a person grew eyes in the back of their head and kept their mouth shut.

As he approached it for the final time the cell where Braburn spent the last seven years gave off a putrid aroma. It was a combination of all the nastiest substances the human body can secrete. Braburn was startled at the fact he never noticed the stench until just now. As he stepped inside the guard gives the "get a move on" sign. He wants the bus loaded before the cellmates come back from the yard so he doesn't have to deal with a crowd. For Braburn it was just as well. There was no love lost with him and this bunch of cellmates. Only one was Rag as they covered each other's asses when locked in and shared a little sex once in a while. The black cellblock housed eight to a cell while the white cellblocks only housed six. Packed that tight there was no way a couple of your cellmates weren't going to be threatening. Everyone figured the idea was to pack the blacks in and let them kill each other. Good thing about it though he didn't have to deal with white cellmates during lockup.

"Leave the denim and use this grip for the rest it. Everything has to be searched before you board the bus so the less you take the better. They will reissue all you need at the check-in station up there. Oh, and be forewarned, there will be a cavity search when you get there so you may want to use the pot before we leave," says the guard handing over a duffle bag, turning his back and stepping out of the cell.

Leaving the cell for the last time left a flood of feelings for someone who lived in an eight by ten lock-up for fifteen years. He was sent up when he just turned eighteen. All he needed now was a few months of good behavior and a continued push with the old white women, then a parole hearing. The whole thing was unbelievable. *Keep your mouth shut, smile when the old women show you off and agree when they talk about Jesus. All it's going to take is playing the role of pet nigger for a while longer.*

"Here Braburn, you can sit anywhere on the bus you want, we never have a crowd on the trip up to Renick. Just remember it will be full when they bring you back though," says the guard chuckling. He did a quick look in the grip and handed it back. It was obvious he really didn't want to find anything and cause a stir.

"Don't look for this cat back Johnny. I'm on my way to total sunshine. I'll soon be a free man," replied Braburn with a smile.

Little Johnny was one of the better guards all through the years. He did not seem to completely hate black inmates like the rest of them. *Black man in here got to watch the guards as close as the other cons. The tension at all times and all around is the thing you have to endure. It reaches the point where its normal. Every moment of everyday is like being in a low-level war zone. The atmosphere of seething hatred creates heavy air and makes it hard to breathe all the time. Most of these guards are Missouri hicks with attitudes held*

33

over from the slave days. They still considered the black man as livestock.

As the bus rolled past the last checkpoint and cleared the gate the sun light glared and brought a squint. The smell of freedom was in the air. There was his first realization it was springtime. On the inside there were no seasons. With three life sentences the time of year didn't really matter. The hopelessness set in years ago with a mind-set that prison is forever. It will take some time to even figure out the date as calendars were not wanted in a lifer's prison cell. Noticing the grass for the first time in years, he figured it to be about April.

Looking through the bus window rolling out of Jeff City and crossing the river bridge, tripped the thought of how many times some cellmate hatched a plot to get across that very stream. They would have it all worked out in their heads but most of them couldn't even swim. Everyone always figured their only chance was to avoid the city with the prison being in the center of downtown. Everyone knew that they would not have a chance on the streets but if they could make the river and the east bank there was plenty of places to hide over there. No one ever got past the planning stage except for the white guy Ray and he couldn't swim. When he cleared the wall he went straight up the tracks on the west side of the river. He lucked out and hopped a freight. Then went off and killed King and ended up right back where he started in prison. *He was a mousey little white guy around the yard but must be King Kong over in Tennessee with his white following. King was a fool all along with his live with whitey attitude. He should have joined the Nation and declared war on the white devils. King got what he deserved.*

The bars on the bus windows still said this is prison but the fact the bus was moving said not for long. His last ride was the one over from St Louis in 1952. He walked straight out of the court and boarded a train for a ride to Jefferson City and the end of a human existence. He couldn't have imagined what was coming that day only being eighteen years old. The harsh taste of white man's justice from the streets stuck in his throat. It was a big surprise that day and he went numb when the court sentence was life for each of the charges. The white judge gave him three life sentences at eighteen years old and he was just days too old to qualify for the juvenile lock-up. It made the old judge's day trying him as an adult and sending him to the Wall. His last words were "I'm doing the people a favor". Those words rung in Braburn's mind all these years. Even a kid could tell the judge was enjoying it and loved every minute. *Well, let the old white motherfucker roll over in his grave now because I'm gonna' walk out after fifteen years in spite of white justice and one thing is for sure, they will never get me back. My mistake was leaving witnesses. Both times the bitches fingered me. Hell, I would have thought the black nurse would have thanked me. She was kind of an ugly bitch. The white bitch was a different story she looked pretty good but dope money was what we wanted that time. Fucking her didn't enter my mind until it turned out there was no money in the place. Had to get something for the trouble.* He pondered many days in prison and thought about how stupid a kid can be when he's full of smack. They went in that day desperate to get money for a fix and robbed a stamp store that didn't even use money at all. That job got him nothing but an additional life sentence.

The gate to the medium security facility at Renick looked modern and halfway friendly unlike the pen in Jeff City. There were windows without bars with light colored buildings and even the smell of fresh country air. When the bus delivered him to the gate at the Wall the whole place smelled like a sewer and just shouted evil before he even got inside. A person just knew right off before even entering demons lived inside and there wasn't a chance of a decent life in the place.

This is going to be a breeze just be careful, keep your cool and smile for whitey.

Braburn settled in to life at Renick with a two-man cell and a free reign during the day. He was given a cushy job of tracking stuff in the supply room so he could devote most of his time to the art classes for the inmates. The art thing become a priority for the Renick warden because of the national press it was receiving from the Missouri newspapers. The old preacher's wife attracted national attention for one of his paintings by entering it in a show in Paris where it won a prize. That went public and got the Governors attention and his interest pulled the chains of every prison employee right down to the guards. Braburn realized for the first time in his life he was in a position of power. Having the old women on the outside pushing the race angle made it easy for him to get about anything he wanted.

"Braburn, you have a visitor" the day officer called out.

"You need to report to reception."

Mrs. Hart entered the reception room so elated she could barely contain herself. She could not wait to break the news to Allen. Her attorney's personal appeal to the Circuit Judge in St Louis County resulted in an agreement to review Allen's case. The argument presented to the court hinged on the fact that when Allen was sentenced he was eighteen years old by only a few days. His accomplice on the other hand was seventeen at the time of the trial and his punishment was dished out by the juvenile courts and was much softer. The accomplice was released years ago. If they could get a fairness ruling the sentence could be set aside and he could be set free immediately. The attorney assured her with public sentiment being what it was, there was a good chance of a reversal. They could claim the art involvement meant Allen was not only discriminated against because of his race but also he was now rehabilitated. She worked on this case as she felt called by god to correct this wrong with every part of her being. Her husband called on his congregation to go out in the community, minister to the poor negro population and help to correct the wrongs society dealt these people. She and Sister Jane picked Allen as their project and shared the legal cost of the lawyers and courts.

As Allen entered the reception room his mood was not good and he immediately noticed the women. *Old white bitch has the goofy sidekick with her. Hope she don't start in with all the praise the lord and Jesus mumbling.* He headed for the table and broke out in a fake toothy smile as the two old women lit up like spotlights when they saw him.

Keep your mouth shut and agree.

"I brought you some more oils; they are the ones you like," the old preacher woman said.

He looked down as he accepted the gift and noticed the logo and words "Arts International" on the bag. The address was Clayton Missouri.

These old rich women don't have a clue. My ass wouldn't even be allowed in that part of the city after dark. If they really wanted to bring me a gift, why not a bag of weed or a fifth of booze. Stupid bitches, all I need is more paint.

"Allen I've got great news. The Judge is going to review your case next week and we will get an immediate ruling. According to the lawyer, you could be out really soon; I mean within a couple of weeks. Isn't that wonderful? Sister Jane and I prayed on it all the way from St Louis and we just know god will answer our prayers. We would like to pray on it with you before we leave," she said.

37

"Yea that's great," he replied bowing his head.

"Reverend Hart is already looking for a job for you because the lawyer said if you have a means of support before leaving the prison it would help. We have some friends from the church that own a print shop in Clayton and it appears they will agree to take you on as a delivery boy, isn't that great news?"

"Yea," he replied as the women packed their things to leave.

You have to be kidding. There was no way I'm going to be some Whiteman's "step-and-fetch-it nigger" after what I have put up with in my life. If I ever get on the streets again, I'll hook up with the Nation and tell these white motherfuckers to go to hell.

"Hey Braburn, they want you in reception again. How come you are so popular lately", the day guard yelled.

"Who is it?" he yelled back. "It's not those old white women again is it?"

"No, there are two big ass black guys in suits. They're not very friendly looking either. Hope you don't owe them money," the guard laughed.

When Allen opened the door to the reception room for the second time in two days he immediately knew who the men were. One of them he recognized from a picture in his cell in Jeff City. They were from the St Louis Chapter of the Black Nation and one was Momar Abdul the leader of the St. Louis Grand Avenue Church. *This has to be big. Hope they don't check my participation in prayers since I arrived. Hope to fuck I haven't done something wrong to attract their attention. These mother fuckers look serious.*

"Are you Allen Braburn", the leader asked.

"Yes," he replied meekly.

"We are here at the behest of our leadership in Boston. They have asked us to come and bestow some honors on you and to elevate you in our religious community to a new level. That of Jalad, are you familiar with that term?"

"Yes, it means chosen I think," he replied.

"That's correct and to serve with that title means you have to swear total loyalty to the Nation and your superiors under the threat of death. You must also take on a holy name and be known by it from now on. You will cast off all things of your white slave masters and live the life of a holy one forgoing pleasures of the flesh. When your superiors ask, you will serve them without question. You will hold an elevated place in the Nation and be allowed to be in the presence of our leaders. Do you agree to these things and wish to accept this invitation to be part of god's chosen few?" the leader asked.

"Yes," he replied.

"With your position in our community you will receive total protection from the white devils and any needs you have you cannot meet yourself will be met by the Nation. Your name will be held with respect and any blasphemy against you will be reprised by the Nation. This head cover is called a Kufi and it is colored to identify you among men. You will wear it with pride. Now we will pray."

As he put the small cap on his head they bowed to the East and the men softly chanted and recited the required phrases. When they were finished the men stood erect and shook hands. This cemented it for Braburn. It meant, when he got out, he would be protected. He could not believe his luck. The problem was going to be faking it as he wasn't a true believer but then again most of the other members weren't either. The enforcement of the rules was lax. The religion was a hedge to scare off white people by professing freedom of religion any time something came up. Between religion and discrimination, a black man could set the stage with the U.S. constitution for any confrontation with whitey.

"Your art gift from above has made you special and given you the opportunity to again be a free man and escape the bonds of slavery. You will be known by the name Malik Jakim from this day forward. Allen Braburn has died today," said the priest.

*   *   *   *

Braburn could still not believe his time at Renick amounted to just two months. The civil rights angle expedited his release beyond belief. The power was in the hands of the old white woman and the courts acted instantly it seemed every time she spoke. All through the processing of his paperwork as they signed him out, he held his breath waiting to wake up from this dream. Now after a bus ride back to Jeff here he stood a free man, all alone waiting for the train back to St Louis. With darkness falling it was just like the moment he arrived. He could recall standing on this very spot fifteen years ago. When he stepped onto this platform he was a scrawny kid and now at thirty-three his hair was even starting to gray. All the time that passed was a blur with accentuated moments of horror and hatred. The hate he carried when he entered prison was nothing compared to the hate he carried now. Even in this train station crowd of lily white farmers he felt the eyes burning through his black body and a low flame burnt deep in his soul with the undeniable desire to strike out.

Suck it up nigger, you be back in St Louis soon. First order of business is a visit to Grand Avenue and some real pussy for a change. No more little white boy punks for this nigger. Just play it cool and get away from these hicks. From now on the key is play it cool. Don't give these motherfuckers a chance to come down on your ass. That's the key.

The train trip from Moberly seemed to take forever. Watching the women passengers in the aisles and smelling them as they passed

40

his seat aroused Braburn sexually. He needed some relief. As they approached St Louis Union station the familiar screech of the trains brakes, a sound he hadn't heard in years, signaled their arrival. He paused to catch his breath and gazed through the window for some familiar sites. Suddenly, they lurched to a stop and he saw Mrs. Hart and her prayer lady friend waiting on the platform. *I've got to lose those silly bitches right now. I'm not spending my first night out talking about Jesus with those two.* Braburn pushed his way through the passengers and headed for the rear of the train car. In the second vestibule to the rear he found a porter sneaking a cigarette between cars.

"Hey man, can you let me out here. Bitch is waiting for me with the law," he said.

The porter nodded and moved over pulling the step levers on the opposite side of the train. Braburn exited onto the opposite platform from the church women and walked to the closest stair enclosure. On the way up the stairs he glanced through the enclosure windows. He could see the old women jabbering and wondering what happened to him. He smiled as he moved out through the station into the city streets. The smell; the wonderful smell of the city enveloped him. He felt in his pocket for the three twenty dollar bills he was given when discharged. *Sixty dollar for all those years. That's less than five dollars a year. Fuck that country fresh air shit, this is where I belong. Now up to Grand to find a liquor store then the raunchiest bitch in the city and my freedom will be complete.*

CHAPTER 4

THE ADJUSTMENT

It was one of those mild Missouri late February days where it's unseasonably warm with a little snow still visible in spots and large clumps of wet green Johnson grass breaking through as if searching for spring. There is the promise that spring is coming but not just yet. The early morning rush was over and the sun felt warm through the car's tinted windshield. The GTO sounded strong as the big block engine purred from its dual exhaust and the interstate rolled beneath the famous wide track chassis. The steering wheel felt good after a year of only occasionally driving ratty assed jeeps on dirt trails in Nam. The car was heavy and sat tight on the road. It was the kind of car one could push five hundred miles at eighty and get out relaxed. When he bought the car the salesman pitched the Pontiac wide track ads as if that was going to make the deal. The guy did not seem to realize he was there looking for that very car and did not need the pitch. He put three hundred down and drove it off, straight to Florida and a new job still stinging from a marriage that just busted in Seattle. Chris never thought the Florida gig would end by him getting drafted. After successfully dodging the draft for years the "suddenly being single" thing caught him by surprise. When the draft came sniffing around he just let the cards fall and halfway volunteered. His life and aerospace job left him wanting something else. He was sick of killing time on the job talking to uninteresting people about irrelevant things. The big thing was the busted marriage and the feelings of failure that go along with it. Maybe there was a broken-hearted death wish mixed in there but whatever it was the Vietnam stint sure seemed to have cured it. Now

43

it was time for another renewal and some time off alone soaking up the peace of it all.

The trip up from St Louis was the typical mundane freeway run where all the exits look the same. Turning north at Columbia leaving the interstate, he noticed the little APCO station at his exit was still there. The only change being the addition of a new 7-11 store next door. That very spot was a pit stop on trips home during his college years. This road was familiar as it was the way home when he was a student. The engineering school in south Missouri was all male so the trips home after a few weeks of studying calculus were highly anticipated to say the least. He was only nineteen at the time and full of testosterone. At that point love conquered all so he married his hometown girl when she finished high school. They settled down as married students to setup housekeeping and finish his education. It was so good they even stayed an additional year for graduate school and got a Masters. He was crazy about her at that point and ready to be an old married man forever. There was never a clue that the marriage vow would become a bit of a scam until she walked out in Seattle five years later.

The familiarity of the road gave a calming effect. This was the old route home back in the college days. Pulling into the convenience store for a pit stop, he decided to stretch his legs as the next part of the trip was a dull two lane road. He decided to pick up a six pack. *It is a little early for alcohol but then again as the old saying goes its five o'clock somewhere. A couple of beers might just be the right lunch da jour for a single man on vacation. Mom will have a fit when I walk in smelling of beer before noon but what to hell I will just tell her I'm fouled up now because of the war.*

The little store smelled of new paint and overcooked hot dogs with a clerk in a company vest giving everyone the suspicious once over.

"Six pack of cold Bud, is that it for you?" asked the clerk.

"Yea, how long has this place been here, good spot for a liquor store", he replied.

"Less than a year, yea this one is always busy. I like your car. Nice day, you should drop the top."

"Little early in the season for the top down. Is the road north of here any better than it used to be?"

"Yea some. They've reworked it as far as Moberly. Where you headed?"

"My mother's place in Maysville, it's been a while since I've been back here. Forgot how quickly it gets flat north of the river."

The road was straight with the prairie flat in north central Missouri. It felt like home even though it was several years since he lived there. Missouri's center was a mix of wholesome country people bound by big cities on both side of the state. There was an unspoken comfort he felt at that moment. The cities were distinct though with St Louis the classic eastern metro area and K C having a cowboy western flavor. Both places were crime ridden and as typical small town folks, the city news stations caused everyone to quake in their boots when they entered the big cities. As a child, his family spent time in St Louis since his sister lived there, but never Kansas City. His old Confederate roots left the whole family with some suspicion of Negros and any time they visited a city as kids there was fear in the air. The stint in Viet Nam cured that as at this point in life he owed many nameless black guys his very life.

The drive between Columbia and Moberly always was dull and long and this time was no different. There was nothing to look at but the winter scene of bare farmland with picked out cornfields and brown foliage. The scene of the frigid winter renewal of the earth with scattered skiffs of snow looked like something out of a Grandma Moses painting. There was an odd familiarity to it. At least the day was sunny and the whole thing was relaxing him. He and his buddies hunted rabbits and roamed farm fields like this all day long in the winter. He could never remember feeling cold though. This time of year, the weather here could be a bitch and change in a minute. *It is time to head west to get over the divide and on the west coast before it changes. This visit home is going to be short.*

The new limited access highway was an improvement. He flashed back to his college days when the road was a narrow 1930's antique two-lane death trap. Keeping his eyes on the road he reached over in the passenger seat and retrieved a cold beer from the bag. By reflex he cracked the pull tab, took a swig and set it between his legs. The cold crisp brew rolled down his throat and seemed to taste better than he remembered, sort of revitalizing him. Something inside him seemed to be returning and he felt better than in a long time. It was a thing he lost track of in the war's turmoil called peace.

As he rolled towards Moberly he could not help but notice new overhead signs heralding the turn off to Missouri's medium security prison at Renick. The name of the town always stuck as it rhymed with the last name of a man from his home who served some time there. Small town gossip made that a hot topic with the kids around home as that man was the only real convict any of them ever actually knew personally. His crimes were not serious really and only involved a conviction for manslaughter during a car accident. The guy's reputation around town portrayed him as a bit wild and out of control. Really though he didn't seem to have a mean bone in his body. He always seemed friendly and harmless like everything in a small town. Just happened to be in the wrong place at the wrong time.

Small town life made him oblivious to the filth in the real world as a child but a few years out in the thick of it and the war experience reset his attitude. After a year in a war zone and a stint as Platoon Sergeant, nothing would surprise him now. He dealt with some of the dredges of society running his platoon of grunts. Some of those ghetto kids were jail bait and given the option to volunteer for military service by a court. It was hard to figure them but it did not take long to realize there was no future in turning your back on them. There was no doubt that they did get the shaft in life. Even in the Nam, any cold ambush would drop the blacks first on purpose just to stir things with the races. Even the gooks were discriminating against them. The whole thing was somewhat laughable as Cotton once joked about wanting to get makeup to turn his face white when they went out in the bush.

As Maysville broke over the horizon he felt this restart is for real and this visit would re-ground his life. The trip down the old hometown three-block main street felt familiar. As he passed, he noticed the afternoon crowd seemed to be in place at the O K tavern. *There must be some news in there that would interest me.* The roar of the gravel was a familiar sound as he pulled into the driveway at the old home place. Immediately his mother stepped through the front door. She lit up like a light. She was waiting for him.

"Did Jody call and let you know I was coming?" he asked as he stepped out of the car.

"Yes, she called early this morning after you left. Come in and let me see you. Thank God you are in one piece. I went to the church and lit a candle every day you were gone," she said.

"Still working the old Irish Catholic voodoo huh? Well I am glad you did because I faced a few close ones over there that's for sure. It seemed dodging bullets was more than luck sometimes."

His mother always was a nervous type of person. Born and raised in a small town she didn't seem to mind the world passing her by. She always agonized over the happiness and safety of her children. She was all heart when it came to people and she could always find a redeeming quality in anyone. The Irish roots made her a natural survivor and those same roots always kept her grounded. The little town life suited her and there was never a desire to go anywhere else. When his father got the fifty-year itch and moved out, she just maintained the old home place as best she could. The love of the locals kept her afloat. Her children were all grown and out of the house when the old man left and she was alone but she dealt with it well. She managed to produce four kids with good Catholic School morals and they all made decent adults. Everyone did leave the old hometown as soon as they could. Chris's failed marriage was the only blemish on the family's scorecard at the local church. The other siblings kept their marriages and religion intact.

"What's new on the local front, I assume the gossip mill is still working. Imagine they all want to hear my Vietnam story with details on the blood and guts of it all," he said.

"Yes, I saw Larry Gurden and he was asking when your time was up. Also heard this morning that Kenny Stevens was killed over there a few days ago," she replied.

"Holy shit, chalk one up for old Maysville. I cannot believe that, he was a lifer. I think he joined the military before we finished our last year of high school. Do you get any of the details?"

"No, just heard it at the grocery store," she replied.

"Kenny was one of the better ones when we were kids. I'll have to go up to the O K tavern a little later and get the dope. Right now an old homemade boloney sandwich with lots of mayonnaise and one of those beers I brought is my priority."

Kenny and his brothers were kind of a hard luck case around town with no father and always scratching for a living. They worked unlike most of the kids in school. Typical of the luck of the draw in Vietnam, the good ones got it first. *There were a lot of pricks over there that I wouldn't have minded seeing get it but they seemed to always make it through.*

Looking around the old place brought back memories of being a kid. The neighborhood children ran the woods and fields behind the house. It was the only family home through childhood. Built on a shoestring from scratch by his dad and grandfather back in the forties after WW II it stood for the meaning of home. He longed for it on some of those nights in the bush in Southeast Asia when he figured he would never return. One particular night he recalled being able to even see the place in his mind. It was a horrible night laying under ten-foot tall elephant grass in Cambodia listening to the dinks jabbering and walking around searching for his platoon. The dinks knew they were in there just not right under their noses. If anyone even flinched the whole bunch would have been dead. They went in to mortar an ammunition convoy on the trail and the news goons got wind of it. Cambodia was off limits to American troops. When the call came in to cancel the mission they announced the extraction would be tomorrow. They didn't want the choppers noticed by the media. The whole platoon lay out there all night as still as hiding rabbits. He asked himself all night long how he could justify giving his life for a country that would write him off for a news story. He promised himself on the chopper coming back the next day never to risk his ass for his country again.

The O K was next to the railroad tracks uptown and had been there for what seemed forever. The front door welcomed those who dare enter for many years. It looked exactly the same with the dirt around the hand hold and the pushed in screen. Amazingly the dilapidated parking spots in front with standing water under your feet when you got out of your car were still there. It was the classic small town watering hole and with all the amenities like the cur dog laying out front. As he entered the pungent smell of a half century of dried beer spills filled his nostrils. Many of the faces at the bar were the same ones sitting there when he left this town years ago. Scanning the bar stools brought back times as a teenage kid. He played pool and watched the drunk's antics in this place. It was particularly fun when a relative of one of your friends was making a fool of themselves and you were going to get to report it to the world. Finally, a call from the far end of the bar rang out. It was Gauffer from his sister's high school class. Around here the guy was a fixture and was the town drunk in training before he left. If anyone would know the news on Kenny, Gauffer would.

"When in the hell did you get back?" Gauffer asked as he excitedly cleared the bar stool next to his.

"Couple days ago. Came back into Fort Lewis Washington. Flew into St Louis to pick up my car at Jody's. Headed west for a little down time to miss the rest of the winter. Needless to say, I'm not used to cold after a year in hell. Nam is the nastiest and hottest place on earth. Could have watered the Linn County's corn crop with the sweat I produced over there," he replied.

"You sure don't look the worse for wear. When did you get so goddamn big? You were small as a kid seems like, but then I have not seen you for years. Sure are in good shape. I guess I'll ask the proverbial question. What was it like?"

"Let's just say it's not like a John Wayne movie at the uptown theater. Was wondering about Kenny. Heard the news from mom but she didn't have any details."

"The word is it was some kind of rocket attack on a field hospital where he was working. You knew he was a medic? Small piece of shrapnel right through his heart killed him instantly. He just re-upped and volunteered for another tour," answered Gauffer.

"Do you know where it happened? Did he leave any family?"

"Seems like it was near a place called Bo Lock. Yea, wife and daughter in the L.A. area. His little brother was in here yesterday and with some details. Said they were shipping the body here for the funeral and burial. City is planning a parade in his honor I hear," answered Gauffer.

"That's classic," Chris replied. "They used to go pick him up and question him for any petty crime that happened around here. Now he's the local hero. Just goes to show you what a bunch of two-faced assholes run the world. Guess the mayor is going to make a speech. I love this place. Glad it's not me they are planting and take it from me friend, it very well could be. It is just the luck of the draw. Watch the turnout at his funeral. Hell, most of these people wouldn't have given him the time of day when we were kids. Now it's good old Kenny I knew him well."

Driving back down the old main street triggered memories of being a kid in the small town. It seemed a person was who they were born to be in places like Maysville and their only hope to beat a dead-end future was to get out. Living there for eighteen years meant there was not a nook, cranny, street, or alley that at some time during childhood he'd not explored. *People in little towns can't imagine what's on the other side of the city limits let alone the other side of the world.* He could really see the difference with the boys in his army unit. They were a mix from the cities and the hick towns, all thrown into a meat grinder together in a life and death struggle and not by choice. The war experience was a lesson in human nature if nothing else. The heat of combat was the glue that bonded a bunch of unlikely suspects and made them a cohesive unit determined to survive. The truth was his bunch did a pretty good job of it too.

*   *   *   *

51

The trip across Kansas was completely uneventful, mind numbing and never ending. The prairie interstate offered nothing but a crosswind and continual tumbleweeds in the road. The only thing that made it tolerable was the thought of getting on a ski slope for the first time in over two years. Winter in the Rocky Mountains this time of year offered the best snow in the world. When he took up skiing in Seattle he never dreamed he would become addicted to it. The drone of the engine and the hum of the tires inducted a bit of a road trance. Thoughts of his days in Seattle and his excitement of a new life with his first job out of college brought a slight smile. How inexperienced and naïve he was when he headed out to conquer the world. A job layoff, a divorce and a year in a combat zone jerked him into the realities of life. He certainly was not the same person that crossed this same prairie three years ago.

As the Denver suburb of Aurora finally came into view, the relief the long road trip was ending gave a feeling of fatigue. The last part across the high plains was ugly and endless. *A cheap motel, a couple beers and a good night's sleep will get the blood flowing for a day on the slopes.*

The end of the interstate dumped onto Colfax Avenue, famous as "the world's longest main street". It runs all the way across the Denver area through the suburbs from East to West. It starts on the prairie and ends at the mountains. He visited the area on business years back and was somewhat familiar with the layout. The place seemed deserted for early evening. The early winter darkness made it feel later than it was so he figured there was no need to go clear into Denver until tomorrow. He would just stay on this side of town. Relieved to finally be out of the flatlands the first priority was a cold beer.

The search for a friendly lounge ended quickly as the strip in Aurora offered plenty of selections. Picking some place well-lit was a must because the area gave off a slight aura of seediness. Writing it off as paranoia, he pulled into a dance place called the "Rest of the Week" and picked a parking spot for the Goat under the lights. Aside from someone messing with the car itself everything he owned was inside it, including his expensive snow skis. They were in plain sight through the windows and it worried him. Scoping out the entrance and the parking lot on the way in he noticed the double doors. They formed a small vestibule area outside the business. As he stepped inside the noise of the crowd hit him with a start and he surveyed the dark room with a squint.

"What will it be?" said the bartender as Chris settled on one of the tall stools near the center of the bar.

"This is Colorado, what else, give me a Coors draft."

The place was typical with a mirrored wall behind the bar and a parquet dance floor with blinking multicolored lights close to the bar stools. One side of the dance floor opened to the bar area with tables on the other three sides. The bar area and the tables were darker than the dance area to highlight the mood and draw people to the floor. There was a fair crowd for early in the evening. The good thing about the set up was a person could sit at the bar and watch the whole place behind them in the mirror. Scanning the crowd, the eligible females stood out as usual making eye contact and trying to get some attention. His romantic interest waned over the past months and after several days of being the road warrior, he just wanted to have a couple of beers before hitting the rack. He didn't feel like dealing with trying to pick somebody up, but it wasn't long before some lounge lizard sauntered up out of the dark from the dance area.

"Is anyone sitting here?" she asked slipping onto the empty stool next to his.

"I guess someone is now," he replied trying not to sound too encouraging.

"Where did you come from and where did you get the curly hair and blue eyes?" she asks with a strong flirt in her voice.

"The other side of the world. Just got back from Vietnam. The hair is from eating the crust of my toast as a kid and the eyes are gift from my Irish ancestors."

This girl was attractive and it was tempting to play this thing as she was looking to hook up for the night but there was something about her that screamed "bimbo". He really didn't feel like fooling with the small talk to make it happen. He wanted to just finish his beer and get a cheap motel. The plan called for ski slopes to be the place for romance. There was always a better class of bimbos around the wine stuebas and bars up in the mountains.

He figured if he bought her a drink it would encourage her so he tried to look away as she fidgeted with her purse.

"Why do they call this place "The Rest of the Week"?" he asked to distract her.

"There is a similar place up the street called "Friday and Saturday" that's real popular and this place opened to compete with it. Guess it's a play off their name. We could slip up there if you want. There's usually a better crowd."

It was a tempting offer but the old sixth sense was telegraphing caution and she seemed kind of anxious and wanting to get out of the place for some reason. Maybe his body was trying to warn him of something. All he needed was to catch a social disease from some local girl his first week back. He avoided that in Vietnam. What the troops called "drippy dick" over there was a real hazard with those eighteen-year-old kids and the prostitutes. The Army dealt with it by passing out the tetracycline like popcorn.

The girl's demeanor was fidgety and nervous. It didn't take long to find out why. Out of the dark at the rear of the dance floor appeared a figure in the mirror. It was a guy stomping toward the bar. As he approached from behind, Chris watched his every move in the bar mirror with the self-defense juices starting to flow. The man walked up next to him and started in on the girl calling her names and accusing her of cheating on him with every other sentence being a physical threat. Unprovoked the man started in on Chris and it appeared by default he blamed him for something. The girl pleaded with the man to leave her alone and finally the bartender intervened. He ordered the guy to go sit down and shut up. The man returned to the rear of the dance floor mumbling something. *This fellow is a pretty good sized boy. If there is trouble I need to drop him right off. The worst case scenario would be if he follows me into the parking lot. Hope this mess stays in the lounge. It's going to take a pretty good lick to stop this guy.*

He suddenly found himself recalling the nickel plated 45 the Army confiscated when he debriefed.

"I'm sorry about that," she said.

"I broke up with him a couple days ago. He is a mean son-of-a-bitch and truly, I'm afraid of him. Has it in his head there is another man and his ego can't let it go. He thinks you are the new guy."

Here I am just wanting to have a casual beer and I'm in the middle of a domestic dispute completely innocent. Before the war, he would have slipped out of the place and avoided the confrontation but now it seemed he wanted to see how it would play out. The war experience seemed to have left some residual pleasure in participating in the fight. Unlike before the war he could now completely suppress fear.

"Will you walk out with me because I'm afraid of him? He's riled up and it will be a while before he cools off. Best thing is to get away," she said.

"I'm not sure walking out together is a good idea. That will just cement his suspicions and he might follow you outside. Truthfully, if you must deal with him it would be better inside than out in the parking lot. This bartender looks like a no-bullshit kind of person but he isn't real big. If you stay inside, the bartender will be the one that must deal with him. Let me ask you something is the guy a veteran?"

"No, he is a major chicken. Mostly picks on women. He has ego and temper issues that take him out of control and he seems to completely lose it. He has a reputation for violence. I think he will leave me alone if you are with me."

"The key word in that sentence is "think". What if he doesn't? Look in the mirror. Here he comes again."

The guy started cussing and yelling as soon as he reached the edge of the dance floor. Of course, that drew the attention of the whole place including the bartender who rotated and picked up the phone at the end of the counter. People could not tell who was the culprit and every eye in the place turned to what was happening. Chris couldn't make a lot of sense out of what the guy was saying but it was sure obvious the rage transferred to him. *What luck, walked in for a casual beer and drew the wrath of some head case over some girl I've never met. Welcome to civilian life.* He turned to talk the guy down again but there was no explaining. The idiot was out of control and on the verge of becoming physical. On top of that, the Irish anger was coming up in Chris and besides being afraid, he was getting mad. One thing was for sure and that was he wasn't going to take an ass whipping over some stranger. If the bartender does not end this, it was becoming obvious he would to have to act.

With the bartender giving his second warning the man turned and headed back to the table. Watching the mirror, Chris could see the demeanor was the same and the man was not calming down at all. It was obvious this thing is not over. He now was the focus of the man's displaced anger and the girl was no longer in the picture. As the guy reached the rear of the dance area he turned and headed back toward the bar. He was losing it and this was not going to be good. Chris immediately felt the self defense mechanisms kicking back in. Watching the guy approach in the mirror he figured he was in a good position to take him out. As the guy crossed the dance floor his face was telegraphing violence and his mouth was spewing profanities. A subconscious message rang through that said this guy could hurt someone. Focused on the mirror image when the man was about two steps away Chris rotated and slipped off the barstool. With his knees slightly bent his feet hit the floor. As he straightened up from a slight crouched position, the timing was perfect and he unleashed a straight right jab that caught the aggressor between the eyes dead center. Pain shot through his wrist and elbow clear to the shoulder joint. He knew from the pain he hit the fellow hard. The scene seemed to be in slow motion as the guy fell over on his back and slid across the dance floor with one of his slip-on shoes coming off in the process. It was obvious the man was not getting right back up. Chris immediately rotated and headed for the double doors to make a run for it but as the doors swung open, there stood the Aurora police. The bartender saw the whole thing coming and already called for help.

Sitting cuffed in the back of the police cruiser Chris felt uncomfortable and immature. The cops were having a good time with it asking stupid questions. They did have his attention though as at that moment he was technically a homeless derelict that lived in a car. They were playing the good cop bad cop roles with the questions. Next to him cuffed was the man that started it and he was bleeding profusely all over the car seat and Chris's good suede coat. The guy's nose was going to need some major attention and the idiot was moaning about his condition wanting to see a doctor. The conversation made it obvious that the cops knew who they were dealing with from prior issues. Chris knew to say as little as possible and the scene didn't intimidate him. He was carrying plenty of money and the cops could tell that he would just as soon avoid any judges.

After all the showboating, the passenger cop turned to him and said, "How much did you drink in there?

"Two and a half beers," he replied

You get across the Stateline by daylight and we'll let you go."

Chris's simple answer was, "Start my car."

As the convertible rolled off into the darkness peace set back in. The decision of which direction to head to get out of state was all that was left. He could disregard the cops and go on up to the ski slopes but they did have a record of the stop and another incident could get him detained for real. He decided to postpone the skiing until he reached California. It was obvious he would be up most of this night at least until he crossed a state line. Mulling it over there was a few obvious considerations. Crossing the Rockies to Utah would take all night and heading back to Kansas was the wrong direction. South would put him in New Mexico and north into Wyoming. Wyoming was the closest and he needed some sleep so that settled it. *Head north and keep it under the speed limit.* With his arm still aching and a slight buzz from the beer, he asked himself what to hell he was doing running from the police in the middle of the night like a thief. Civilian life so far wasn't a whole lot different from the turmoil of the life he just left.

Enveloped in the darkness listening to the engine hum, he recalled the last time he made this trip. It was four years ago when he and his ex-wife took this route to Seattle. They drove to their new life after graduation with a completely new world at their doorstep. The realities of life taught a harsh lesson since that trip. Maybe this thing in Aurora was karma to send him in this direction. At that point he made a decision to go on up to Seattle and get it out of his system. He always knew there was going to have to be a face to face with her to settle it once and for all. *There should be an interstate rest stop just over the line in Wyoming where I can pull in, roll out a sleeping bag in the back seat and sleep some in the car.*

*   *   *   *

After the trip to Seattle the Arizona desert was a refreshing change. The altercation in Denver combined with the tense meeting in Seattle made for a long week to say the least. It was time to take a deep breath and kick back so a stop at the Grand Canyon was in order.

The meeting in Seattle got halfway physical when his ex's new boyfriend decided to be heroic and protect his new girl from her lunatic ex-husband. The whole scene was ugly. All he asked was to speak to her. When the guy called him a stupid son-of-a-bitch he lost it and kicked the guy in the crouch before he could slam the door. The result was another sprint for a Stateline. This time he needed to run as he was guilty of assault. Three days of driving down the Pacific coast highway through California helped tone down the nerves and for the first time since getting back his insides seemed completely calm. No stomach knots to hold down. Taking the side trip to see her first was the right thing to do. This episode gets her clear out of the picture. It seemed amazing after two years of living in Seattle and working at Boeing he felt no attraction for the place.

It was a good two years but typically a divorce leaves a bad taste for everyone and everything involved. *A visit to Vegas might be just what the doctor ordered now. Maybe a show with all the girls and bare skin would get me back into the simple pleasures of life.*

*　　　*　　　*　　　*

The stopover in Vegas wasn't the right match for his mood. The hype and hoopla of the place was too much and too phony for the inner peace he felt from the time alone on the road. One night of ringing slot machines and tip hustlers was plenty. The road down across Boulder Dam dumped the convertible out near the south rim but too far from the Grand Canyon to make it before dark. He stopped at the dam area for a short water fix on the shores of Lake Mead and just walking in the desert seemed to have a healing effect. It was as if the desert dryness was killing the mold that accumulated on his soul from a year in the damp Asian jungle.

Coming up on a National Park it was pushing midnight so he decided to just find a place to park and curl up in the backseat for the night. He figured he'd get a room at the canyon tomorrow night and really relax. The temperature was dropping as the night passed so he rolled out his sleeping bag, dropped his shoes and slipped inside it with his clothes on. The comfort of the makeshift bed amazed him as he dozed off. With the rear floor of the car packed level with engineering books and the passenger seat folded completely forward he could stretch out and actually sleep sound.

As the sun broke the horizon the sound of a truck leaving the park woke him. His first thought was that he forgot to fill his thermos with coffee before going to sleep. It was still winter and the desert was cold so he tucked the sleeping bag around his neck and snaked past the driver's seat to start the engine and hit the heater switch. He figured he would let the car warm up before leaving his cocoon. Then the priority would be a hot breakfast because dinner last night only consisted of three left over warm beers from the day before and his appetite was definitely nagging. The bright sunshine and smell of the conifer pines in his nostrils gave a positive feeling as he rolled out of the park.

The little cross roads café at the turn to the canyon entrance was typical. Navaho window dressings with an aged clapboard wooden curio shop for the tourist next door. *A greasy spoon like this is usually either horrible or great with no in-between.* He slowed to scope it out and the smell of bacon from the vent fans seemed to nudge the car into the parking lot involuntarily. *Guess this is going to be it for morning chow.* As he entered the small café, it wasn't particularly crowded and he picked a window table away from any other people. *People in these types of places tend to seek conversation.* He wasn't in the mood for any mom and pop chitchat. Ordering up breakfast, the menu didn't have much of a meat selection. As he queried the waitress about it, he noticed a glance from the attractive one of two girls sitting together at a table across the room. She was listening to what he was ordering to eat for some reason. As their eyes met she quickly refocused on her friend and continued eating.

The breakfast was good and filling and after paying he decided to stop in the curio shop and maybe get a souvenir of some kind. The restaurant and store seemed to be Indian owned and he felt like he should buy something. Maybe it was his great grandmother's Cherokee blood bubbling up. Shopping was not his forte so it didn't take long to spot a small hand-made copper cross on a neck chain that fit the bill. Cashing out and exiting the store his religious roots crossed his mind as he pulled the chain out of the box and put it around his neck. As a kid in Catholic school he wore a religious

61

medal under his shirt most of his life so it felt natural. The wooden covered sidewalk in front of the store was slightly elevated and as he headed for his car, he scanned the lot. He noticed a light blue Volkswagen Beetle with the rear end hood raised over by the cafe. The two girls from the restaurant were standing next to it, looking a bit distraught. They were talking to a man and his little boy. He noticed the man spot him and turn to approach just as he stepped down off the porch.

"Do you know anything about cars?" the man asked.

"Yea some, what's wrong?" he replied.

"Well it cranks and there is gas in it but it won't start. That's about as far as my knowledge goes," the man shrugged.

Walking over to his convertible and opening the trunk he retrieved a screwdriver from a small toolbox he always carried with him when he traveled. It was just a dead car and that was a relief. At first, he thought the person was going to try to mooch a ride somewhere.

The rear engine Beetle was easy to deal with since there was not much to it. Pulling the coil wire and shorting it to the engine block he instructed the girl that seemed to own the bug to go crank the starter. A short whine of the starter yielded no spark.

"That's good," he barked. "The ignition is dead. Do you have a finger nail file?"

"I have an emery board," answered the attractive girl as she retrieved her purse.

She seemed to fumble some trying to open her purse and when she handed the emery board over their eyes met. He felt a sudden attraction for this girl. It was a feeling he hadn't felt in a while. Her long dark hair casually fell to her shoulders and her gray eyes absorbed him. She was wearing a black pants suit that fit perfectly with a white blouse that showed her assets both modestly and boldly.

He noticed her perfect proportions. As her fingers raked across his palm when she gave him the emery board the skin-to-skin contact felt like an electric shock for a second.

Collecting his thoughts, he focused his attention back on the engine, unclipped the distributor cap with the screwdriver and pushed it aside.

"Turn off the key," he called to the girl in the driver's seat of the V W.

There was something about the girl standing next to him intently watching his every move that was mildly arousing. It was as if he could feel her breath on his neck but she was not close enough for that to be the case. Inserting the emery board between the surfaces of the ignition points, he sanded the crud off with a slow back and forth motion. Her intense gaze and the motion of the file were oddly erotic and he lost his train of thought a second time. When he finished, he reassembled everything and called out to the driver.

"Now try it," he shouted.

The little engine sprang to life with the distinctive Volkswagen bug sound so he reached up and gently closed the hood. There was almost an audible sigh of relief from the crowd. Everyone realized the crisis was over and started heading for their cars.

"How did you know to do that? Are you a mechanic or something?" the dark-haired girl asked.

"No, I'm a brain surgeon," he teased with a straight face. "That little black thing I took apart was the cars brain."

Her response was a knowing smile and it was obvious she knew he was flirting.

"Actually, I'm a Mechanical Engineer but I could have fixed that problem when I was ten years old. You need to take that car in when you get home and have a set of points put in it. It should be o k today but if it quits again tell someone it's the points."

"Are you headed for the canyon?" the other girl asks as she approached the rear of the car.

"Yea, first time for me. I have never been in this part of the country. It's a pure sightseeing trip. You might say I'm a tourist," he answered.

"Follow us up and we will buy your dinner. We owe you one. We booked a room at the South Gate Motel. It's just before you enter the park gate. It has a great restaurant. Are you going to stay over?" she asked.

"Yea, I planned to. Do you think this place would have a vacancy?"

"Surely they will. It's the slower part of the season. We didn't have any trouble booking yesterday."

The little Volkswagen pulled out and turned north on the narrow canyon blacktop. He fell in behind and stayed close intent on not losing them. Following them he couldn't help but notice the eyes of the girl that was driving the Volkswagen cutting over to the rearview mirror intermittently. That was a definite sign that he was the topic of conversation at that moment in the Volkswagen. It was funny they never even exchanged names before leaving the restaurant parking lot. It was as if names didn't matter and their meeting was karma.

The motel was high-end southwestern architecture with all the amenities and the room was a little pricey. *What to hell you only live once as they say.* As he settled into his room and thought about it, he felt he definitely wanted to get to know the dark-haired girl better. There was a strange quiet magnetism between the two of them that didn't require any words and she seemed to relay her attraction for him as well.

The south canyon rim was a tourist delight with overlooks and easy places to stop and talk casually as they strolled the sidewalks and took in the views through the afternoon. When they returned to their rooms to change for dinner he fumbled with the room key. He realized his focus was entirely on the girl. After only the short afternoon she totally enamored him. He couldn't recall ever meeting someone that captured his attention in this way. Spending the time on the canyon rim gave them a chance to get acquainted and the majesty of the canyon scene just added to the whole romance thing. Everything about her was positive. Even her name, Jeannie, seemed to fit. She was single, a registered nurse and worked at a hospital in Phoenix where she lived at home with retired parents. Her family relocated to the desert from Michigan because of her father's lung issues. This evening was going to be a good one and he felt he would finally get some real rest.

It felt good dressing for the dinner date. The plan was to meet right about dark. He thought about how he could justify diverting to Phoenix for a few days. The truth was the way he felt at that moment any excuse would do. Checking his clothes, he wanted everything to be just right. Along with a sweater he figured he would need a coat as the desert cools quickly when the sun goes down. There was an issue with his good suede coat with blood spatter on it from the mess in Denver. He wanted to avoid having to explain that mess to her at this point. Using a washcloth, he worked on the spots and finally gave up. He decided he would have to wear it anyway. *Maybe she won't notice.*

After a decent but not exceptional dinner with both the girls, Jan the Volkswagen's owner excused herself politely. It was obvious that the girls agreed that three would be a crowd. It was a nice moonlit night and a drive along the canyon rim was in order. Jeannie changed for dinner and was wearing a full-length light beige colored loose fitting dress that looked a little light for the cool desert air. She wanted to see the canyon after dark so after fetching their coats, he dropped the top on the convertible and they drove to the best and most deserted overlook. The spot rather jutted like a platform into the canyon with a view on three sides. The whole canyon scene was magnificent. It seemed to glow in the dark with the colors distorted by the light of the full moon. It was a clear night and in the dim light it was remarkable how much of the canyon was visible. The overlook setting offered a rock outcropping near the edge that formed a natural bench so they sat together and took in the view. The majesty was a little overwhelming and seemed to demand silence. There was not much conversation. After a long silence, Jeannie stood up to face him.

"I'm a little chilly. My wardrobe anymore is geared to Phoenix weather and most of it is light weight," she said.

"Yea it definitely cools off at night in the desert. This coat has a zip out lining plus the suede is warm by itself," he said.

He stood up and pulled back the lapels of the unbuttoned coat with both hands to show the lining. As he pulled his coat open by the lapels she moved forward and walked into his outstretched arms. With her arms around his waist beneath the coat she rested her face against his chest. He pulled her close and closed the coat lapels. Her soft breasts heaved against him and the erotic rush of the moment overwhelmed him. It brought back something he didn't realize was lost. It was the tenderness of the feminine touch and the feeling like someone cared for him again. They held each other silently and the two bodies seemed to melt together and resist separation for several minutes soaking the companionship up like two sponges trading water.

Pulling back into the motel parking lot, she spoke for the first time since leaving the overlook. "Let's go check out the pool. It is supposedly something special, at least that's what I've heard. It's in the basement under the lobby and heated all year. I haven't even seen it yet," she said.

The pool entrance was a spiral staircase that descended from the lobby to a full windowless basement. As they went down the smell of dampness and chlorine immediately made it obvious they were entering a pool area. The pool was large for a motel and the place were bright. The underwater pool lights emphasized the crystal clearness of the water. It was after midnight so the place was completely deserted. As they descended the stairs the warmth of the heated water vapor in the room replaced the chilly desert night air. He watched her intently as he could see she was thinking about something as she approached the pool's edge. Without saying a word, she pulled off her coat and tossed it aside, then reached around and unbuttoned the dress at the back of her neck. With one swift move, she pulled the dress over her head, dropped it to the floor and there she stood in her bra and panties. Her underwear was a matching set, paisley print, with low cut bikini panties and a skimpy bra. There in front of him stood a perfectly built twenty-five-year-old female in all her glory completely uninhibited. She took two steps and dove into the warm water, swimming underwater to the other side of the pool before surfacing.

"The warm water is wonderful. This is the way to end a perfect evening," she said as she surfaced and turned to face him.

The water swept her hair back to expose her high cheekbones and the gray eyes. He could not restrain the rush of emotion inside him. Without saying a word, he dropped the coat in his arms to the floor, shimmied out of his Levi's to strip down to his plaid sport cut boxer shorts. He walked over to the pool and dove in to join her. Swimming up to her they held each other with their almost naked bodies intertwined and kissed for the first time as the warm water extracted every ounce of tension. He thought to himself how natural it was and how remarkable to feel this way with someone he only met this morning. He knew at that moment they were going to make love eventually and when they did, it was going to be really special. Suppressing his arousal, he wanted to postpone it until they were in a place that was more intimate and private. He could feel deep inside she felt the same way so after a few minutes holding each other they climbed out, grabbed towels from the poolside rack and dressed.

As they walked back to her room she stopped at her door and reached up to gently kiss him goodnight.

"You know you have to come to Phoenix, don't you?" she said in a low husky voice.

"Why don't you let your friend go back and we will stay here for a while tomorrow and drive back later in the day," he replied.

"I'll talk to her. Surely she will agree."

CHAPTER 5

THE CRIME

Arts International was the perfect setting for a small high-end art gallery. It was the last store in a new strip mall running along a downtown side street in the upscale suburb of Clayton. The high-rise office buildings in the center of the city cast some shadows on the street. The shade made the summer afternoons bearable for the customers that wanted to sit outside at Jenson's café next door. The small trees that lined the street complimented the step stone sidewalk that ran along the front of the whole strip. The low rod iron fence around Jenson's outdoor seating combined with the tablecloths gave the place an international look, kind of "Parisy".

The café was a special draw for the art store with its name being Arts International, especially in the summer. It made the whole area fit together warm and welcoming. All the businesses in the mall seemed to complement each other and drew the same high-end clientele. There was women's clothing and designer furniture on the far end of the mall and specialty food and beverages in the center. The liquor store's specialty imported wine's prices matched their reputations. The whole place blended into the environment yet maintained its own character. When one observed the shoppers along the block it was obvious they were well moneyed. This was the best the St Louis area offered. Clayton bordered Ladue the highest of the high-end city suburbs. Ladue was the residence of families with names like Anheiser and Bush of St Louis brewery fame. When sweeping the store's sidewalk in the morning it wasn't unusual to hear someone's personal helicopter pass over the store delivering an important person to their office in downtown St Louis.

69

The inside of the store was small with the walls completely covered from floor to ceiling with art works of various sizes for sale, most of it very pricey. There was an odd combined feeling of coziness and luxury at the same time. Some of the works were from prominent artist with international connections. The marketing concept of the business was to overcharge a well-healed clientele by using the privilege of ownership as the hook. Floor stand easels filled the center of the room setup back to back for easy viewing of the various framed works. The whole place reeked with the slight rich smell of oil paints.

The organization of the works attempted to give each individual painting equal attention. Proper presentation was a must with lighting naturally from the glass storefront. The egos of the artist that the works belonged to were fragile so the company policy was to strive to give everyone equal attention to keep the peace. Despite efforts to please there were occasional complaints from visiting artist. At the rear wall, there was a door to a small mostly empty storeroom with a restroom and an exit to the alley. Next to the storeroom entrance door a small nook with a raised counter created a private open window for monetary transactions. In the front of the counter were shelves stacked with oil paints and supplies for retail sale to local artist. Behind the counter was a built-in desktop such that the setup formed a small private office space for the phone and a chair.

Accepting the job was a godsend for Jody. Just in the three months since she started it renewed her attitude and self-image. Dealing with the public on this level was a new and refreshing experience. All that was on Jody's previous resume was a job at a hometown five and dime as a kid. This job was a real boost to her self-esteem. She dumped the self-doubt she carried when she started and was comfortable with it now in a natural way. These local old rich women were a snap to sell to and with her looks, if they brought their husbands, it was even easier. A little Irish charm and a suggestive smile could put a sale over the edge and yield a commission any day of the week. She was gaining a little insight and experience with human nature and the real world. Doing her hair and getting dressed every day to meet the public fit her needs as looks were always a high priority for her. New clothes were also easier to come by with the extra paycheck. She shed the homemaker slavery doldrums and for the first time in years noticed the sunshine again each morning.

Starting the day with sweeping the sidewalk there was always the opportunity for a conversation with one of the waiters next door who seemed to time setting the outside tables with her sweeping. He was a negro kid named Byrd who was working his way through school and seemed to think flirting with an older white woman was a great sport.

"Hey Jody, why you sweeping today? It rained last night. The side walk can't get any cleaner," said Byrd.

"Creature of habit Byrd. Not looking for dirt just some morning exercise to get the juices flowing. Us old women must keep in shape you know. Never know when our husbands will run off," she joked.

"You get in any better shape and us young boys will explode. When are you going to sneak off with me? I won't tell your old man. I tell you girl, you're putting us young guys in cold shower territory."

"You better watch it. I'll tell Brenda and she'll have your butt," she replied.

Byrd's girlfriend Brenda usually stopped to chat when she picked him up and was as sweet and innocent as they get. They planned to marry when he finished school and the young woman was bubbling over with enthusiasm for building a life and family. She would come early to pick Byrd up, park in the alley and slip into the art store through the back door for some one on one with Jody about marriage and children. It made Jody feel good to think someone valued her opinion. The truth was Brenda was the first friend of Jody's that was a negro. It felt natural to sit and relate and the girl soaked up Jody's advice. All through her childhood in a northern white small town there were not many blacks to get to know. Byrd and Brenda broke the stereotypes her Virginia ancestors passed down. She was proud to be this young woman's matriarch.

"Hey Byrd, run in and swipe me some tomato from the kitchen. I brought a turkey sandwich for lunch and didn't have one in my refrigerator at home. Can't get it down without some tomato on it," she said.

"O K as soon as I get the setups finished. What will you do for me in return?" he replied.

"I won't tell Brenda what a flirt you are, how's that?" she laughed as she headed back into the shop.

Sitting at the small desk updating the stock reports in the morning light felt good. The commission from that sale yesterday was going to be the saving grace for this month's bills at home. Morning was a good time to update the stock reports as the customer traffic was usually light and the paper work went smoother with no interruptions. As the chimes on the front door rang her first thought was that must be the tomato and without looking up she called out, "just set it on the counter Byrd".

With no reply, she glanced up with a start as it wasn't Byrd at all but some strange negro man. "Oh, I'm sorry. I thought you were somebody else. Can I help you?"

"It's free to look at these ain't it?" he replied. "I paint some myself. Need to get some oils while I'm here too."

As he strolled around scanning the art he seemed to make comments to himself about various things as if he's trying to emphasize the fact that he really knew something about art. With a short afro hair do and medium skin he was well-dressed. His demeanor seemed self-assured but there was a dark aura about him. He wasn't from this neighborhood that was for sure. Jody's skin began to crawl as he continually shifted his eyes from the art work to her as if sizing her up. She felt some comfort in the fact that the sidewalk café was full of people at that moment and they were visible through the store window. As he circled the gallery she kept her eyes on the paperwork on the desk and then suddenly felt his presence at the counter.

Dropping four tubes of oil paint on the counter the man tried to make small talk.

"These are a good brand of oil. How pricey are they? I really like these folk's base colors. Blends better than any other brands I've used."

"Forty cents a tube", she replied as she watched him peel off two one dollar bills.

Picking up his change he turned without a word, strolled to the door and glanced back over his shoulder and half smiled. She felt a tinge of guilt at the relief she felt and blamed her feelings on residual prejudice from childhood. *He was probably just some poor working stiff from St Louis trying to make a living.*

As the morning passed with paperwork at her desk the chime broke the stillness again. It was Byrd's voice saying something about how good a morning tip-wise it was.

"This place has good tippers and if the restaurant stays this busy for a couple weeks I'll have my next tuition money in a snap. Where do you want this tomato? I could only swipe a half so it's kind of messy."

"Set it on that napkin," she replied pointing to the desk.

Byrd walked over to the napkin and suddenly his demeanor got serious.

"Let me ask you something." he said. "What did that black guy that was in here this morning want?   I noticed him stay a little while."

"Said he was an artist and bought some paints. First time I've seen him. Why do you ask?" she replied.

"He caused a stir over at the café couple weeks ago about his bill. Seemed unstable. They asked him not to come back in and he seemed to go off in the head. Scared the hell out of me. Apparently, he works at the print shop up the street. Take my advice; don't trust project trash like that. Don't turn your back on him. He gives off nothing but negative waves."

As Byrd trips the door chime on the way out, Jody relaxes at her desk for a lunch break. *This sandwich is going to be a good interlude to a slow morning. Hopefully no one will stop in and interrupt me. The only negative with this one-person operation is can't completely relax. Always anticipating the door bell ringing. Can't even take a pee in peace.* Opening the desk drawer Jody fished for the little paring knife that was the combination letter opener and tomato slicer for the store. As she sliced the tomato she made a mental note to bring in a better knife. The dullness of this one was obvious but it would suffice as a smooched tomato slice would be better than no tomato at all.

*　　　*　　　*　　　*

The Missouri August heat was smothering as she made her way out of the house to the car to head for work. *Even this early in the morning it's hard to breathe. Thank god for good air conditioning at the store.* Her new light sweater and matching skirt would be bearable once she got to work but in a hot car they were a bit heavy. Fridays were usually slow with light foot traffic at the store and Jen, the gallery owner, always worked Saturdays. Jody's mood was exceptional as she headed off in the old Ford looking forward to the weekend off. Things with the kids and the car worked out perfectly as the children loved their sitter Cindy like a big sister and Tom could walk across Olive to his work at the lab. Her job was great all the way around not to mention the extra money it provided at home.

The car was slow to cool off with the age of its air conditioner so the heavy traffic was extra annoying on the way down to Clayton. By the time she reached the shop she was in a hurry to get inside. The shop thermostat would be turned down because of the oil paintings and it would be cool inside.

Putting the key in the shop's back door she was mentally starting her day as her mind mulled over the four artists she needed to call to give good news regarding this week's sales. One of the pleasant tasks of the job was calling the starving artist on Fridays to tell them one of their works sold and to come pick up a check. Most of the artsy types were not very good with money or managing their lives it seemed, but they were mostly kind and gentle people and rewarding them felt good. The checks should all be ready on the desk as the store owner Jen did the books on Thursday evening and dropped everything off after closing time. On the floor in the store room she couldn't help but notice six new paintings with a note from Jen. Scanning the note, it simply said, "put these up today if you can." *Jen must have a live prospect coming in tomorrow that she thinks might go for one of these.* As she walked past the lavatory she unconsciously grabbed the hammer off the store room shelve. She would need it later to hang the new stock. The only spot available for them was the west wall. She'd have to hammer in some wall hooks and move some things around. Mounting the paintings would be a good way to kill the morning as that time was slow anyway. Reaching for the broom she glanced at the clock and headed for the front door. With the August heat, sweeping the sidewalk would not be very pleasant today so she was kind of dreading it.

"Where's Byrd today?" she asks the new girl that was working at the tables next to the door as she stepped outside.

"He's down at the University registering for next semester. Took the morning off," she replied as she sat and rolled loose silverware.

"I think he is actually just trying to stick you with having to prepare all those place settings. School is probably just an excuse," Jody laughed.

The muggy August morning gave off a moan as if its own personality knew how miserable and unpleasant it was making daily life. To the east of the city the sky was orange with late summer haze from pollution, dimming the low morning sun. There wasn't a sign of a breeze and the pungent smells of car exhaust and factory smoke mixed with humidity made being on the street repulsive. Jody gave the sweeping job a quick lick and a promise so that she could get back inside as fast as possible. She sure didn't want to work up a sweat at the start of the day. Maybe it was exhaustion from the work week but whatever it was her mood was a little down for the first time in a long time. She just didn't feel right. *It must be the weather. Cooling off and hanging the new stock might get some creative juices flowing and pick things up.*

*　　　*　　　*　　　*

"Where's Allen?" asked Mr. Kelley as he entered the production area of the copy shop.

"He's late again," answered his wife. "Third time this week and it's getting worse."

"Hate to say it but this isn't working out. This guy is not who Reverend Hart and his wife said he was when they ask us to give him a chance. He's going to have to go. I am afraid to deal with him anymore. His temper and reactions scare me. When I correct him his face and eyes don't look normal. I knew it when we agreed to hire an ex-con it was going to be a mistake. He flies into a rage with any little criticism. I can't live in fear in my own business. I'm going to call the Harts. We need out of this arrangement. This guy's a Jeckle and Hyde."

Mrs. Kelley shook her head and replied. "Sometimes I wonder what he is thinking. He seems a million miles away. Took a delivery of handbills out yesterday to Jones's dealership and went to the complete wrong address. Don't think he is listening anymore. His mind seems to be on something else. Then when he did make the delivery he lost us a customer, because he flew into a rage when their office manager asked him why he was late. The customer called to request we don't ever send him to their store again. Hope he is not back into the drugs. You remember his history. It might be smart to call his parole officer before talking to him. Let the officer take his wrath if he flies off the handle."

Braburn's night was a bitch and waking up late for the stupid job was going to get him called out again. *That old motherfucker and his wife at the print shop are about all I can deal with always praising Jesus and carrying on. Their phony assed sympathy for the poor black boy is enough to make me want to puke. Here I am some white man's step and fetch-it nigger. At least in prison I had some respect. These people didn't seem to even know my religion and that I don't even believe in Jesus. Hell, I don't really believe in the Nation's god but at least faking that pays off. Going to their St Louis church and kneeling on a rug has reaped some reward. It seems like "the man" is afraid of the Nation both inside and out of the joint. It feels good to be part of it.* In prison Allen made his bones with the black population by stabbing a white boy who was working a protection shakedown con on the black inmates. The blacks protected him from there on in prison and they still were on the outside. He could definitely relate to the Nation's religion with its base being hatred of the white man and violence. Prison time was the best training for membership there was and it was basically a school for tuning up the hate.

Now that he was out the streets were beginning to beckon him again and keeping the parole and the job going at the same time was about all he could do. Thoughts of making a run for it haunted him day and night. The alcohol and pot were starting to lack the kick he needed and the heroin was starting to sound good again. He went out a little last night to look for some sex and some white hooker working Grand Avenue clipped him for his last twenty dollars. The curfew thing was a real problem and having to live with his mother made it even worse. The old prostitute was always his problem and she hadn't changed since the day he left for prison. He thought many times about how much better off he would have been if the mean woman would have died when he was a child. Nobody would have been a worse mother not even an orphanage supervisor. She would use her kid to attract a type of johns that were head cases and throw the kid in the pile. He couldn't count the times as a child he was slapped around and fondled along with his mother for an extra buck or two by some brutal whacko she picked up off the street. He finally stopped it one night at about fifteen when some pervert insisted he do his own mother as a show and he stuck a butcher knife through him. That honky limped off with a hole clear through him and either never reported it or died. Allen's only regret was that he was too young to know to not just stick the john but to also turn the knife at the same time. He'd learned that in prison. Like Rag used to say, "you never be fingered by a dead man".

Allen felt sick on the bus trip down to Clayton. When he dropped off he leaned on the bench back and took some deep breaths as the blast of the summer heat hit him in the face. The bus ride down from the north side was slow and it seemed the air was heavier up there than here in this white town. As he recovered some and started for work he passed the fancy shops on the strip. His resentment for life stirred even deeper. *Even white folks air is different and better. These rich ass white people are the reason we live in the north city. They want to keep us in nigger town. This headache is about all I can stand. That was some bad shit I smoked last night. I should just skip work and find a place to sleep it off. I'll bet that old bastard climbs my ass when I reach the shop. Think I'll stop at the art store and scope that white bitch out. I need to get juiced for the day.*

Not being particularly mechanical using a hammer was a little clumsy for Jody. She didn't have the ladder in the best spot so she stretched out to reach the portrait hanger she just nailed to the wall. At that moment, she felt a presence in the gallery. *If I'd known I was going to hang paintings today I would have worn slacks.* Pulling down her skirt she rotated on the step ladder, looked around and the room seemed empty. Then suddenly from behind the large paintings on the easels in the center of the room, there was some motion and out stepped the negro artist from the print shop. The look on his face was a sardonic grin and he appeared to be touching himself. *Dear god he has been looking up my dress.* The man rotated and went out the door without a word. She felt a slight dose of fear and the feeling made her skin crawl. *How did he get in without setting off the door chime? Byrd is right about this guy.*

The print shop's putrid chemical smell turned his stomach every morning when Allen entered the place. With the hangover from last night this particular morning the smell was even worse. It reminded him of the disinfectant they used to clean cell floors in the lockup. *Hell of a note to have a job where the first thing each day is a reminder of my years in prison.* Still a little excited from the confrontation with the white woman in the art store he settled in to stacking some boxes that were obviously ready for delivery. *Looks like this old motherfucker is going to send me right back out in the heat.*

"Allen those boxes have to go over to an attorney on Delmar as soon as possible", old man Kelley said as he came out of his office.

"You expect me to carry both of those clear over there?" he replied.

"No Mrs. Kelley will take you in the truck. It's just they need to go right now."

Having talked to the parole officer, the Kelley's decided not to mention it to Allen and to just tell him the officer wanted to see him. Letting him leave early might get him out the door before he realized what was happening. Being Friday he would be paid up so hopefully they would not see him again. They wanted to avoid any confrontation if possible because at this point it seemed it could get violent.

"Oh, by the way your parole officer called and he wants to see you this afternoon. You can leave early to make it over there," Kelley said.

"What does he want I ain't scheduled till next week," Braburn replied.

"Didn't say, probably just needs you to sign something," Kelley lied.

Riding in the delivery truck with the reverend's wife Braburn was sullen. *This meeting don't make sense. There is no way they would want a meeting on Friday with one already scheduled in two days. This old white fucker is lying to me.* He glanced over at Mrs. Kelley as she drove. *Her ass is in a knot and she ain't acting right.* He began to seethe as he realized the Kelleys were sending him packing. *I've only been out three months and now no job. With no job and no reference my ass is in a crack. No matter what they decide I'm not going back to prison, that's for sure.*

*   *   *   *

If this keeps up it's going to be one of my biggest tip days yet thought Byrd as he quickly cleared the sidewalk table so he could seat two of the four waiting couples. He came in late today but this five o'clock rush was going to make up for the lost tip revenue from this morning. The Friday afternoon happy hour crowd always tipped good although he would earn it today. The summer heat was a drag when working the sidewalk tables. As he glanced over at the art store he wondered where Jody was as she usually waved out the front door before locking it when she left. Maybe he missed her. As he picked up a tray to head for the kitchen a scream from one of the far tables pierced the rush hour traffic sounds. He rotated and looked up to see a large red and white object fall through the art store door and crumple on the sidewalk. As he dropped the tray he realized it was a person wrapped in a blood-soaked sheet. It was all surreal. At first he thought it was someone redheaded then he realized it was bloody hair. From the rear of the crowd someone yelled out, "Oh my god it's Jody."

*　　　*　　　*　　　*

The St Louis county police headquarters was throttling down for the weekend. Lieutenant Westburg wasted most of the day stuck in the office trying to unravel a bureaucratic paperwork mess down in the evidence lockup. As he mumbled something under his breath regarding the lockup supervisor's mother the phone rang with a mic patch to a street cruiser.

"You better get down here Buzz we got a bad one. Arts International in Clayton, assault and probably a rape. Woman about late twenties. Don't think she'll make it. Massive head injuries. They just loaded her, taking her to County hospital," said Sergeant Johnson the scene supervisor

"O K, any suspects or witnesses," he replied.

"No, looks like the son-of-a-bitch just strolled out the back door. I've already got the print guy on the door knob. It's a bad one Buzz. Matter of fact as bad as I've seen."

"Have you secured the area?　Isn't there a restaurant next door?"

"Requested witnesses and emptied it. The rest of the stores are closed. We have men around the whole strip mall. I've already called county to see if they have any "possibles" on file."

Westburg picked up his service revolver from his desk drawer and headed for his car. *That "bad as I've seen comment" is pretty strong. Johnson's been around a while.*

Arriving at the scene he could see what Johnson meant with blood pools on the sidewalk in front of the store and a bloody sheet still lying at the front door. Johnson was inside directing the evidence personnel as the Lieutenant entered. A trail of blood lead to the rear of the display area and continued around behind the service counter. It appeared the assault took place behind the counter and she apparently come-to enough to stagger out the front door.

82

Westburg couldn't help but notice that none of the paintings on easels near the front of the store were disturbed. The man obviously completely surprised and overpowered the woman.

"This one's a mad dog Buzz. I've never seen anyone whose head was in that bad a shape, at least not anyone still alive. Looks like he used the hammer on her skull, face was unrecognizable, mouth full of loose teeth, identified her with the driver's license in her purse. Soles, lives on Watson Road near Olive. Already sent someone to get her old man and take him to the hospital. At this point we're assuming it was a rape. The cash box was still in the desk and there was some cash still in her purse," said Johnson.

"Looks like he waited to jump her until she was out of sight of the windows. There doesn't seem to have been a struggle out here in front. That means the son-of-a-bitch was worried about drawing attention from the restaurant," replied Westburg.

"Along with the hammer we also found a kitchen paring knife on the floor behind the counter. Looks like he used his fists on her during the rape then beat her unconscious and finally decided to finish her off with the hammer and the paring knife. Funny, it looked like he used the knife on her eyelids. Also stuck her pretty good in the chest and the stomach. The eyelid thing is kind of odd," Johnson remarked.

Buzz returned to the cruiser to call in. He couldn't believe how unlikely it was someone from the café next door didn't notice or hear anything. Suddenly the radio came to life. It was the sheriff's office calling back on the "possibles" request. A female voice from the speakers broke the silence.

"Lieutenant, there is one here that might be of major interest to you. Name is Braburn. Allen Braburn. Negro, thirty-four years old, three life sentences for two rape convictions and a robbery, paroled three months ago after fifteen years in Jeff City. Works at a print shop about three blocks from your scene. I've also got a Northside address for him. Apparently lives with his mother up there."

"Good get everything you've got over to our office as soon as you can. Give those details to Johnson," he replies as Johnson approaches the car with an armload of evidence bags and envelopes.

"Did you get her clothes? The Lieutenant asked.

"Yea, there's a white sweater that's covered with blood. Looks like he stuffed it in her mouth to silence her," said Johnson.

"Good chance this Braburn is our boy. Get the hammer over to prints ASAP. Address is his mother's place up on the Northside. Get someone in plain clothes up there to watch the house as soon as you can. He may have something he wants to take with him when he runs. Send Sergeant Rush if you can. He's the right color and knows that neighborhood. Fill Rush in good on this boy's history. The son-of-a-bitch could be dangerous. Remember as far as he knows he thinks he killed the woman and has nothing to lose.

As the radio crackled back to life it was the dispatcher calling with the report from the ambulance.

"Just wanted to let you know the last we've heard from the hospital Buzz. The woman went straight to surgery for the head injuries so she's still alive. Should we send someone over there?" he asked.

"Yea, get some uniforms in the hall and tell them to park the black and white at the emergency room dock. Make it obvious we are on the scene," he replied.

"Now that I think of it, also maybe should get some surveillance of the woman's home too. This boy was locked up in Jeff for quite a while, good chance he is wired with the Nation."

*   *   *   *

Dr. Stricker pulled the scrubs shirt off stripping down to his tee shirt as he walked down the hall headed for the family conference room. It was extra cool in the surgical unit and the rest of the building seemed a little warm. He was exhausted and slightly light headed from operating on an emergency assault victim for three hours. As he walked, he thought about his own daughter and the fact she was walking the same streets as the animal that administered the punishment to the woman they just finished in O.R. three. It was unthinkable someone could do that kind of damage with their bare hands. Speaking to a family was always a tough thing for him but at least this time he wouldn't have to break bad news. The patient was perking up, vital sign wise. He checked on her before leaving recovery. He wouldn't have given her a chance in hell when they rolled her in and he pulled the sheets. The head injury was almost as bad as the car wreck victim he lost in surgery a few weeks ago. It was hard to believe someone did this with their bare hands. The stress of the two hours of picking bone splinters one piece at a time was showing in his face and as he entered the room, he was thinking about the martini that was waiting for him at home.

"I'm Bob Stricker. I assume you are the husband; Soles is it?" he asked.

"Yes. I'm Tom Soles," was the guarded reply.

"Your wife's in recovery and her condition right now is still very critical. She has several small wounds but the big thing is the head trauma. The right frontal portion of her skull is basically missing. It was pulverized and broken into small shards of bone. The issue with this type of injury is bone splinter penetration of the membrane that covers the brain between the brain itself and the skull. After I removed the bone fragments I examine the membrane with magnifiers before closing the wound and could not find a single incidence of compromised membrane. That in itself is a miracle.

There is a small stab wound just below her navel and one to her chest very near her heart both missing anything vital. There were also slight stab wounds to her eyelids but they were not very deep. Of course, the facial trauma to both cheeks and her nose can't really be evaluated until the swelling goes down. We packed her nose temporarily and it could require attention once we can see what we are dealing with. Basically, the cheek bones are intact and the nose can be fixed so her appearance should restore very well but it will take some time. Most of her upper teeth where loose and some were so bad they required removal before we could even intubate her for the respirator. The dental will have to be evaluated by an oral surgeon later. The bottom line is she has an excellent chance of recovering physically from this but there is no guarantee there will be no permanent residual effects to her brain. The missing skull may warrant a plate after she completely heals but actually now the missing bone is a good thing. She has some brain swelling and the organ itself has a little room to expand with the bone gone. They will keep her for a while in recovery then take her to the I C U. She will be on a respirator at least for a while as they will sedate her. Best thing for you folks is to go home and try to rest as you are going to need it in the next few days. She is young and strong. The indications are that her vitals are moving in the right direction. I personally think she has an excellent chance."

As he exited the room and headed down the hall he couldn't help but notice the uniformed policeman in the hall near the intensive care unit. *For Christ sake, guards in intensive care. That woman has four small children. What to hell are things coming to. Maybe it's time to buy a gun.*

CHAPTER 6

THE PROJECT

"Hey, Captain this is the Skipper, were in the hell have you been? I called everyone trying to locate you, including your mother. She gave me this number in Phoenix," the urgent voice on the phone barked.

"Jimmy, what to hell are you doing. I haven't heard from you since Florida and leaving for the service," Chris replied.

"I know man, miss my old diving buddy. Got a project here that requires someone with a secret clearance. Ballistics related. That is all I can tell you on the phone. I need somebody right away; somebody just like you. How would you like to move to Tennessee for a while?" Jim asked.

"What's the deal?" he asked.

"I'm wired with the Feds these days. I left Florida when the engine project ended right after you left and started a grant mill here in Tennessee across the street from the Arnold Research Facility. You remember Arnold where we ran the jet engine test a few years back. Started my own business. Just won a priority grant to do some work for the FAA. Highest of priorities but I need an engineer that's a free thinker. This is a problem they want solved right now. It will require some original design. It fits you perfectly, needs an idea man, can't discuss it over a phone. Can you come down here ASAP for a sit down? I'll make you an offer you can't refuse."

"O K, get me a ticket to, I guess Nashville, and reserve me a car. As I recall the damn airbase is in the boondocks and we got there through Nashville.

"Yea, that's right. Got a great office setup though. If I can produce this thing will be a money machine," Jim replied.

"I'll drive down from Nashville to your place. Call me back with the arrangements," he replied.

"We will try for day after tomorrow. You should make plans to stay here couple of days. We'll have a couple of cold ones. I have already checked and your security clearance from the old days is still intact. They will only have to check your days in the Army to renew it. Please tell me they won't find anything. You didn't knock-up some Generals daughter or go AWOL or anything did you?" teased Jim.

"Not to my knowledge but you never know," he answered chuckling.

"We need to hit the ground running on this thing and the sooner the better. I will have my girl here confirm at this number as soon as she has the travel arrangements nailed down. Ticket will be waiting for you at the airport in Phoenix," replied Jim

"Alright I'll see you then," Chris said attempting to hang up.

"Be good to see you buddy. We can catch up on lost time when you get here. I wasn't sure you were still out there. Still got all your body parts?"

"Oh yea, they cut me loose about three months ago. Picked up the GTO in St Louis and have been bumming ever since, mostly in the west. I missed my old skiing partner when I went through Squaw Valley a few weeks ago and got a snow fix. It's been a good run and a vacation. I also have some new adventure stories you'll enjoy. We will sit down over a beer or two and talk about the old days. See you in two days," Chris replied hanging up the phone.

The days in Phoenix were getting a little slow and Jeannie was getting more and more clingy. He was not ready to settle down and she was, so the whole affair was getting awkward. *Maybe it is time to move on. I hope this doesn't get messy.*

88

He worked with Jim at aircraft companies in Seattle and Florida when he first left the University and they formed a friendship. They were entry-level engineers together. In Florida, they would spend the weekends together on the beaches and boating. They both invested in boats to enjoy the gulf stream waters. Jim's was a sailboat and his was a powerboat, thus the nicknames Skipper and Captain. Those were good days as kids before life started dealing out reality. Besides getting some real-world work experiences at the wind tunnels around the country, they spent most weekends out on the salt water and learned to sail and navigate in their boats and deal with the sea.

He would tell Jeannie it was strictly a friendship trip since he did not want to stir her suspicions. With this opportunity, it might be a good time to make a move and break it off with her. In addition, the desert was getting kind of old and he was ready to do something productive. *This might be the right thing at the right time all the way around.* After all, it was three months since his discharge. A big plus was this sounded like a project job of pure engineering design and it would be short term. The duration appealed to him. He still wanted to see some more of the country before completely settling down to a career type position. This could be a good interim project and a little money would not hurt either.

The weather out of Nashville delayed his flight so he was late getting to the Air Base. Pulling into the parking lot at the research building, he couldn't help but notice how tranquil and nice the facility looked. Jim's company sign and logo high on the front of the white stucco single story office building gave off a professional aura. A nicely landscaped courtyard with a concrete pedestal near the front surrounded the entrance. On the pedestal three separate flagpoles stood up in the brisk southern breeze. From left to right there was Old Glory, the Tennessee State flag and the Company logo. According to Jim, NASA built the building for research and then gave it up to the University of Tennessee for small business military oriented research. The University now managed it and rented floor space to independent contractors for grant based research geared to Aerospace. It backed up to a large lake that supplied cooling water for the rocket test facilities down the road at the Arnold labs. The cleared site opened with a lawn out to the road. A heavy woods surrounded the building but hid the lake behind it. The rear of the building bordered the lake with a view of the University campus on the other side. There was a long asphalt lane that served as the entrance to the parking lot and the lot was full of cars. The place gave off good karma. It appeared something important was happening there. The work setting fit scientific people and pleased him. *This will certainly do for a while.*

The fresh Tennessee air brought back something that was missing in the desert as Chris walked up to the reception area of the building. As he stepped inside he immediately saw Jim bouncing up the hall with a grin.

"Hey Captain, saw you pull in. How was your trip?" he asked.

"Good, wasn't sure I could find the place anymore", Chris answered as they shook hands.

"Marg, visitor badge him and take him to the conference room and I'll get a couple of coffees. Black, right?" Jim asked.

"Yea," he replied.

"Oh, I got the clearance stuff on you from the bureau already. They sent it over by courier this morning. That should give you an idea of how hot they are for this project. No problems with that stuff so we can discuss this thing today. Why didn't you mention you got a bronze star over there in Viet Nam? That will help with the follow-up grant proposals on this project. Government agencies love that type of thing," Jim said.

The conference room's large heavy oak table surrounded by a dozen blue upholstered chairs with wooden arms looked official. The room jutted out from the main building into the courtyard. Frosted glass blocks floor to ceiling formed the arc of the outer wall in a continuous curve. With the maroon drapes open, it was very well lit but at the same time no one could see through from the outside. There was a door from the hall at each end and between the doors on the inner wall there was full-length black board. The glass bricks captured some heat from the sun so it was a little warm inside. He shed his sport jacket, loosened his tie, took a chair at the end of the table and retrieved his note pad from his briefcase.

When Jim entered the room he was alone and his demeanor was of someone that was under the gun and in a hurry. He appeared flustered and on the edge of having too much going to do.

"I never mentioned it but my old lady ran off just before I left Florida. Bitch got involved with the guy she was working for right under my nose. We divorced a little less than a year ago. Honestly, I'm still getting over it," Jim commented.

"Gotta go on down the road buddy. I'm living proof of that. I kind of wondered about her before I left. You know the old saying "husband's the last one to know". Take it from me it will end up being the best thing that ever happened to you."

"I hope so. O K, here's the deal. Remember in the old days when we were flying back and forth from Florida to the Langley wind tunnels in Virginia every week? They were hijacking about every other flight to Cuba. Well, this project is geared to solving that problem. The FAA wants us to develop some concepts to neutralize a hijacker inside an airliner's cabin while in flight. Our company won the grant for the ballistics side of the proposal some other group got the chemical side. In other words, we are looking for a way to put a bullet in a hijacker inside an airliner without him knowing it and most of all without compromising the skin of the bird. A hole in the skin could mean an aircraft decompression and blowout resulting in a crash. That is not an option. The number one design specification is to ensure that could not possibly happen. This starts with a blank piece of paper buddy, the more original the idea the better. The FAA figures they are going to have to ice one of these clowns and make the news to stop it. Tell me you're in so I can settle my staffing issues with the feds today and tell them we are in motion. These government types are paranoid as hell and have their nose up your hind end constantly. It kind of drives me crazy putting up with them," Jim said.

"I haven't followed the hijacking since I left, is it getting worse? I remember we used to call National Airlines "Air Cuba" when we were shuttling back and forth from Palm Beach to Langley and Hartford. I was nervous as hell because I was usually traveling with a briefcase full of classified wind tunnel data and they seemed to be taking a plane a week there for a while. When I mentioned it, the brass said I should eat the wind tunnel data papers if it happened. Remember I carried that salt shaker in the briefcase as a joke."

"Yea I remember that, the old man didn't think it was funny as I recall but the rest of us did," Jim replied.

"Alright, I'll go back and get my car. Everything I own is in it so the move will be simple. Give me about three days max. Got a little baggage there that I will have to deal with but it's been coming anyway. I'll go ahead and fly back this evening," he said.

"I'll put you on the payroll as of today and get you a travel advance. You just start thinking about the problem. The agency people will be in here the first of next week so they will want a concept or two laid out for them. My secretary will go ahead and get your security credentials and permanent I D badge in process. I will introduce you to the rest of the staff here when you get back. You'll be the senior man on this project and of all the different things we are working on this one has priority. Anything you want or need modeled will go to the head of the line in purchasing and the machine shop," Jim said.

As his flight approached Phoenix airport the view out the window was of the mountains that surrounded the city. All the days and nights with a special girl connected him and Jeannie at the hip. He probably should have cut this off sooner. He knew all along there was no way he was ready to settle down. There was hopefully some way to announce the fact he was leaving without all the unpleasantness of a face-to-face breakup. Undoubtedly, she was the best female experience of his life but hooking up permanently with a wife right now was not in the cards. One thing he knew though, he did not want her hurt. He hoped they could have one last night together but if not he really didn't have much to get together to pack and head out.

Jeannie was waiting on the airport arrival ramp and she slid over so he could drive home. Pulling off the ramp and merging onto the interstate, there was deafening silence in the car. She broke it with the standard question.

"How was your trip? I thought you were staying two days."

"Things changed when I arrived. Some of the people I needed to see were called away," he lied.

"You don't have to lie," she replied. "I figured it out lying awake last night. You're leaving aren't you?"

"Yes, I accepted a job with these guys. I am going to Tennessee for a few months. You know I've told you all along I would eventually leave. I'm just not ready to settle down," he answered keeping his gaze straight ahead.

"When?" she replied.

"In the morning or right now, that's up to you", he answered as he made eye contact for the first time since entering the car.

"In the morning, I want one last night together. I always knew you would eventually leave. When I fell in love with you, I accepted it wouldn't be permanent. You are a very romantic episode in my life and truthfully, I don't regret our time together. I will miss you though," she said tearing up slightly.

*　　　*　　　*　　　*

The summer seemed to pass in a flash but the late summer Tennessee heat slowed the prototyping and production of the device. The design rolled off the drawing boards smoothly but the physical logistics of getting the device produced was full of the usual people problems. Everyone on the staff was dragging from the intense pressure of the project all summer and tempers occasionally flared. All in all, things clicked off smoothly and the progress pleased the management. The staff set the deadline to demonstrate the device but hadn't completed all the FAA required proof tests. There was no way to make the completion date other than to put in the time so the whole place went into an overtime project completion mode for several weeks. The summer was pleasant as even the weather seemed to cooperate. The intense engineering work and pressure felt good after being away from it for so long but Chris was definitely ready for some relief.

The chosen design consisted of a thin plastic form fitted breastplate an individual could wear strapped to their chest. A specially designed shirt concealed it. The device was small with a shallow chamber the length of a thirty-two caliper bullet in the center. A miniaturized firing mechanism concealed between the pectoral muscles of the wearer would fire the cartridge. A well-built man could wear it under the loose fitting shirt almost completely undetected. The firing mechanism was a remote transmitter activated by either the shooter or an accomplice. The concept was for the assassin to walk up to the target either from the front or the rear, take aim using some body position parameters and put a bullet in the target's chest or back hopefully hitting his heart. With the kill shot not guaranteed the slug, made from a powdered metal could be laced with cyanide. The powdered metal composition of the slug insured it would not penetrate the fuselage of the plane in case it passed clear through the target or completely missed. The whole idea was to get close enough to drop the hijacker in his tracks while smiling or even giving him a kiss. The conclusion was there would have to be some training for the operator but the lab tests were promising. The final proof tests scheduled for mid-August left only three weeks to get everything finished. In addition, the FAA wanted three working prototypes supplied with the final design report so the shop was on overtime. The tight lead times made for strained nerves. Things moved through design and prototyping and a live test with the actual device scheduled for the weekend looked doable. The weekend test time would minimize the "looky-lous" that firing test always attracted from the offices. This was a "need to know" project and less people meant less gossip.

As Saturday morning rolled around a small group gathered at the crude firing range set up on the edge of the lake. Chris stopped by his office on the way to the range and picked up the device and the test ammo. He couldn't help but be somewhat aggravated that the word was out and so many people were present. *Guess everyone wants to see someone kill themselves. Human nature never ceases to amaze.* As he strolled out the back door to the test range he was a little aggravated with the commotion at the firing site.

"Settle down gentlemen. Show time," Chris said entering the range.

"Did you bring the tit sling?" asked Jerry the lab tech.

The formal name for the device was the ballistic breastplate but the crew nicknamed the device "the tit sling" because it did closely resemble a woman's bra.

"I've only got five rounds of ammo so we have to make 'em count."

Everyone was a little nervous, as up to this point all testing employed body mannequins salvaged from a local clothing store. Today was the first scheduled test with someone wearing and firing the device. The crew's apprehension showed and the moment reminded Chris of other projects when the time came to employ a design. Typically, all his engineering insecurities bubbled up as this was the moment of truth. Those feelings were nagging at the back of his mind at that moment. The question was always what if there is something no one considered and what could be the consequences. All the tests so far came off without a hitch but everyone was antsy about firing a live round next to their body. If something fouled up there could be some injuries.

Yanking his polo shirt over his head he unfolded the sling and slipped his arms through the straps. "Who's first in the barrel?" he said jokingly.

He wasn't about to let anyone else take the first risk and besides all the positioning and targeting calculations were his numbers. He turned around asking for help to fasten it in the back.

"O K you sons-a-bitches, no photo's. I don't want anyone passing around pictures and accusing me of being a cross dresser and wearing a bra," he joked to ease the tension.

Everyone laughed as he buttoned the dress shirt that was specially fabricated to cover the device. The shirt button positions insured they would not interfere with the projectile. The shirt cloth was a pressed powder of cellulose that would disintegrate from the bow shock of the moving slug. The accuracy depended on the slug making a clean exit from the device. With the short little barrel only as long as the cartridge itself, controlling the projectile path was the main issue. As he stepped up to within about three feet of the mannequin, he positioned his body then turned and grinned yelling "fire in the hole". Turning back, he hit the remote button and the small caliber bullet went off right on queue. His first response was to note that there was very little recoil against his chest and no sensation of heat at all.

"Good shot", yelled Jerry as the rest of the crew broke out in applause.

The small slug entered just to the left of the mannequin's heart area and would certainly have been a kill shot especially with the cyanide considered. The bullet disintegrated as designed when it passed through the target model and hit the sand bag backstop. It only left a gray spot on the bag and performed just as designed. *This thing will work but it's going to take a cold-blooded son-of-a-bitch to use it. Better hope the hijacker doesn't have bad breath because you are sure as hell going to be close enough to smell it.*

As he removed the device he barked off instructions to the crew.

"Alright guys get some more ammo pronto. We will need probably fifty rounds to do all the qualification tests. Call the supplier and tell him to get on it and have it shipped airfreight. Write up a test schedule. We will test around the clock until finished. I want all tests completed and the reports written before the FAA engineers show up in two weeks. If you want to fire it go ahead and take a shot but save one of those four rounds just in case something comes up before we get more."

The tests could not have come off any better but the actual firing did point out one flaw in the design. The device needed a manual trigger in addition to the hand held remote. Something that would fire the round in an emergency. Something fastened to the sling itself that could hand trigger the firing of the cartridge. As he walked back into his office he mentally worked a possible design for the trigger modifications in his head. What he visualized could be part of the cocking mechanism. It would not require any major changes and was simple enough to allow revisions to meet the deadlines. When he entered his office to close out the day he noticed two white plastic capsules a little larger than a jellybean in a small box marked secret. He dialed Jim's office for an explanation.

"Hey Skipper, did you leave this classified stuff laying open on my desk," he asked.

"Oh man, I walked out of there and it slipped my mind. Glad you are the one that found them," Jim replied.

"What is it?" he asked.

"Those are samples of the real ammo that will be used for the application. Less the cyanide that is. Those two aren't lethal. Just for show. The capsules pull apart and the bullets are inside. Lock them in your desk and give the box to Mary," Jim replied.

The August humidity hit him as he headed to his car to end a bitch of a Friday. It was two weeks since the live fire tests and the last of the FAA sign offs. The last week was hectic trying to follow up on the live firing test results and he was ready for some down time. Walking to his car, he could not believe how well the sign off meeting went. Everything was in place to answer the FAA's questions right on queue and the whole government bunch seemed really pleased with the design and performance of the device. There was a slight glow of accomplishment emanating from his crew when they left the meeting. The engineering was original from concept through production and everyone knew it. Jim was on cloud nine, as the completion bonuses would make this project very profitable for the company. At least it was Friday and this weekend would be his first one off all summer. With the pressure suddenly gone he couldn't help but think about Jeannie and wonder what she was doing. He was missing her suddenly and wondering if maybe it was a mistake leaving her like he did. He thought about planning an evening out to try to get back into the social world. The best thing was he could sleep late tomorrow. As he neared his car Jim yelled out the door, "Hey Captain, there is phone call for you. It's your brother. Says it's an emergency."

As he jogged back to the reception desk he felt a slight adrenalin rush because he knew this wasn't good. His first thought was something happened to one of his parents. He picked up the receiver with a sudden knot in his stomach.

"Yea, John what is it," he said.

"It's Jody she's been assaulted. They are not sure she is going to make it. They have her in surgery right now. Guy jumped her at work and caved her head in with a hammer. She is in County Hospital here in St Louis. I just got here and realized no one called you. Think you need to come up because it is bad, really bad. Mom's a basket case," his brother replied.

"O K let me think a minute. What happened? Was it robbery or rape or do they know?"

"Rape, but the guy tried to kill her and left her for dead. They already think they know who it was and supposedly they are looking for him. You won't believe it. She is beat to a pulp. Tom didn't recognize her when they called him to the hospital. He told them that's not Jody. Can you come? This bunch is going to need you if she doesn't make it," John replied.

"Alright I'll catch the next thing out of Nashville. I'll call you from the airport when I know the flight. You can pick me up at Lambert. Will you be at this number?"

"Yea, I'm at the house with the kids and will be for the night. Get this, it looks like the son of a bitch belongs to the Black Nation and the police told us to watch the kids. Can you believe that? "John replied with tension in his voice.

"You got a gun?"

"No."

"O K my old 20-gauge rabbit gun is in Jody's closet and there is a box of shells in the garage on one of the shelves. I left it when I picked up the car. Load it, put the kids to bed all in one room and stay up with your eyes open all night. Shoot first and ask questions later. Those shells are bird shot so you will have to be close to kill someone but you will at least knock them down and they will wish they were dead."

As he ran across the parking lot to head for the airport he vowed to himself "if my sister dies I'm going to kill this guy".

CHAPTER 7

BOSTON

"Elija it's Malik. I'm hurtin' man," he says softly.

"Yea, we were wonderin'. You all over the T V news. Where you right now?" a low voice asked.

"Pay phone on the east side of the river. It's Crenson Street near the river under the bridge."

"Ok that's a good spot. I know where it is, just stay put. Our people say every police motherfucker in St Louis is looking for your ass. You got no chance in hell here. We must move you right now. I'll send someone. Look for a green Fairlane. It will be Shab Abdul. He will bring you a change of clothes and put you in his trunk. He will have some hair clippers so cut the fro down to the bone and don't shave your face for a while. Be about ten minutes so lay low till you see his sheen. Have you talked to anyone else?" asked Elija.

"Just my mother," he replied.

"You didn't go by her crib did you? asked Elija.

"No, I caught the bus and came across the river. Figured I could blend in better over here where no one knows me. Where can I go?" he replied.

"It will be Boston or Oakland. We haven't decided yet but you be safe wherever it is if we can get you out of St Louis."

Standing near the phone booth, it was still daylight. Braburn couldn't stop shaking as all the horror of his years in prison flashed before him again. Right then it was him against the rest of the world just like when he entered prison. As he glanced down he could see his hands were purple and swollen. At least his mind was starting to settle some. Taking stock of his situation he looked down at the skinned knuckles on his right hand. There was also visible blood on

101

his shoes. If he's stopped these things would be a dead give away. When he left that store, he went out the back door and washed the blood off his hands in the lavatory. *How could I have been such a dumb nigger? My prints will be on the facet handles. It won't matter much cause the bitch is still breathing so she will finger my ass anyway. They will have me cold and that's it.* As the events of the day raced through his mind he feels there is no way out. He vows to himself he will not to be taken alive.

*   *   *   *

The cramped ride in the old Fairlane was coming to an end. They were approaching Boston and the lights of the city gave off a low glow on the horizon. He could smell of salt air once they crossed the river into Connecticut and it was new to him. The traffic seemed heavy for predawn but this highway was the major route around Long Island sound. They were on the road solid for over two days with Abdul doing the driving. Lucky there were enough bennies to keep everyone awake but Abdul seemed a little edgy. Malik was ready to get to the safe house in Roxbury before the cat started coming down from the dope. He knew people on Benzedrine come unglued when the juice starts wearing off. The trip out of St Louis was tense with trying to change clothes and cut his hair in the car. They relaxed a little when they reached Indiana and called in as the street reports from St Louis said the cops were still concentrating on the local area. His appearance changes with the bald head and the three-day beard would help. He heard reports that the Nation owned the Roxbury district with the Black Nation center being there. The Boston authorities stayed away for political reasons to keep the peace. The riots all over the country when they killed King put the fear of god in most local politicians. Plus, the leaders of the Nation knew how to shake their trees and use the fear factor of Black Power

102

by getting in the papers. The whole thing was a source of pride to hear of a place where the black man ruled. He was starting to breathe easy for the first time since leaving St Louis and was beginning to think he might be safe here.

"You gonna' like it here man," said Abdul as they approached the community center.

"There is some righteous pussy hanging around this place. The kind that the onlyist thing they want is to make a man from the Nation happy. To tell the truth, I volunteered for this run cause of that. I'm gonna' stay up here a few days and get some of the action. Thought at first they was gonna' send you to Oakland and I wasn't for that at all. You a lucky man today."

*　　　*　　　*　　　*

Malik could not believe how things shook out. The Nation settled him into a waiting apartment with everything prearranged. A place to live, a full set of I.D.s and even a beautiful eighteen-year-old girl were all ready and waiting. The power of the organization made him, for the first time in his life, feel invincible like no one could touch him. The people in charge of the center never even questioned him. They just seemed to know his needs and hand him a complete new life without saying a word. They gave him a paid job organizing the petition drives which amounted to getting people together to collect thousands of signatures on blank petition sheets. The Nation filled them in as needed and it gave them the power to produce a petition protest anything they wanted at a moment's notice. The whole thing impressed him. The planning and design was pure genius. Combining religion and race provided a double edge sword against the law. The Nation could plaster any issue they wanted to push in the papers and the television news with immediate maximum exposure.

The St Louis leader decreed his place in the organization. No one in Boston ever asked him any questions regarding his past. The Nation owned the streets in Roxbury and at the same time paid for it all with cash from government grants issued under the guise of community service work. There were very seldom even any cops around especially near the Center. He felt so comfortable he even let his fro and goatee grow back out. Allen Braburn was dead. Malik Jakim roamed the streets at will and everyone knew him and catered to his position. It was a little difficult playing the holy role but he was getting better and better at that all the time. His woman worshiped him and even secretly supplied a little dope on occasion because she knew he liked it. They would spend their nights together high and having sex. She was intrigued and motivated sexually by all the deviant things he learned in prison. His art was a required interest as it made his original bones with the Nation. He was doing some classes at the Community Center and for the first time in his life he resembled a real citizen.

*　　　*　　　*　　　*

The months passed and Jody healed. With the exception of the missing skull, her hair and face were back close to normal. Working the hair-do just so-so, covered the head scars and her teeth were repaired with bridges, compliments of the art store owner's insurance. It was remarkable how little work her nose required and it was a godsend she didn't have to endure the pain of a complete reconstruction. She did suffer from headaches occasionally but they were tolerable with pain medication. Although physically healed the mental agony of the memories of the rape and beating, and the continual fear of seeing her assailant again on the street, were always present. When out on the street driving she was petrified at every stoplight to look over and see who was in the next car for fear it would be Braburn. She couldn't shake the fear and could not go out alone. The police didn't even have a sniff of a clue on Braburn's whereabouts and the officers did not give much encouragement and mostly just made excuses. The police tried to convince the family the chances of Braburn being in the St Louis area were very slim but that didn't provide peace of mind. The only one who offered her any encouragement was Buzz. He would call and give her a rundown on things that were in motion at the police department. Both he and Sergeant Rush genuinely seemed to have a personal interest in catching Braburn and there was some security for the family, knowing it was a priority for the two of them.

The months came and went and the fear issue finally forced a family decision to make a move and get out of the city. So when an opportunity to take over a small business in Jody's old home town of Maysville presented itself, the family decided to take it. Contributing to the decision was the fact in a lily white town of three thousand people, any negro strangers would be noticed immediately unlike in the city. That provided some comfort. The move went pleasantly smooth and they settled into their new hometown with minimal hassle. The whole thing brought some new peace to her life. They rented a nice older two story and the kids settled into school and already made friends. The small community fell in behind her and the church family was the same as when she was a kid. The Catholic Church and school were a local institution and served the whole community as well as it parishioners. She attended it as a child so the familiarity helped relieve some of the constant anxiety she felt since the incident. She was finally comfortable with going out alone again and the whole environment provided some freedoms that were stolen.

The sound of the phone broke the silence of the afternoon as Jody stood in the winter sun from the windows in the living room and ironed waiting for the kids to come home. When she answered it, she was surprised the local priest was calling.

"Jody, this is Father Dollet down at the church. I was wondering if you could come down and talk to me. I have a problem over at the school. Mrs. Fratman has been diagnosed with cancer and she is going in for treatment. She can't finish the semester and I was wondering if you could take her classes through the end of the year."

"You know father, I only have two years of college and no certificate," she replied.

"Don't worry about that we can get around the state as a parochial school in an emergency. Her classes are first and second grade and we just follow the diocese guidelines so the lesson plans are laid out in black and white. Guarantee you won't have a problem with it. I can't pay a lot but your kids tuition will be thrown in."

"Let me talk to Tom and get back to you at the rectory this evening," she said hanging up.

"This might be divine intervention. It is dull during the day at home without the kids and we could use a little extra money. Surely, Tom will not object, I'm going to do it.

Redialing the phone, she felt a rush of confidence that hadn't been there since the assault.

"Father, it's Jody. I will do it. When do I start?" she said.

"Tomorrow, when you pick the kids up this afternoon come in the office and fill out the paperwork and I'll give you the keys to the classroom," he replied.

It was a nice sunny Saturday morning with the May sun promising a Missouri spring day free of any sever weather. The tornados were in the area the day before and things were a little tense at school. The kids were out playing in a yard up the street and Jody was doing the morning dishes trying to get the house ready for company. She was looking forward to some girlfriends coming over later in the afternoon to catch up on the local gossip. Tom was at the business working and she was enjoying the peace of it all. *Maybe things could be normal again here in the small town.* As she looked out the small window above the sink, she noticed a strange black car with what seemed liked exceptionally large black wall tires turn the corner. *That car doesn't fit this town.* It pulled up onto the side street next to the house and stopped over on the grass in the shallow ditch near their sidewalk. Out stepped two large men, one white and one black both wearing suits and looking grim. A chill ran through her as she watched intently. When they started up the sidewalk toward the back door of the house there was a flood of relief when she recognized one of them as Lieutenant Westburg from the St Louis County P.D.

"Don't tell me you finally have news for me," she said as they entered the back porch.

"Yea, looks like we got our boy," he replied sitting down at the large round dining table.

"This is Sergeant Rush from County. He's one of our lead investigators on this case," the Lieutenant said opening a file folder from his briefcase.

"Nice to meet you Jody, although I feel like I already know you. Your case is very close to my heart I want you to know," said the Sergeant.

"Braburn was caught applying for a passport under an alias in Boston. He was headed for Europe to go study art on a government grant. Can you believe it? Apparently, the Black Nation has been hiding him there in the Roxbury district under the name Malik Jakim. The Feds noticed him from a hot sheet when they reviewed the passport application and sent two men to pick him up. When they went to arrest him, he made a run for it and jumped out of a third story window at the community center where he worked. He tore the ligaments in both knees when he landed so they have him in the medical unit at the Suffolk County lockup in Boston. At the moment he can't even walk but regardless he is definitely off the street," said Buzz.

"Thank god. Where does this thing go from here?" she asked.

"Next step is extradition and the prosecutor's office is cutting that paperwork as we speak. Then we will bring him back to Missouri and put him on trial," the Lieutenant answered. "I'll personally go to Boston to get him myself."

"Then we will send him back to the cave he came from and never hear from him again," Sergeant Rush added.

"I've never been involved in any type of legal stuff so I don't know what to expect. How long will all this take and what will I have to do?" she asked.

"It depends on if he cops a plea. We have a lot of evidence so his lawyers will probably try to get him a deal. There is a good chance they will just try to save his life. This charge is eligible for the death penalty and we are going to ask for it to force their hand. I can see him pleading so it might be all over in six months. If that is the case I can't see the chance of any more paroles. He will never get out again. I know that's what you want to hear."

"There is one complication though Jody," interrupted Sergeant Rush. This person has elevated himself with the Black Nation. I hate to tell you this but they consider him special and may try to pull some strings to protect him."

"What do you mean pull some strings?" she replied with alarm.

"Well, they have been known to try to intimidate witnesses with threats and the like to get them to back off. I'm not going to lie to you. The Nation is a scary bunch. We will have your back of course but for the next few days you might want to watch your kids. Our intelligence should know within a few days if they intend to push back for him or let him go back up the river. We will be watching everything very closely. It is good you live here now because I do not think they would risk coming into this small town. It's not as if they would not be noticed but they are bold and know how to manipulate the law with their religious and racial claims. We will contact your local law enforcement and put them on alert," answered Rush.

As the black sedan drove off Jody was overwhelmed with fear again not for herself this time but for her children. *My god, what kind of people would harm my children especially after what they have already done to me. I'll call Chris. He'll know what to do.*

$$* \quad * \quad * \quad *$$

"I'm Eli Shabaz your attorney. The Nation has assigned me the job of defending you. I am here to tell you the way this will work. First of all, you will keep your mouth absolutely shut unless I tell you to say something. Second, when I do tell you to speak you will repeat my words exactly. This is very critical. You do not have to deny anything. We will deny it for you. The plan is to get you back out on the street and to pursue the race issues to keep you there. When you get out you will be tempted to run. If you do we will find you and you will go back to the pen as an orphan of the Nation. You know what your future will be then. There is only one way here and it is our way. You are just going to be a player not a thinker. Do you understand?" he asked.

"Yea," replied Malik.

"Alright listen up man. Your bond hearing is scheduled for next week. You have to get up on your feet before then, so even if it hurts get your ass up. The request for bond will be based on our claim that there is no proof Allen Braburn and Malik Jakim are the same man. We've been able to hold off your prints so it will be based on lack of evidence. At the hearing character witnesses will tout the great things Malik has done here in Roxbury. We have the Judge so you will definitely be released. You do not have to worry about that. You will be bonded out and back on the streets. The problem will be staying out. Once you are on the street there will be a newspaper campaign bragging on your work here in Roxbury with the kids and such, so be visible and paint with the kids at the center. I think the news will be friendly but watch your mouth. The big thing will be the petition we will present to the governor's office. It will be submitted with five thousand signatures requesting the governor not sign the extradition order. We are threatening to riot and burn Roxbury if he does sign it. Governors all over the country are running scared with the cities burning down around them. Their political asses are on the line and at the mercy of the black man. Until he signs it they cannot take you back into custody. We will have warning if anything is going to happen and we will get you out. Otherwise, you just stay on the street and act normal unless you hear from us. Do you understand?" he asked.

"Do I just live where I been living?" he asked.

"Yes, right back to normal man. Don't change a thing till you hear different. You need to call in twice a day though for any news or changes. That's about the only difference. I guess I don't need to warn you to do as you are told. If you fuck something up the Nation will be very unforgiving."

The warning set in as intended. There was no doubt in Malik's mind he would be protected if he maintained his loyalty and if he didn't he would be as good as dead.

110

* * * *

The office at the front of the small parochial school looked out over the off street parking area that ran along the sidewalk out in front. The sun warmed the room in the late May afternoon as Father Dollet sat at the principal's desk tallying the book bills he just received from the diocese publishers. The frustration of all the errors in the book counts frustrated him to the point of taking the lords name in vain. Paperwork was not his thing anyway and he was going to have to find one of the teachers to do this from now on. As he stood up, he noticed a green sedan pull into the front parking area and out of it stepped two large black men in suits and ties. As they headed up the sidewalk toward the front door, he stood up at the counter so he would be noticed and waited for them to enter the school. The men avoided eye contact as they passed the windowed office and headed down the hall toward the classrooms.

"Can I help you," called Father as he hurriedly exited the office to intercept them. "You have to check in at the office for any business in the school."

As the men stopped and rotated he could see they were not smiling and a wave of fear swept over him. A feeling of total helplessness overwhelmed him as the phone number for the local police instantly surfaced in his mind. It was obvious these were not local people and these men were seething with hate. He could feel deep in his soul Satan was in the building.

"Yes, we are looking for Jody Soles," was the answer.

"I'm sorry Mrs. Soles is in the classroom and won't be available until school's out. She cannot be disturbed at this time. Do you have school business with her?" Father asked nervously.

"We want to talk to her about a friend of ours. She has made some false charges against him and we are here to ask her to explain her racist behavior and request she drop the charges against an innocent man," replied the larger of the men.

"I can't disturb her. Maybe you can talk to one of our local attorneys or the police or somebody about this. There is a law office up on the main street in town. Perhaps he can arrange something," Father replied trying to vie for time.

"Just tell her we will be in touch and give her our request. She is attempting to persecute an innocent black man for purely racist reasons. Tell her we will not allow it."

The men turned with no further words and walked out the door, got back in their car and drove off. As his stomach churned Father immediately slipped into the office toilet and threw up. The whole confrontation felt overwhelming and he thanked god it ended the way it did. It was the first time in his religious career, he felt he confronted the devil himself. Now the problem was going to be telling Jody about the event. With her fragile state of mind god only knew how she would react.

"Chris, can you come up?" The fear in Jody's trembling voice was obvious.

"Man, you don't sound good what to hell is it?" her brother replied.

"I'm scared to death. I am just standing here trembling. Two black men showed up at school today looking for me. They were from the Black Nation from St Louis. They told Father they wanted to talk to me about a friend of theirs I falsely accused. They came right into town and walked into the school bold as brass. Father stopped them at the door and I didn't have to see them thank god," she said.

"You need to call St Louis County and tell them. Go on record right now. This is an open veiled threat. Did you get any names?" he replied.

"No, they just came and were gone before anyone could even catch their breath. Father waited until after school to tell me. Scared him so bad it made him physically ill," she said.

"O K Jody, this is not good. I need to make a trip to the coast so I will go ahead and come your way. I'll drop off in Kansas City tomorrow and drive over. They probably won't show up again for a while. They will let their appearance on the scene soak in. Their objective was to scare you. They are trying to force you to drop the charges. The problem is going to be down the road if you stand your ground. Then it could get dangerous. We'll talk about it when I get there. I'll see you tomorrow," he said.

As she hung up the phone she heard the kids coming in the door. This was the first time she was calm enough to collect her thoughts and think about the kids. They went up the street after school to play with the neighbors. She should have kept them in the yard where she could see them but she was not thinking straight. Her heart sank as she immediately noticed the youngest girl was missing.

"Where's your sister, **Where's your sister**," she yelled as she shook the oldest boy.

"She wasn't outside with us," answered the oldest son starting to tear up.

As absolute panic set in, Jody faced the reality the five-year-old was missing. She ran out the door yelling the baby's name. The absolute terror of the thought of these men having her child was more than she could handle. She ran down the street crying uncontrollably not really knowing where to go or to look. She needed Tom so she ran back to the house and picked up the phone. When Tom heard her voice and she said the baby was missing, he dropped the phone and headed home in a dead run. He was already tipped off by some of the locals the black men were spotted in town. He knew without being told what was going on. The turmoil in the house was a complete state of panic with the kids crying and Jody in shock. As they sat in the living room preparing to call Lieutenant Westburg and trying to collect their thoughts, Jody glanced out of the corner picture window. The flood of relief was instant as there in the middle of the next block with her blonde curls blowing in the wind was the baby. She was nonchalantly walking toward home on the sidewalk licking a soft-serve ice cream cone without a care in the world.

Jody ran out of the house to retrieve the child from the street. She dropped to her knees, embraced the child and asked, "Where have you been?"

She knew to suppress the emotions of the moment for the sake of all the children. There was going to have to be an explanation of the dangers to them but this was not the time.

"I went to see the puppy," replied the little girl showing her confusion.

"The men bought me an ice cream and let me pet the puppy. They said they knew you momma and it was O K."

The gripping fear of knowing that these armed men picked up her baby a block from home, completely unnoticed, made her stomach turn over. How could anyone in her household ever go to sleep again or take their eyes off of any of the kids? She knew the peace of living in an obscure small town was gone, never to be felt again.

*   *   *   *

The trip up to North Missouri was the typical hassle with the air service only into the major cities. It always required at least an additional two-hour drive from the airport. Both the brothers were supposed to meet at Jody's house so John was on his way from St Louis. The reports from Jody that the intimidation was starting and listening to her on the phone indicated it was working. Level heads were required here and that was going to be a problem as this bunch weren't experienced with life or death situations. The less they knew the better. The bottom line was it was probably going to be up to him to deal with Braburn. He was the only one in the bunch that was not still completely influenced by the goodness side of their upbringing. The war experience exposed him to the other side of evil and forced him to participate in dealing with it. The kids being involved put the whole mess in another dimension. Having thought it through several times he always reached the same conclusion. The conclusion was there was no way to stop this without some type of offensive action. Defense was not going to be an acceptable way of life for his family. The big question to be answered was why would the Black Nation place such emphasis on this obscure little criminal? What was their motive? Would they back off with his demise? Those questions needed to be answered first.

As he rolled toward Maysville he decided to lay the groundwork for a contingency plan to go on the offensive. The first thing he would need is a place to hide in plain sight. The police were as big a problem as the Black Nation. They would come straight to him if anything happened to Braburn. That meant he would need to be able to turn into someone else to maneuver at will. The answer was a legitimate set of false identification. This meant finding someone from his past who was dead and applying for and compiling that person's identification. It needed to be someone his same age that he knew well so he could answer any questions. Someone who spent their childhood in Maysville and was raised with him as a kid. The only candidate was Kenny. He knew the date of his death and his family member names and addresses. He decided he would stop at the cemetery in Maysville and collect any information he could on Kenny's legal name and birthdate before he headed back. Also, the local V F W office might have some file information that could be helpful. If he could get Kenny's original birth certificate the rest of it would be easy. With a fake I.D. he could operate at will without detection. It would be a lonely old task because this project must be secret and kept even from the family members. The only chance of success here was to not tell anyone anything and keep the family out of it.

Pulling into the side street at the corner of his sister's house, he couldn't help but notice the cars. It appeared his brother was there along with a white four-door sedan with black tires and an antenna on the roof that was obviously a cop car.

Looks like the St Louis County boys are here.

As he entered the dining room, the ashen faces of his brother and sister made it more than obvious the subject of discussion was not pleasant. Seated at the table were the St Louis County policemen looking confused.

"Lieutenant this is my brother Chris from Tennessee," Jody said.

"Yea, I remember him from the hospital," answered Buzz.

Shaking the policeman's hand, Chris asked, "Why are you up here today?"

"I've got bad news. A Judge in Boston bonded Braburn out before we could get the extradition papers up there. We are still trying to get an explanation as to what happened. Apparently, the ruling was that there was insufficient evidence that this was Braburn at all. You know he has taken the Nation name of Malik Jakim and they let him loose based on that. We are being stonewalled in all directions including the fingerprints. The court was presented with

116

a petition of five thousand signatures attesting to Braburn's work in the community. The Judge is obviously in the bag for the Black Nation and the local politicians are afraid of trouble. This is going to have to go to the Massachusetts Governor's office to get past the local level corruption. Our boy is walking around as a free man on the streets of Roxbury strutting his stuff and referring to us as "Missouri hicks" in the local papers," answered Buzz.

"What about the Feds? Can't they take him into custody? It's just a matter of time till he runs you know that," Chris replied.

"Yes we know and really all we can do at this time is cut the paperwork and wait for the Massachusetts Governor to sign it. We are working every angle we can but the truth is with the riots all over this country the past year or so all these local politicians are afraid any conflict with the black community will result in their city getting burned. The people that are protecting Braburn know this and they are capitalizing on it. In short they are holding the Roxbury neighborhood hostage," replied the Lieutenant.

When the policemen left Chris stood stunned at the results of the meeting and peered out the window watching them drive off. *What are the odds in this political climate they will ever get their hands on Braburn? The answer is slim and none. This guy will get early warning and bolt. They will never catch him again.*

117

CHAPTER 9

THE ESCAPE

As the months passed Malik roamed the Roxbury district out on bail, completely free. The locals held him as a hero for the belligerence he showed during newspaper interviews. He would spew racial rant and tout his complete innocence. His attitude helped the Nation show its power to the local residents and engrained the organization as the rulers of the community. The St Louis prosecutors hit a complete blank wall with every attempt to force extradition back to Missouri and six months passed with no progress. The prosecutors were searching for an angle to force the Massachusetts authorities' hand. All standard avenues came to simple dead ends. The stonewall was the Governor's flat refusal to sign the extradition order. The threat of a local riot and the veiled threat to burn the city kept him at bay. As long as the Governor held out the extradition would never happen.

Finally, a threat to circumvent the local political establishment was issued when the Missouri prosecutors proposed filing a suit on behalf of the victim under the new federal civil rights law. This was an untested process and required claiming the white victim's civil rights to due process were violated on the federal level. There appeared to be no alternative but to try to get the extradition decision out of the hands of local Massachusetts politicians.

The call from the Missouri prosecutor to the Governor's office in Boston pulled the right chain. It was election season and a civil rights action on behalf of a white woman as the lead story in the Boston Globe on Sunday, could shake the white community's support at the polls. Signing the extradition on the other hand could set off the black community so for Governor Sorgant it was damned

119

if he did or damned if he didn't. Either way his chances of reelection would be in jeopardy. As he mulled over his options the realization the political answer for him would be for the problem to go completely away. As he picked up the phone he justified what he was about to do in his own mind by telling himself "maybe the man is really innocent".

"Janice, get me the attorney for the Black Nation. I think his name is Eli Shabaz," the Governor instructed his secretary.

As the phone rang the Governor thought about what he was about to do. In the scheme of things, it did not set well, but it was a political reality for his survival.

"Yes, this is Governor Sorgant, as I understand it you are the attorney representing Malik Jakim. Is that right?" he asked.

"That's correct," was the curt reply."

"O K, I'm only going to say this once so don't ask me to elaborate. Today at four-thirty, I will be forced to sign the extradition order for Braburn to be sent back to Missouri. It is nine right now so you have a seven-hour window. Do you understand?" said the Governor.

"Yes," was the simple reply.

Shabaz hung up the phone quickly. He knew there was little time to get the right things in place for Malik's escape. As he mulled it over in his mind he concluded the Nation's connections in the Caribbean would probably be the best avenue on short notice. As bad as St Louis wanted Jakim the only safe bet was to get him out of the country. The Governor's "seven-hour window" comment implied they needed to move fast. The Nation's connections to the communist factions in Cuba and the surrounding areas of the Caribbean, would be served by a good soldier like Malik. The first issue was to get him out of Boston then deal with taking the pressure off later. If the white woman in St Louis could be spooked to back off, then he could return. The plan would be to get him offshore then work on the woman. Their harbor connections would have to be it for this escape. The Nation could call on their smuggling friends in the merchant marine down on the docks. That connection was established years ago and there was no way these people could refuse to help. The Nation just completed a deal for drugs with a group on a steamer that was slated to leave today. There was no way they could refuse to smuggle Malik back out with them. Feeling the pressure of time, he dialed the center first.

"Malik, you gotta' split right now. The man's comin', so don't go home just leave where you are and take a bus over to the harbor. Don't say a word to anyone or go anywhere else. Gotta move your ass right now man. There is a tramp steamer called the Caribbean Palm at pier 31. It's leaving at two. Be on it. Ride the bus over there and ask for Reggie when you find the boat. Don't take a cab they can trace that. He will set everything up and show you where to hide till you're out at sea. Just do as he says," said Shabaz.

"Alright, where am I going?" was the startled answer.

"You don't need to know in case you get stopped. Just go there right now."

As Malik hurried down the street and shuffled through the alleys to find a place to catch the bus, panic began to overwhelm him. Everything was turning in on him and the impulse to make a run for it and tell the Nation to go fuck themselves tempted him. The time in Roxbury was the best life of his life and now he was being forced to leave it. The whole thing made him light headed and his chest tightened making it hard to breath. *All my life I've been forced to live according to the white man's wishes and now some white bitch from St Louis has me running again. How could I have been so stupid to not see to it she was finished before I left that art store.*

She will always be out there from now on. Rag always said, "Dead men don't testify". This situation is living proof he was right.

The Nation made him and now was breaking him but he didn't have a choice. Defying them amounted to a death sentence. They were more dangerous than the white law because they didn't have courts or forgiveness, their reach was inescapable and their judgement final. In some respects, the only thing that really changed for him was he now had new bosses with the consolation being at least the new ones were of his own race.

The overcast winter sky and the fact the pier area was deserted made the place look and feel sinister and cold as he jumped off the bus. The smell of salt air mixed with creosote from the piers, the sound of the gulls and the seediness of the whole dock area only made the chills go deeper. As Malik started down the pier toward the ship's gangplank he noticed a crumpled bearded figure in a blue pea coat and stocking cap coming out of one of the dock's warehouse doors toward him. At that moment, he thought about not having a weapon.

"You Jakim?" asked the man.

"Yea," was the reply.

"I'm Reggie. You bring any money?"

"Just the walking around money in my pocket," Jakim replied.

"Let's have it and follow me," said Reggie.

As Malik emptied his pockets and handed over his cash there was a sinking feeling.

The ship seemed deserted with no one else in sight. This white sea-tramp was obviously dangerous and couldn't hide his hatred for blacks. Climbing through the gangways and descending into the bowels of the ship, one deck at a time, the stench from the bilge increased with each metal staircase they descended. With each breath the increasing sensation of wanting to gag made him realize it was going to be all he could do not to puck. As they reached the bilge of the ship they were forced to stand on the edges of the cold steel bulkheads of the hull. With just the beam of a flashlight for illumination it was obvious this bilge was the nastiest place on the ship. Covering the keel area, the standing stale seawater combined with oil and rotting plankton made the floor invisible. It formed a thick putrid whitish soup that reeked of rotting dead sea life. The slim filled the keel area about a foot deep and the only place to sit in the dry was on a superstructure beam on the side of the hull. At that moment his admiration for the Nation sank to a low. Up to this point everything from them was top drawer but this set up was even worse than any of his prison experiences.

"You stay here till we are out past the limit. If the port authority boys check us and board they won't come down here so just sit and keep your mouth shut. Someone will come get you when it is safe. Let's get something straight right here mate. I don't like niggers and neither do most of this crew. Any shit from you and we will throw you over the side and tell your friends you jumped off. Do you understand," said Reggie as he glared at Jakim.

The seaman pivoted, turned and left with the light, leaving only the sound of the ringing trail of his footsteps ascending the metal stairs.

Malik sat in the stench and total darkness just like instructed. The tension filled his body and it was all he could do to resist running from this whole scene. They dumped him in the bilge and left him in the dark maybe to rot for all he knew. The darkness was overwhelming and it was all he could do to overcome it. On top of everything, taking orders from that white Reggie stuck in his craw.

Finally, after what seemed hours, the ship's hull began to shudder beneath his body and there was a feeling of relief. They were casting off. Maybe he would get some light and air soon.

Solitary in the Wall was a better place than this. At least there the only stink was your own body.

The horrors of the unknown nagged at his gut again as his life once more completely turned sour. It was a low feeling. A feeling that only fueled his hatred for the white society that has slapped him down time after time all through his life. The scum seamen on this garbage scow would make certain this trip would be a rough one. He was cursing himself down deep for not at least carrying a knife.

*   *   *   *

Chris stayed on with the group in Tennessee mostly because of the great work environment and the interesting projects. The productivity of his time over the last two years and his status in the group insured he got his choice when new projects came online. In addition, his time was pretty much his own if he wanted or needed to take off. The money could not get any better and he was now financially flush. The company was branching out into some new technologies particularly the application of emerging digital electronics and the introduction of minicomputers. Having employees with backgrounds in writing aerospace computer programs made the company a natural for software development as the need arose.

The pursuit of his sister's rapist reached an impasse several months back and every day the family waited for any news from St Louis County. It seemed nothing ever developed anymore and Braburn had fallen off the face of the earth. The last reports of his capture and release in Boston combined with the frustrations of the months of watching him work the extradition system, only to skate out the door, left a bad taste in everyone's mouth. There was total disgust with the whole system of justice along with a desire to get the family settled down. The regret of not acting when the man was

124

living in Boston was gnawing at Chris now with the way it turned out. Leaving justice to the law seemed to be a fading fantasy. His sister's life was still one of continual fear and her mental state seemed to be continuing to deteriorate. Apprehension about the children's safety ruled the whole family's daily lives and caused their mother's continual crying jags. As a unit her family was coming apart at the seams. She was dependent on her brother's opinions and called him almost daily to try to prop up her courage to go on. It was reaching the point where it appeared if anything was going to change he would have to change it. Suddenly his thoughts were broken by voices in the hall. Jim popped in the office door with a stranger beside him.

"Chris, this is Dave Morgan of International Investments in Nashville. He is looking for someone to build a financial software package for Radio Shack's new T R S 80 microcomputer. Told him you are the guy to see since your math and programming background is the strongest we have on staff," said Jim.

"Hi," Chris replied shaking hands.

"What we are looking to do is develop a computer tool for sale to financial planners that will predict what type of return on present assets a person will require to reach their retirement objectives. In addition to using it ourselves for planning purposes with our clients, we want to license and market it to other financial planners," Morgan said.

"O K, I smell some type of iterative solution here and the computer is definitely the way to do it. Can we meet this evening after hours when we can get some peace and quiet? Right now, I am jumping through ten hoops trying to get something out the door before quitting time. Say, stop by my office about five thirty," he replied.

"Will do. See you then," Dave answered as he turned to leave.

The evening meeting was a success with the parameters for the project being spelled out and the two individuals hitting it off forming what seemed a natural bond. Dave was a big city person with the moxie to deal in the financial world. His formal education was limited and it was obvious he came from the city streets. Dave's intrigue with the technology and natural interest helped things click and as the evening progressed, the two men became more and more personal trading life stories and such.

They decided to work together during the evenings through the next week for the privacy and late one evening the story of Jody's assault came up. As Dave listened, it was obvious the whole scenario really disturbed him. Finishing the story with the fact the rapist walked out the door and beat the extradition topped the whole conversation off with the unfairness of it all. As Dave absorbed the story his astonishment with the whole thing became more and more obvious. It was apparent his basic human instinct for justice was being pumped. With that, the conversation rather died and the rest of the evening was spent working on the software running test cases trying to finalize the computer system. Shutting down and getting ready to leave for the night, Dave turned and made a proposal that was a total surprise.

"You know, I have some friends in Chicago that can find that guy for you," he blurted out.

"What do you mean," was the reply.

"Just that. I was raised on the streets of Chicago and attended Catholic schools in the city for twelve years. Lived on the Near Northside. It was an Italian and Irish area and several of the kids I ran with were the children of underworld figures. Hell, they talked about it openly and most of them grew up to fill their father's shoes. I've known these guys all my life. Truthfully, these are the wiseguys that run the place now. My connections with them are the reason I left the place. I was in the loop for a while and it was getting dangerous," Dave answered.

"How can these guys find him?" responded Chris.

"Believe me they can find anybody, anywhere. Their tentacles reach into places like the FBI and the CIA clear to Interpol. They are wired world-wide. Nobody can escape them if they really want to find a person. They have access to everything and everybody. The fact that your boy was in Boston would probably make it easy for them. That's home turf for the Irish families. They will have relatives there. However, let me warn you, if they help you, they might show up some night at your door with a request that you put some stranger in your attic for a week, and you better do it. They will never forget you owe them and they will eventually collect. Something this simple probably won't even require money, just a favor someday. Hell, they might do it just because the guy is black. There is definitely no love lost between them and the niggers," Dave answered.

As he drove home in the dark, Chris could not stop thinking about what Morgan told him. How simple it would be to just tap these Chicago people to locate Braburn. The real advantage would be Braburn himself would not be tipped off and realize what was happening like he would if the police were looking for him. This way he would not be as likely to get wind of it all before it was too late for him to run again. He would be a sitting duck, fat and happy, when the action was taken to bring him down. The fact that these people and the blacks were so estranged also meant there was a very good chance the Black Nation would not pick up on the hunt for Braburn. That could make all the difference in surprising him. There were many positives about the whole proposal right up to the return favor thing. That could be a problem as having these people in your life could be worse than involvement with either the Black Nation or the police.

The next morning as he shuffled through the pile of stuff on his desk trying to get a starting point for the day the door swung open and Dave quickly stepped in and closed it behind him.

"I thought you took your software diskette with you last night. Don't tell me you came out here because we missed something last night with the software tests," Chris said startled.

"No, I made a special trip to talk to you personally. I talked a friend of mine in Chicago earlier this morning and told him about the situation with the nigger being on the run. He owes me a favor or two and, after thinking about it last night on the way home, I decided to see if I could call one in. I presented the whole thing as if it were me that wanted to find the guy so you and your bunch won't be in the loop at all. Anyway, he said he would put out some inquiries and see what comes back. I used to tend bar in a joint on the North Side where his competition hung out. Information I picked up in there made him and his bunch a lot of money," Dave replied.

"My sister can't deal with anymore crap. I just pray you have us insulated," Chris said.

"Yea, I do. Don't worry. I did not get serious about it when I talked to my old friend. Just indicated I was interested and didn't give him a reason why. Your name never came up. Good chance their Boston connections will come up with something and it won't have to go any further. Give it a day or two and don't worry. I'll let you know when I hear back."

Locking his desk to leave that evening he thought about the events of the day. Skepticism about the ability of Dave's Chicago connections made it difficult to take this approach to finding Braburn through the underworld seriously. After all, he really did not know Dave that well. Down deep he questioned whether Dave was really wired up with the Chicago hoods or was it just talk. Also, the fact that this unsavory element would be getting involved with his family could be a big problem. These people were probably better left completely out of the picture for the sake of the family. Then again the status of the hunt through law enforcement channels was at a total dead end. Maybe this could get things off dead center. The question was what to do if they did locate Braburn. That decision would be the next big bridge to cross. It would depend on where Braburn was hiding. There was no urgent need to worry about what would be next at this point in time. He put the chances of anything coming of it all as pretty slim and headed home to relax. It was time to let down as the very thought of Jody's situation always made him tense.

Several days passed and as the end of the week approached Chris figured he owed himself a weekend so a call to the receptionist over at the airbase guard shack was on the agenda. He had had a couple of drink dates with her on previous occasions and really enjoyed her company. As he fished through his phone directory for her extension the phone on his desk rang. Answering it, the voice on the other end was immediately recognizable as Dave.

"Anybody with you," Dave asked.

"No," was the reply.

"Can you meet me over at the officer's club at the airbase at five thirty? I've got something for you from out of town," Dave said.

"Yea, I guess. What is it?" he asked.

"It's your Christmas present. I am going to give it to you early. Keep this meeting hush, hush," Dave replied.

"Alright, I'll see you there."

The officers club at the base entrance was actually a private club for military personnel but the brass let that slide and just left

129

the door open to business people. There was so much commercial activity with the test area being on the base that a watering hole with a social setting was a necessity. They just let anyone come and go from the club without question. It was a high end cocktail lounge and a good private spot where no one would notice the meeting. As he took a window table in the rear overlooking the lake and ordered a scotch and soda Dave came through the door looking like the cat that just swallowed the canary. He was smiling from ear to ear and as he passed the bar he called out a drink order to the bartender. When he sat down he was kind of chuckling to himself.

"You are not going to believe this one," he said.

"O K lets have it."

"The Chicago boy's connections in Boston have really come through this time. They zeroed in on your man's ass almost immediately. Your friend is in South America in a place called Guyana. He was shuffled out on a tramp steamer to Cuba and the islands through his Black Nation connections. Word is the crew that gave him a ride were not his best friends though. Scuttlebutt is they considered drowning his ass on the way down and completely solving your problem. Guess he's an obnoxious bastard so everyone was glad to fink on him. We were lucky he went out through the harbor because nothing happens on the Boston docks that's not mob connected. They came up with dates, places and names without barely lifting a finger. Get this, your man is now a member of the local military defense force down there and is using a Swahili name or some damn thing. Pretending to be African as a cover. Lives in a military barracks in the capital city. Place called Freeport. Even wears a uniform. Apparently he has the full passports and identifications and looks completely legit on the surface," Dave said.

"How in the hell did Braburn finagle this? Who in the hell is this guy?" Chris replied.

"I don't know but you don't get the paperwork he's got at the five and dime. Looks to me like there are some hard knockers backing him up. This kind of cover smacks of government stuff, at least that is what the Chicago boys mentioned. FBI, CIA kind of thing and let me tell you my friends would know. That is where they get their fake paperwork.

"How in the name of god can someone of this caliber be hooked up with U S government agencies? The man's a rapist and a cold blooded killer for Christ sake," he replied.

"All I'm saying buddy is tread lightly till you know a little more. Chasing this person could be hazardous to your health if he is wired to one of the agencies. Let me put it this way, the only thing worse than having my Chicago friends down on you is having the agencies down on you. These are the only people the hoods actually fear."

As Dave scooted his chair back to leave he suddenly interjected, "Five grand, that's what they quote to solve the problem".

"What do you mean", Chris replied.

"Just that, for five thousand dollars he will disappear forever. But then again you would be in the loop because I will not get in the middle. You will have to deal with them directly. This is as far as I go."

Driving through the deserted airbase headed home with the top down, the cool evening air felt good. The smell of the southern lodge pole pine forest at dusk in the early fall signaled that the summer humidity would soon give way to cool crisp fall air. It was a funny thing but the airbase offered a certain calmness. It seemed it related to the secure feeling of being surrounded by the military.

Thoughts of the mess with Jody and all the issues involved seemed to eat at him constantly anymore. Worrying about the safety of the children was always in everyone's face. The nagging question now was should he talk to the St Louis County police about the information Morgan just relayed or should he keep his mouth shut. Telling them would lock-in their suspicions that he was pursuing the investigation outside of their control. If anything should develop like Braburn suddenly dying they would come straight to him. In addition, considering the way they handled the whole thing so far, he seriously doubted they could deal with Braburn being overseas and possibly wired to some type of government conspiracy. The truth was just Braburn's political connections in Boston proved to be bigger than the St Louis County bunch. He was captured there and they could not reel him in. Now this thing was an order of magnitude more complicated than the Boston episode.

It was time to clear his mind and let down for the date with the girl from the guard gate. Thinking aloud, he could not remember her name for the life of him. It started with an S, maybe Sharon or Susan. He needed to make sure and look it up before leaving the apartment because he did not want to insult her by calling her the wrong name. Since Arizona Chris' love life was empty, he sometimes wished he would have stayed with Jeannie. She was one of the few girls he ever met who could always fill the empty spot that needed a woman's soft touch. At times like this there seemed to be something missing in his life.

CHAPTER 9

GUYANA

The skiff rocked from side to side through the rough sea and the wind driven warm salt mist drenched the occupants of the small boat for what seemed an eternity. He left the small island where the freighter dropped him and was in the skiff at sea for two days. It now seemed they were moving along a coastline looking for some landmark but he was still too sick to even be interested. Finally, the small engine slowed so he raised up to look over the side. In the dark he could barely make out what was happening but he could see they were finally turning inland toward an estuary. Braburn breathed a sigh of relief for the first time in two weeks. Finally, he would get out of the open sea and on dry land to stay.

Climbing into the tiny boat and shoving off, not knowing his destination, took all the guts he could muster. The two Jamaicans manning the skiff laid in each end of the boat and jabbered back and forth. Through the whole trip the sea was up and he just lay in the floor of the boat sick as a dog, baling water, vomiting and trying not to be thrown overboard. The Jamaicans laughed aloud at him. They seemed to enjoy watching him squirm for two days. Their diet at sea was dried fish and Cuban rum through the trip and it was now impossible for him to hold anything down. At least now, the trip seemed to be over as the smell of brackish water was unmistakable. They were heading into the mouth of a fresh water river.

The river quickly narrowed and with the sounds and smells, even in the dark, as things closed in around them, it was obvious they were going into a jungle. The dark foliage on the banks looked impenetrable and forbidding. *What in the fuck am I doing here? I've*

133

never even camped out in my life. Now I'm alone in a jungle on a moonless night with two spooks that can't even speak English.

His trip from Boston was a total bitch, every bit as bad as any of his prison experiences. Being captive on the steamer out of Boston was just like prison with the constant threat of someone jumping him. The crew was white scum and down deep every one of them wanted to get credit for killing the nigger that was onboard. He spent six days in total terror with no sleep and kept his back to the wall of his cabin just waiting for one of them to make a move. The threat of being thrown overboard was almost unbearable as he never learned to swim. Being unarmed only made it worse. When they finally dropped him ashore, he felt a little better as most of the people on the island at least were black, but they couldn't speak English and were not very friendly. He just went along with his handler without understanding what was happening. He finally scrounged something to eat and was able to get a few nights sleep but none of those local islanders could be trusted. It was obvious they were all smugglers and any of them would sell a person out for a couple of bucks. He followed the instructions from Boston, assuming they were coming from the Nation, but under his breath he cussed them for sending him off with no weapons and no money. The truth though, was someone would have taken them from him anyway. He could only hope that things were still under the Nation's control. The Nation was silent since leaving Boston. There were no instructions or communications of any kind. All he could rely on now was faith and that was a word that left his vocabulary years ago.

The bump of the skiff against the bank jarred him and he rose up out of the floor to look around. There was absolutely nothing but the darkness and strange sounds. The larger of the two Jamaicans said something and motioned for him to step ashore. When he hesitated, the man made a threatening move towards him and it was obvious he was to get off at this spot. As they handed him his things they quickly shoved off and instantly melted into the total darkness with only the slight sound of the skiffs wake against the river bank. He felt completely enveloped in isolation and the surroundings poured in on him like a liquid drowning him in a frozen state. Fear was never been an issue with him in life but this was different. Visions of being killed and eaten by animals entered his mind and he suddenly got a new picture of what the world could offer. The city streets were nothing compared to this. No instructions combined with the strangeness of the environment locked his mind up. He couldn't even think for several minutes. The splashing in the river and the rustling in the bushes were sure signs he was surrounded by living creatures. Making any kind of a move would be a mistake. At that point the thought of just what might be happening hit him. He was overcome by a dose of paranoia. *The Nation has dumped me here to get rid of me. Of course, that's it. I could never survive trying to walk or swim out of here.* A sudden swell of anger filled his throat.

Just then the bounce of a flashlight's beam broke through the jungle foliage and the sounds of voices pierced the dank air. Over to his right someone was coming and he could only hope they were friendly and looking for him. If not, he knew he was in big trouble. The sound of his name washed the darkness back and cleared his throat so that he was able to answer. There was a flood of relief as the accent said this is definitely a black American.

"You Jakim?" asked the larger of the two strangers.

"Yea, who are you?" he replied.

"Davis man. We been sent to get you man."

The flashlight put off enough of a glow to silhouette the men and it was obvious they were both in uniform. They looked like police but they sure did not act like it. The one calling himself Davis seemed to be in charge and was packing a holstered sidearm. The other one was carrying a rifle. The fact they were armed felt good and for the first time since leaving Boston he was breathing easier and felt like he was among friends. Davis exuded confidence and his demeanor was that of an American black man. The reassurance the Nation was still covering his back allowed Braburn to take his first relaxed deep breaths for weeks.

"I don't know how much they told you man but here's how it is. You in South America. Place called Guyana. We gonna' hide you from the man for a while. Got everything here you need including wine, women and song. You now a member of the Guyanese Defense Force called the GDF. All you gotta do is what you told. We work for the man who runs the place. Black cat named Durham. We do his bidding and keep shit straight if you know what I mean. We brought you all the stuff you will need including your GDF threads and a new I.D. Your new name is Odwalla. That's African Swahili and means something, I don't know what, but if anyone ask, you from Africa. And, by the way, learn the name as fast as you can. Don't want you fuckin-up and answering to something else. We got some wheels so follow us out and you can change cloths in the car. And another thing, if you are smart you will step where we do on the way out. There is a lot of unrighteous shit in this jungle and most of it bites," said Davis chuckling.

On the drive back to Freetown Davis explained the whole layout to Braburn. It seemed the Nation's arrangement with the Government of Guyana was to supply enforcement muscle in the form of black American fugitives to keep the existing government in power. The communist were pushing for elections all through the Caribbean and trying to unseat the powers that ruled and those powers were pushing back with force. The government controlled the local military and used it at will. The black Americans were for special assignment and posed as GDF officers to do special jobs. As

136

Davis explained with a laugh, the whole thing was covertly sanctioned by the United States to squelch Communism in any way possible in that part of the world. They conveniently overlooked the fact that most of the Americans were wanted in the States and kept other agencies noses out of it all. The whole thing was an arrangement between Durnham, the Nation and the C.I.A. There was security in it if one did as instructed but the whole thing could turn at any time.

"Hope you have a strong stomach. Some of this stuff gets a little messy," said Davis.

"What does that mean?" answered Braburn.

"Occasionally have to draw some blood or break some bones but that shouldn't bother you from what I've heard. Heard you beat a white woman to death with a hammer. Fucked her first though," replied Davis with a grin.

"Not exactly. Where did you get that?"

"We get the scoop on all our men. Gotta be able to take a life to do this job," said Davis.

The trip into Georgetown was rough with the unpaved roads rutted from the dried monsoon mud. With the windows down the air smelled of mildew from the rains. The only thoughts going through Braburn's mind were of the comforts he left in Boston and how he was going to get back there. After what seemed hours of endless jabbering by Davis, the lights of the city broke over the horizon. The realization they were back in civilization brought some sense of relief. As they drove through the city streets at night Braburn got his first look at his new home. The brightly painted houses and shanties and the open sewers in the narrow streets screamed poverty. Worse than anything in the states. Nothing compared to it. Things improved as they reached the government section of the city and finally the military base. There were security guards at the gates as they entered the military base and just seeing the facilities enabled Braburn to finally completely let down.

As he settled into his barracks room and unpacked he thought to himself how good a full night's sleep was going to feel. His new rank of Lieutenant qualified him for a private room with a door that locked. Davis gave him a reefer so a few drags and it would be lights out. The disturbing thing with the whole scene was the control issue. These people seemed to know a lot about him and were in complete control of his future. He would have to get some dirt on them for insurance or his future here was questionable.

$$* \qquad * \qquad * \qquad *$$

Waiting anxiously for the mail to arrive at his desk, Chris sipped his morning coffee and noticed a slight tinge of indigestion. He guessed the whole false identity thing was causing the worry. If he were caught applying for someone else's birth certificate through the company, there could be a stir with the security clearance people that could be a nightmare. When he requested a copy of Kenny's birth certificate from the state, he laid it out as needed by the company for federal clearance purposes. He made the excuse he hired the man and needed it quickly for a passport application so the new employee could travel. If anyone in the agency picked-up on the fact the applicant was in reality a dead man he would never be able to explain it. Then again, if he could get the birth certificate he could easily apply for all the other I.D. without question. The good thing about government systems in this case was the ineptness of the employees. If they picked-up on it he would just plead ignorance and they would most likely forget it. The federal security clearance people could explain away anything with no questions asked. Anyway, it was too late to worry about it now. He could only hope the charm he laid on the female clerk on the phone would work some magic and get her to expedite the application without looking too deeply. He felt his pulse quicken when he heard the voice of the young mail clerk in the hall as she approached his office door.

"Hi Jenny, any mail for me today?" he asked.

"Just clearance stuff," she replied as she tossed the envelope on his desk.

There was a tingle of excitement as he split the envelope and watched the certified document fall out on the desk. *I've pulled it off.* He felt like a little kid putting something past their parents. There on his desk was Kenny Steven's birth certificate for the entire world to behold. Next steps were driver's license, social security card and passport. Those would be easy. It would be simple to cover all his tracks now. His first objective in the pursuit of justice for his sister was accomplished. From now on when he wanted to be someone else all needed was his other billfold. The goal of being able to hide in plain sight was achieved.

*　　*　　*　　*

Two weeks passed and Braburn settled in with the military unit. For the first time in weeks he was fully rested. His initial fears of the whole arrangement never materialized and his comfort level was up several notches. No one asked anything of him yet and he just spent his time getting the lay of the land so to speak. He was not required to drill or assemble with the other members of the Defense Force and since arriving, he was mostly left alone. He was military in name only but he did have to wear the uniform. The best thing was his rank allowed him to carry a side arm at will. His pay arrived every Friday like clockwork and with the weekends off the local bars and whorehouses were a real treat. Half of the people in his new country spoke English and were black so adapting to the culture was simple. Actually he realized, it was too simple. As he prepared to leave for the weekend, the catch arrived, when Davis entered his room carrying some knives and a short saber in a sheath.

"Cancel your weekend. We workin' tomorrow," said Davis.

"Say what?" Braburn replied.

"There's demonstrations tomorrow at the city center in Freetown to protest our man's rule. We gonna' bust it up. The group is the biggest pain in the ass. Wanting communist to rule. Their head man is a little white priest. He's the party leader. We been told to bust some heads and break it up maybe more if we can cover our tracks. This priest is our biggest problem," answered Davis.

"How do we play it?" asked Braburn.

"The whole show will be covered by uniformed GDF guys. We just blend in and look for a chance. You can know the priest because he wears a white straw hat and he's little. People will be all around him. Our man's biggest wish is for this cat to disappear. No guns though," said Davis.

A protest demonstration at government square was scheduled to start mid-morning the next day. The opposition party wanted it to look spontaneous but it was fully planned, and there would be a crowd. The GDF intelligence plants inside the communist organization knew their plans down to the smallest detail. Braburn and his comrades were to position themselves near the priest and watch for a chance to strike. Braburn immediately recognized the opportunity this whole thing would present him. Just like in prison, he needed to make his bones with this group. This was his chance to perform and move to the head of the list with the group. If he could kill the priest, his credit would go clear to the top and even the president would know about him. As he laid in his bunk there was a rush just thinking about killing some white holy man. *I'll kill the little white motherfucker right there in front of the rest of the group and they'll know who they are dealing with from this point forward.*

His mind wandered back to some of his actions in prison as he recalled what it felt like to draw blood with a knife. It all seemed to go back to gigging the white john when he was a kid. The excitement aroused him sexually and he couldn't sleep so he wandered out for a visit to the red light district near the camp.

The morning was clear and the day promised to be hot. The government complex was a group of stone buildings that were fenced and formed into a square fortress looking arrangement. As the hit squad pulled into the gate and parked behind the barriers that held the crowd back from the entrance and out in the streets. It was obvious the demonstration was going to be large. Braburn knew that in the crowd his GDF uniform was going to be like a target on his back. Killing someone while wearing it wouldn't work at all. There was going to be people around to witness it. Before leaving the barracks Braburn dug through his things and pulled an old loose fitting taupe colored long sleeve shirt from his locker to take with him.

"Hey man, give me the long knife," he said to Davis as they exited the car to enter the street.

Davis smiled knowingly and handed the short saber over.

"You smell blood huh man? I knew you was the man we need," said Davis.

The streets around the complex in the center of Freeport were packed with people. It was obvious the communist group was large with a significant following. Braburn trolled through the crowd alone searching for the leaders of the protest particularly the little priest. Dressed in his uniform he attracted attention and most demonstrators lowered their signs and stepped aside when he approached. The unspoken power of authority was juicing him. The streets on all four sides of the government complex were shut down because of the crowd. The priest was not where Braburn expected to find him, which meant the leaders were probably lying low and expecting trouble. That meant surprise was not going to be to his advantage if he decided to strike the priest.

In the third block the priest came into view on the southeast side of the complex. He was smiling, talking to a couple of followers and not paying a lot of attention to what was happening around him. *This is good, he's comfortable and will be off-guard.* Braburn pulled off this type of attack in prison a couple of times. To make it work it needed to happen fast. The key was for it to be over before any witnesses could process the scene, hit and run. Slinking to the back of the crowd unnoticed he stepped into an alley and pulled out the old shirt he brought from the barracks and the long knife from under his military blouse. Pulling the shirt on over his uniform blouse, he tucked the knife and scabbard in his belt under it. Then he buttoned the front of the shirt. Setting his military hat and sun glasses up on a window ledge he reentered the street and blended in to just look like one of the demonstrators. The crowd was flowing down the street in the direction of the priest so Braburn just joined the chant and went along with the group, slowly working his way to the side of the street near where the priest was standing. The noise rose in his ears and his heart began to pound as he neared his mark. Braburn knew at that moment he was going to act and a natural high engulfed him. When he was about two steps from the priest the man raised his arms and waved to his followers with both hands. At that second Braburn lunged, pulled the saber and in one move shoved it in the front of the little man's rib cage. It sank to the handle in an upward direction and his eyes met those of the man he was killing just as the knife entered his heart. The priest went limp and collapsed. Leaving the saber in the body Braburn jumped over the dead priest and disappeared between the buildings. It was over before the stunned crowd even knew it was happening. He retreated through the alleys, pulled off the shirt as he ran and discarded it. He then circled around to pick up his hat and sunglasses. Reemerging into the crowd from the other end of the street he yelled orders to the crowd around the dead man. In his full uniform he took charge of the scene and began dispersing the crowd. As he gave orders and restored calm he smiled to himself at his success. The memory of the event aroused him sexually and he knew on his way back to the barracks he would have to find a prostitute.

Back at the barracks there was jubilation with the news that someone killed the priest. The word was not out as to who did the killing, but everyone in the GDF knew it was big. Whoever it was would be rewarded from the top. Everyone in the defense force knew that for sure. On the way back Braburn decided to walk and visit one of his favorite whores on the way. He needed to come down from the high induced with the killing. When he finally arrived at the barracks he avoided the clamor in the building by going straight to his room and shutting the door. He was still high from the events earlier and he felt really good. There was something in his nature that couldn't be explained going all the way back to his childhood. Drawing blood, especially white blood, always made him high. It was like a drug. There seemed to always be a rush and he always wanted more. He could still see the look on the little white priest's face when he realized he was stabbed and dying, particularly the look in the eyes. Braburn chuckled to himself. *Let him talk to his jesus now*. As he changed out his clothes, a knock on the door sobered him up. When he opened it there stood Davis grinning from ear to ear.

"Man, the Colonel wants to see you. It was you, wasn't it? Give it to me straight man. You did it didn't you?" said Davis.

Braburn didn't answer but smiled knowingly. *They will never get out in front of me. I'm the smoothest motherfucker in the GDF. Even my own people didn't see what happened.*

A meeting with the GDF commander was a big thing in the group. Most of the top echelon of the defense force did not associate with the troops unless they could not avoid it. As Braburn walked into the commander's office there stood a strange man in a suit.

"Lieutenant Odwalla this is President Durnham the leader of all Guyana. He has asked to meet you," said the Colonel.

"Lieutenant Odwalla what is spoken here will go no further than this room but I just have to thank you personally for what you have done today for the nation of Guyana. The subversives that are constantly trying to overthrow my regime have eaten at the very heart of our nation. Today one of the worst has been silenced and I want you to know this nation will not forget who is responsible for the welcome silence," said the president.

Braburn knew at that moment his spot in Guyana's political power structure was cemented in place. Maybe this would allow him to finally accept his new name and start thinking of himself as Odwalla. With this kind of pull he would be able to get out of this god-forsaken place and back to Boston.

*   *   *   *

The Tennessee fall weather set in and the cool crisp morning air felt good as Chris pulled into the office parking lot. After working for several months to complete the false I.D. set so he would have it if needed to deal with his sister's situation he was a bit frustrated. Everything was in place but the passport. It would be the key if he were required to travel out of the country. He filed the application with Kenny's birth certificate with one of his own photos. Waiting for the reply made him nervous. The big worry was a cross-check by the passport people. If they checked military records they might stumble on to the fact the social security number was deceased or that the signature did not match. The whole thing could get somewhat sticky to say the least. All the other pieces of the false I.D. package were a cakewalk after obtaining the birth certificate. Drivers license and all went off without a hitch. He considered skipping the passport all together with the risk but decided to apply for it earlier in the month. It would really nail down the false documentation. The danger was it could bring some real heat if processing the paperwork fouled up.

"Mary, I need a favor," he said as he passed the receptionist headed for his office.

"I want you to call the passport office and see if you can determine the status of a passport application for me. Name is Kenneth Stevens. Tell them he is a new hire and we need to send him out of the country ASAP. Make up anything just see if you can get it finished. Lay a sob story on them."

As he walked away listening to the receptionist talk to the passport people he realized he needed to stay out of any of these conversations. That way if this thing went haywire he could plead ignorance. The nervousness he was feeling was probably more related to the conversation he with his brother-in-law last night than to the passport thing. Tom called and relayed the bad news that his sister was back in the hospital with her mental condition deteriorating. Her fear and anxiety were getting the best of her. Chris's dilemma was should he tell her Braburn was not in the country. It might comfort the situation, but the question of where he got that knowledge would have to be answered. There was no way if he let anyone else in on his information from Morgan's friends there would not be a leak. Once the St Louis boys got wind he had information that they did not, it would destroy his desired perceived position as a bystander. These people were still cops and they suspect everyone about everything just by nature. The less they knew about his role in anything related to the investigation the better. The last news from the police was months ago and as far as they knew, Braburn was still on the loose in the States. Mulling the whole thing over and over was getting nowhere and the thought entered his mind that maybe the easy way out was to cough up the five grand to Morgan's Chicago connections and solve the problem. One way or the other something was going to have to be done. All the psychiatric evaluations of Jody's condition pointed to the fact the only way to cure it was for her assailant to be captured or killed. The general consensus among the doctors was that as long as Braburn was on the loose she would continue to deteriorate. As he thought about it, the anger rose from within just considering the bad luck of this guy crossing his family's path in life. He never really hated anyone before but this was different. Visions of his sister laying there with her head beat to a pulp filled his mind and down deep the thought of delivering Braburn's scalp to his sister in the old Indian tradition entered his tormented thoughts.

*   *   *   *

Odwalla's bold behavior paid off more than he could ever have imagined. Orders from the top immediately got him promoted over all the other special force members and now he called the shots for the group. They moved him out of the barracks and into his own air conditioned apartment in Freetown with even a full time woman to serve his every need. There was no more red-light district in the middle of the night to quell his passions as well as no more sweaty nights in the barracks. Best of all there were no more military rations plus they issued him his own phone. It seemed if he wanted something all he needed to do was think about it, and it would appear. The only requirement of his new job was to be on call for special assignments and stay close to the phone. He could dress anyway he wanted and spend his time as he pleased. The truth was he was free again almost just like life in Boston.

He resurrected his art interest and was dabbling in local native art. As a dealer he opened a small shop in an out-of-the-way street market. Surprisingly he was making a little money. The people in the streets now recognized him on site and they respected and feared his reputation. That part was comparable to his last days in prison and in Boston. The whole experience just reinforced his belief that people are the same sheep anywhere and the meat-eaters will always rule. The way things worked out in this little country he quickly become one of the meat-eaters. The last couple of months were dull and the scene was starting to bore him. His only instructions were to stay close to things and be on call. There was the rumor of a mess developing in the western part of the country with an American church bunch that was trying to break ties with the United States. A big stir was supposedly coming down with a California Congressman investigating the American commune. Supposedly it was in the remote western jungle and was ruled by an American preacher. Odwalla had no desire to even visit that part of Guyana as it was wild. His experience in the jungle the night he arrived in country was enough for him. His hopes of avoiding the whole thing were shattered when the call came down to pick two men and catch a bus to the edge of nowhere. He was also instructed to arm everyone with rifles so the thought a possible long range killing was being planned entered his mind.

CHAPTER 10

BLUE WATER

The time at the research facility was starting to drag for Chris and, more and more, thoughts of Jeannie and his days in Phoenix seemed to occupy his mind. There was something about her he just couldn't put his finger on and he could not shake her constant presence. There was never a woman who left that kind of impression at any time in his life, including his ex-wife. The inner peace he felt when she was with him seemed to refill his body each day. It made getting up in the morning a rejuvenating thing. There was just no way to explain it other than some clique' like "soulmate" or "life partner" and yet that did not do it justice either. The girls that passed through his life since he left Phoenix were all great people but making love to them was an empty bag. He was always glad when they got up and left after a date. The urge to call Jeannie was becoming overwhelming but the thought she may have moved-on paralyzed his dialing finger. *What if she has met someone? What if I call and a guy answers the phone?* The truth was he needed to know one way or the other so he decided to call her when he got home. As he finished the final performance reports on the latest design project and was closing his file drawer Jim bounced in his office grinning from ear to ear.

"Tit sling project just bought us a sailboat, what do you think of that?" he remarked.

"What do you mean?" Chris replied.

"Just that, I've decided to buy a thirty-five-foot Hunter sailboat with the bonus check from the project and it's all your fault. You're the main reason we are getting the extra money,"

"All my fault your ass. You've been looking for an excuse to get back to sea since the day you left Florida and besides where you going to keep it, on Woods reservoir here on the base. The pressure must be getting to you man. When are you going to go sailing?"

"Got it all figured out. Dock it over at Kentucky Lake during the hurricane season and motor it down the Tennessee river out through the Tim Tom waterway in the fall. Raise the sails in Mobile and disappear. Already have a slip lined up at a marina in Charlotte Harbor down on the tip of Florida. Fly back and forth out of Fort Meyers and sail the Bahamas at will all winter long. You should see this boat it's fully equipped and ready to go. This baby is a total chick magnet. Fixing to change my life and start having a little fun with some of this money," Jim answered.

"Better watch what you wish for because there are some guys in this organization who will actually use that boat and you're looking at one of them. Besides you couldn't sail your way out of Charlotte Harbor without my help," he replied chuckling.

"They are bringing it up day after tomorrow. Do you want to ride up to Grand Rivers with me for a shakedown cruise on the lake this weekend?" Jim asked.

"Guess so. Was planning to run up to my sisters next week. I can catch a flight out of Paducah over to Kansas City when we are finished. Need to go check on her. She's not doing well," he replied.

"Still the assault thing?"

"Yea the thugs from the black Nation are still trying to spook her and it's about to get her down. It's working too. Bastards showed up at her husband's business unannounced and made an appearance just for show couple of days ago. Never said a word, just ordered a burger and fries and sat there staring while they ate. Whole thing has her clear down in bed," he replied.

150

"Why are these people so hot on this ex-con anyway? Looks like they would drop him like a hot potato with the pressure that's on him," Jim said.

"He was designated somebody special like a black jesus or something years ago by the organization. When he was in prison, the top man from the Nation actually visited him and decreed him special. It appears the power structure running the group now can't back off. They have to save face. At least that's what the St Louis County police bunch are professing. Easier for the Nation to intimidate my sister than to change a policy I guess," he replied.

"Scary bunch buddy, watch your ass," Jim answered as he turned and left.

Driving home Chris was mustering the courage to call Jeannie. Maybe after all this time she would be gone or have a different number so she would not answer. He figured he would pick a time that was early enough to be sure to catch her alone but late enough for her to be home from work and settled for the evening. The sailing thing could be a good diversion from the pressures he endured lately with both his sister's situation and the job. Maybe he could put together a trip with Jeannie so they could spend some time alone and really sort things out. Lately he felt life was only bouncing him around with no clear purpose. A few days of solitude and swimming in the sun with a most special person might help put some priorities in order and eliminate some of his confusion.

He could feel the apprehension on the drive back to his apartment. Stopping at the store to pick up something for dinner, he couldn't clear his mind enough to seriously shop. This thing with Jeannie made him nervous for some reason. Just a beer and a deli sandwich would have to do it for supper. His mind was still reeling when he pulled up to his apartment. He unloaded his things and settled in for the evening. After downing a couple of cold beers to take the edge off, his excuses to postpone the phone call ran out. *It's now or never. Gotta know one way or the other.* The odd combination of the sense of anticipation combined with the sense of dread made him hold his breath involuntarily as he dialed the number and the phone rang on the other end.

"Hello," answered Jeannie with a meek tone of voice.

He knew at that moment with one word from her that his timing was just right. That single word flowed over him like a warm shower on a cold morning and instantly soaked in to his core. He suddenly and inexplicably felt better.

"Thinking about you babe. Need to see you. Not doing good here alone," he replied.

"I know. Seems like it's been a million days we've been apart. It hasn't changed with me. How about you?" she replied

"No just stronger," he answered.

"What about your work?" she asked.

"Beginning to get draggy. You know me, I can't stand the routine," he replied.

"I love you Chris and think I always will. This separation has just made it stronger," she said in a low husky voice.

"What's your schedule? Can you get away for a while? Could you meet me in a few days?" he asked.

"Yes I can, even if I have to quit my job. I've got some vacation built up. I'm still in love with you. You are in my thoughts constantly."

"O K, let me see what I can arrange," he replied.

As they both hung on the phone the time passed quickly until he noticed the clock and realized they were on the line for over an hour. They filled in the time since they parted and he unloaded about the situation with his sister's assault. He even admitted to her that he was considering paying for an assassination by the underworld.

The whole conversation was so soothing as these secrets were held completely within all these months. The relief of just telling them to another person felt good and the things he was telling her meant he trusted her with his life. There was certainty in his mind she would keep it all secret. Finally, the realization that he was talking on an open phone line set-in and he decided to end the conversation.

Gathering his thoughts afterwards he realized that truthfully he couldn't pursue this killer without some kind of behind the scenes help. She would be a good choice for that kind of support. It would also be easy to get her off the hook if something fouled up. With their relationship the denial of any prior knowledge by her of events would be believable because he could limit her knowledge and not warn her in advance if he decided to act.

$$* \qquad * \qquad * \qquad *$$

The arrangements for a gulf sailing trip took some finesse particularly since the boat was so new. Everyone wanted to use the new boat so Chris pulled some rank to get it for a couple of weeks. The deal clincher was that all the other employees were novice sailors and Jim didn't trust them at the helm particularly taking it down the river. The Tim-Tom waterway was narrow in spots and the barge traffic was heavy and dangerous. It all worked out first of all to get the boat to Florida for the season, then to allow a few days with Jeannie alone in the islands and finally to leave the boat at the slip in Florida for the next lucky guy in the organization. He decided to meet Jeannie in Mobile.

The river trip was a boring engine run with no sails for miles and miles winding down the crooked river finally ending in Mobile Bay. The mast was lowered to clear the river bridges by the dock crew at Kentucky Lake. It was tied to the deck of the boat for the river trip. He made prior arrangements to have it raised at Dog River

Marina when he got to the coast. Jeannie was scheduled on an evening flight and would meet him at the marina. The rest of the time would be blue water sailing down to the Bahamas and the vacation of his dreams.

The river trip was a bit taxing without any crew due to having to deal with the locks and anchoring single handed in small tributaries at night. The anxiety gnawing at him from all the things that weighted on his mind made it hard to sleep. Worst of all were the mosquitos combined with the splashing of the feeding alligators at night. There was some relief when he exited the river in the city of Mobile and entered the bay. It was mid-morning and with luck he hoped to get the mast up before the marina's dock crew went home. To make it happen he needed to hurry the last few miles. He kicked the engine up a notch even though the bay was rough. As he pulled in under the dog river bridge a tip seeking kid from the marina instantly showed up on the dock to help him tie up and let the bumpers out.

"Where's the boss," he asked the kid.

"Gone for the day," was the reply.

"Anyone here that can put up my mast?" he asked.

"I can," answered the kid enthusiastically.

"Tell you what, get it up before quitting time and there's a case of beer in it for you," he said.

"Untie, start the engine and I'll take the boat to the tender pier right now," answered the kid.

The kid quickly stowed everything, took the helm and left Chris standing on the pier. He watched the boat as it motored away for a minute until he was at ease with the kid's ability at the helm. *This will put us in a position to leave before first light. That's sure as hell well worth a case of beer. I'll let them get started on the mast and get something to eat.* Walking across the street to the local burger joint he realized he needed to find a phone and check Jeannie's air connections. First he would have lunch and a quick beer then find a phone and a place to sit out of the sun to wait for her arrival. He was tired and seemed to recall a bench at the tender dock where he could relax and watch the kid reinstall the mast.

The slow rhythm of the river wash lapping against the boat's hull lulled him as he relaxed on the Bright Star's bridge. The bridge gave him a vantage point to watch the street in front of the marina as he waited for Jeannie's cab. A cool gulf evening breeze bathed his body and he could feel himself dozing slightly. The gentle contact of the boat's bumpers against the dock created a rocking motion that added to the peace of it all. The fading light of the evening and the fatigue of the solo river trip contributed to his heightening euphoria. The marina returned the boat and re-secured it at the pier quicker than he expected. The whole experience was a testament to the beer incentive plan. When he fetched a case of canned Bud from the cabin's storage area to pay the kid he reflected on the boy's attitude. *This is what I wanted in my unit in the bush, smart and aggressive.* Suddenly the calm was interrupted by the roar of tires on loose gravel. It gave him a start as a taxi appeared through the maze of the boat yard next to the marina office. His heart sprang to life as Jeannie stepped out. The realization the wait was over hit him and excited anticipation filled his body.

*   *   *   *

Breaking out of the bay into the open gulf was like a rebirth. The gulf water under the deep blue sky, the aqua glow and the infinite scope seemed to just beckon a sailor to disappear into it. Last night with Jeannie docked in the marina was a dream come true and there was no way he could ever feel any better than he did at that moment. Getting out before daylight and motoring down Mobile

Bay put them at the outer marker buoys before noon. With decent wind they would make one of the dry islands off the Florida coast by dark. On those islands there was no fresh water supply and which meant there wouldn't be any bugs, so they could anchor close-in. They could spend some time completely unmolested and with any luck spend the night on the deck in the moonlight. As he set his heading and hoisted the mainsail, he felt it catch and the wind was perfect, just off the starboard stern. After the jib was up they would probably be doing better than twelve knots so they would reach their destination in time to swim and relax with a cocktail hour. The boat was a dream to handle having all the newest whistles and bells. It was his first experience with power wenches and one person could sit in the cockpit and manage the sheets single-handed. As things settled down, with the sea at about three foot rollers, he tied the tiller on the heading and took a deep breath. Jeannie emerged up the gangway from the cabin wearing only a bikini bottom. The marvel of the perfect form of her white breasts outlined by her jet-black hair and desert suntan on the rest of her body was a sight to behold.

"Are you trying to even out your tan or seduce me? You can get a serious burn out here in the Caribbean sun and I don't want those babies tender and untouchable this evening if you know what I mean," he said.

"It's your call. After last night I figured you might be out of steam. Time for some sun. I'll be careful. You need to pay attention to the road and drive the boat," she answered.

"Gonna' have to teach you some sailing jargon I can see. You don't drive a boat you sail or pilot it," he replied.

"Looks like driving to me," she teased.

"Alright directions first, the front of the boat is called the bow. The rear is called the stern. The right side is starboard. The left is port."

"What if your port is on the right side, do you have to back the boat into the dock, "she laughed.

"It has nothing to do with a port. They just call it that."

"That doesn't make sense," she replied.

"It doesn't have to make sense. Most things in this world don't make sense. Now here is how you remember it. Right has more letters than left and starboard has more letters than port. Compare the number of letters and that will keep it straight. You'll know which word to use. You have to talk to me like a sailor out here on the water. I think that's called maritime law," he joked.

"How about tonight when we are making love, do you want me to talk to you like a sailor then," she smiled.

"Cut it out, I'm serious," he laughed and turned to check the helm.

This sense of humor was the thing he liked most about Jeannie. She was usually one up on everyone around her. The independence and the brains made the difference. As he leaned back against the cockpit rails, he raised his bare feet to the instrument dash to relax. Jeannie gingerly walked out on the foredeck and spread a towel to lie down and soak up the sun. There they were rolling out across the gulf with nothing but water and sun in all directions with the rhythm of breakers against the hull for their music. As Jeannie raised up and unsnapped the lid on her sunscreen bottle she glanced his way and smiled knowingly. She dispensed it in her palm and rubbed it suggestively on her upper body. The vision of their evening destination and a nude swim to cool off entered his mind as he closed his eyes to doze off.

*   *   *   *

Odwalla sat in his art shop fooling with a saxophone someone dropped by for him to try to sell on consignment. He learned to play the sax a little in prison but it was long ago. He figured it would be a waste of his time to try to pick it back up. *This motherfucker is total shit. I'll never unload this. Don't know why people never bring nothing decent. Always junk.* As he set it aside he surveyed the other instruments and noticed a guitar with a broken G-string.

He set up the art shop as a cover for the covert activities of his job with the GDF but to his surprise, it was paying off a little. He was making a little money with it. The urge to paint something of his own was eating at him as he considered the stock in shop total crap. So far the stuff was mostly local from people who were descendants of the original African Guyanese settlers. The African influence was prominent in the works and the crudeness of it all actually turned him off. The thought of someone running in the jungle in a loincloth carving some kind of trinket out of wood was demeaning to him. Tourist seemed to eat it up though. The music side was a little better as the locals would buy the guitars and horns because there were not a lot of places to get instruments in the city. Fidgeting a little for some reason he decided to change the guitar string to relax his tension. Besides a customer might walk in and want to test it so the guitar needed to be ready to strum. He retrieved a new string from his desk and sat down.

The shop was in the older part of the city on a narrow street only wide enough for foot traffic. There were little shops all along both sides and the street would be very crowded on a busy afternoon. Mornings were slow though and he could paint and put things in order. The shop was one of the few places where Odwalla was unarmed which made him very uncomfortable. The order to stay unarmed when in the shop came down from the top and he was suspicious of it. Supposedly, the leaders did not want the least hint to the locals he was anything but a citizen businessman or so they said. He was leery of his vulnerability not just from some outside enemy but mostly from within his own group. Anyone that wanted his job or any superior that suddenly wanted him dead knew he would be unarmed in the shop and would pick that location to hit him. All those years in prison taught him something about surviving.

As he strung the guitar a thought came to him. He could take one of the larger guitar strings and cut a couple of pieces of broomstick for handles and make a garrote. It was a common prison weapon. The thing would go unnoticed on his desk but in an emergency he could use it to defend himself if he were jumped by someone in the shop. Retrieving the broom from the corner and a saw from the toolbox, he cut two pieces of handle about four inches long. After tying the wire to the center of each piece of broom handle he looped the wire over the corner of the desk and pulled the handles to test the connections. *This will work. If I can get this wire around someone's neck he a dead motherfucker.* He rolled the wire around the handles and stuffed it in the top drawer of the desk. As he closed the drawer Davis came through the door looking kind of spooked.

"Word came down we goin' up north to deal with the church group that's out of control. Don't really want nothin' to do with this shit man. These people from the States. Our black asses be hangin' out big time if this mess goes down bad. Hell man the cops are jonesin' for me in Cleveland. Word could get out I'm down here. These people are goin' shit in our nest here," Davis said wide-eyed.

"What's the word? What's the job?" Odwalla asked.

"Shut some people up before they can get out. Shoot their asses I guess. Hey man, I don't like that nigger Jaywil you pick to go with us. He a crazy motherfucker," Davis replied.

"The cat's alright. We need someone good with a long gun for this job and I hear he the man. What's our orders?" Odwalla replied.

"Catch some bus in the morning up north to a jungle camp where they livin' and wait for a contact. God forsaken god damn place, alligators and shit all over up there. Word is it's worse than around here. I want nothing to do with no animals. Jungle spearchucker I ain't. Just a street nigger from Cleveland, that's me," answered Davis.

"Don't worry about it I'll protect you. Pack the weapons in one of those artifact boxes in the back. Don't want any attention on this bus we takin," he answered smiling.

*   *   *   *

Arriving in the village of Catoma, Odwalla could not have imagined the surroundings. They was nothing but jungle for what seemed like hundreds of miles and only a single lane red dirt road all the way. The trip was miserable and slow with the temperature hot and sticky. The rickety old bus stunk from unclean human bodies and the jungle mildew in the upholstery. As they unloaded everyone had a disgusted look on their faces. *I hope someone is planning to come and get us when this is over. There's no other way to get out of here unnoticed.*"

Listening to Davis bitch all the way put his nerves on edge and strained the situation. Everyone's tension was high. Wondering to himself, Odwalla was uneasy about this whole mess and he could just feel something wasn't right. As Davis exited the bus he didn't seem to be himself either.

"Man, I got the bubble guts. Must be that shit I ate when we stopped. What was that meat anyway? Gotta find a can right now." said Davis.

"Good luck. You probably need to just go behind the building and drop 'em. Sure don't see anything that looks like a toilet. Tell

Jaywil to get the duffle bag with the rifles out of the bus. I'm going to check inside," he answered as Davis turned and trotted off.

Odwalla didn't like this Jaywil either. The man seemed spaced out like maybe he was doped but if he were he sure covered it up. Odwalla could usually spot drugs. Maybe the motherfucker was just crazy like Davis said. Considering the situation, he decided if there is any gun play it might be smart to stay behind this guy and keep him in sight.

CHAPTER 11

THE DECISION

The sailing trip was the interlude Chris needed to clear his mind. The nights and days on the sailboat and the freedom to roam the islands at will could not be equaled with the peace of mind it offered. After two weeks of sailing the islands, the tension from all his life issues disappeared. The time passed too quickly and the fact Jeannie returned to Phoenix was a bummer but all told, the vacation was a raging success. He forgot what a vision the live reefs were and the scuba everyday helped tone his body and put him back in a decent physical shape. He taught Jeannie to use the scuba tank and she appeared natural in her black bikini trailing flowing black hair under the water as her perfect legs cranked the flippers. The time spent teaching her to sail got more laughs as her playful teasing nature tweaked his seriousness about the process. She turned out to be apt with handling the boat so the objective of making her a decent skipper was reached. The scenes of the trip would stay in his mind and be available for recall when things got rough. The two of them couldn't seem to reach a conclusion on what to do about their relationship in the long term. She still was tied to her family with her mother in Phoenix even though her father died the previous year. There was a good possibility her sister would pick up the load and move the mother to Michigan in the next few months. That would free Jeannie up for a move to Tennessee. Upon parting, they left it at that, but both knew they could not stand to be apart for long.

When he dropped the boat at the marina in Florida there was a phone message to call his brother. It appeared the St Louis County police boys requested a parley regarding his sister's case and were coming to her home to talk. They wouldn't reveal the news on the phone but supposedly it was big. They were scheduled for Saturday and his sister wanted him to be there to talk to them. There was so much back and forth over the last few years Jody was at the point where she did not trust anyone except her own blood. A diversion for his return trip through Kansas City was going to be required as he wanted to talk to the detectives personally about the status of things.

The drive over from the Kansas City airport was the same drag as usual and as he pulled up to Jody's house, he could see from the cars in the drive everyone was already there including his brother.

The excitement around the dining table was obvious as Chris entered the room. Everyone was already seated and Sergeant Rush rose from his chair to extend his hand.

"Sorry to say Buzz couldn't make it today due to a family issue but I came anyway. This latest stuff is big news," he said shaking hands and sitting back down.

Settling into a chair, Chris observed how haggard his sister looked. Her weight was visibly down and her hair was uncharacteristically unkempt. The hollowness in her cheeks and the circles under her eyes were a testament to the misery she was enduring. Just the sight brought the anger up in his throat and he could feel himself starting to sweat a little.

"That's alright. What's the story?" he replied.

"Braburn has turned up in South America. You possibly saw the news about the killings of the Congressman and his staff down there at an airport in Northern Guyana. Our boy was one of the shooters. Story is he works for the dictator of Guyana as a hit man and enforcer. Apparently there are several American fugitives that are hiding down there doing the same thing. Braburn has been hiding in the Guyanese military under an alias name. In addition to his military duties Braburn also has an art and music store in the capital city of Georgetown as a cover. This has all come out since the shooting incident a few weeks ago. The Congressman went down to investigate reported abuse of some of his constituents by the American church group and was murdered along with several others. The connections that placed Braburn in Guyana are still unclear but it appeared it was all arranged by the Boston HQ of the Black Nation. He still holds the special status with them," said Rush.

"Will the feds go get him?" John asked.

"Well, that's the fly in the ointment. The extradition treaties with this country leave the decisions to their president. Fellow named Durnham. Right now he is stonewalling all the U.S. authorities and will not even allow the FBI into the country. He says local people will handle the investigation and prosecutions. The only American law enforcement on the inside right now is CIA and god only knows where they fit into this. They are notorious for letting things ride to get favors from the locals. Their objective is to deal with the big communism issue in that part of the world. They will go along to get along to avoid upsetting the apple cart if you know what I mean. Don't see the Guyanese government doing much about Braburn since he is now one of theirs. As far as bringing him back, to be truthful, I'm not optimistic," he said.

"So what you are telling us is you know where he is but you can't do a thing about it, just like the episode in Boston. Is that right?" Chris responded with his face turning red.

"Basically that's it. There is some scuttlebutt in St Louis about going after him but I'm afraid it's related to the election that's coming up. Prosecutors like to get into the newspapers right before the election. They want the exposure. This story would put them on the front page of the Globe for weeks, so color me skeptical of their good intentions. If they do move on it one requirement of theirs will be that Jody agrees to testify against Braburn when they bring him back. That means a face to face at a trial possibly and truthfully with the clout the Nation bunch has, he might squirm his way out again. How do you like the thought of him being turned loose on the streets again back in the states?" said Sergeant Rush

"I can't handle this," answered Jody breaking into tears.

The officer got a stern look on his face and replied, "If they approach you to testify I want you to promise me Jody you will not agree unless they guarantee that the officer they send after him is me. Work it that way and if they do send me your problems will be solved. With this guy and me it's personal. I really want him. I know damn well he will resist arrest and I'll leave his ass down there for the local buzzards.

As the meeting ended Chris casually asked, "What is this guy's name in Guyana? What does he go by?"

"Odwalla, supposedly it is Swahili. Not sure how they spell it though. He's capitalizing on the black issue with the art store and all. Knows where his bread is buttered you might say. Apparently he has a small store that sells native art and music instruments."

*   *   *   *

Conferring with his brother after the meeting, they agreed John would watch Jody closely as suicide was a concern for both of them. He left her some cash to take the money pressure off but her state of mind was scary. As he drove back to the airport a million thoughts were flowing through Chris's mind. What he just learned was old news. He knew about the overseas connection well over a year ago. *For Christ sake, Morgan's mob buddies had this information a month after Braburn skipped Boston.* The ineptness of the cops just disgusted him. He did learn some things from Sergeant Rush though namely a city and an alias name. Even if the authorities say they will get this guy there was no way to factor in the influence of the Black

166

Nation. That unknown could change anything from over the local authority's heads. The Nation was notoriously well connected and unpredictable. Based on experience he didn't expect any better results from the law than there were to date. The more he thought about the whole mess the angrier he got. The whole thing dragged on and on and now seemed to be right back at square one. The only thing that wasn't sitting still was his sister's condition. It was continually deteriorating. To end this thing and save his sister and possibly her children he was going to have to act.

Just the thought of confronting his family's nemesis filled his body with adrenaline. This was how he felt in Viet Nam and he didn't know if it was good or bad. There was just the familiar feeling he was back to a place he left a long time ago. It was remarkable how clear his thoughts were and what his mission would require. The self-doubts that plagued him since the assault were suddenly gone. He decided right then he was going to solve this problem. He needed to drop Braburn like the animal he is and free his family from any more pain.

*   *   *   *

Odwalla's life was totally turned upside down since the mess at the airport two weeks ago. He couldn't stop blaming himself for it all because he knew the kid Jaywil was unstable from the moment they met. *How could I have been so stupid? I should have picked another man for the assassination of the church people. The whole thing was a paid job and was supposed to only involve dropping a couple of defectors from the church group. The crazy motherfucker Jaywil lost it when the shooting started at the airfield and just started killing everybody. There is no way this thing isn't going to bring the law from the states down on all of us. There is no way the Guyanese authorities will be able to stonewall the killing of a U.S.*

167

Congressman and a news crew. Even the Nation won't be able to stop this freight train. Hell the whole episode was filmed and it's almost certain everyone involved will be fingered. Where can I run now? Certainly not into the fucking jungle. Surely there will be some instruction from Boston on what to do. That stupid Davis and the others are coming unglued and reaching the point of total panic. I have to deal with them in addition to saving my own ass. All I can do is sit, wait and hope the Nation don't decide to throw this whole bunch to the wolves. Maybe I can get back to the states and leave this hellhole of a country. Haven't heard anything from the states for months. All I can hope for is the Nation has scared the white bitch enough to get her to back off so I can get to fuck outta here. As he lay in his bed in his apartment the door broke open and in walked Davis.

"Been told to lay low and shut-up," said Davis excitedly.

"Is that it? Who'd that come from?" answered Odwalla.

"The top, man, the top. Word is the whole thing is handled. Remember that C.I.A. cat at the village? He has the big dick in this place and there will only be the local fuzz involved in this investigation. They guarantee we gonna' skate. Said just sit tight."

Odwalla watched as Davis shuffled out the door still talking to himself. *He a dumb ass nigger of the worst kind. Dumb enough to believe that shit for sure. No way this thing is just going to be forgotten. This is a con to get the guard down and Davis is going to suck it up like a hog at the trough.*

Odwalla had to admit he didn't know if this news was good or bad. At least if the U.S. Feds entered the scene it would force him to get up and do something different. The thought of Guyana now made him want to puke. *The people in this place are dead from the neck up. African niggers to the core around here and mostly dumber than dirt.* Dealing with the native art through his shop only lowered his opinion of the natives. The other half of the people in the country were East Indians. They were uppity as hell and didn't want blacks around at all. It seemed like they were worse than the whites in the States. Things here were totally segregated. All he really wanted was to get back to Boston where the Nation was in control. Ever since he left Boston they kept promising he could come back. Always the same promise that they would scare the white woman and she would back off. He considered running off but the complication was his new I.D. It was for an African and he couldn't fly anywhere but Africa without other paperwork. He knew he didn't want to go any deeper in the African culture than he was in Guyana. The whole thing got down to still being in a prison just in a different way. He cursed his circumstances and decided to go over to his shop and do some painting. That always seemed to take the edge off.

*   *   *   *

On the flight back to Nashville thoughts still swirled through Chris' mind at the speed of light. After all the wasted time over the last few years he needed a way to get to Braburn in Guyana. Chances were good Braburn wasn't going to show back up in the states. There were some positives about killing him over there and one big one was any investigation would probably die a natural death quickly. In addition, immediate suspicions would be on his local enemies and a guy like Braburn was sure to have several. The snag was operating in a foreign country and pulling it off unnoticed then coming up with an air-proof alibi for the time. Making an overseas trip and covering all the tracks would be tough. He felt certain the St Louis cops would suspect a family member if they got wind Braburn was suddenly dead and the one at the top of their list would be him. The cop Westburg made some remarks through the years that related to his suspicions the family wasn't satisfied with things. One comment at one of their last meetings "that murder for vengeance was still murder" kind of said it all. Bottom line was if Braburn turns up dead, the St Louis County bunch would probably come straight to him for some answers regarding his whereabouts during the timeframe. He could not involve anyone else without jeopardizing them and he refused to do that.

With his false I.D. he could make a clean entry into Guyana using the airlines but getting out would be different. Once they found Braburn's body the locals would be checking passports and watching the airport. The question then was getting out of Guyana. As the old military combat mentality kicked in things started flashing through his mind. The fundamental plan was obvious and would revolve around taking minimal risk. This action clearly shouted "cold blooded ambush". Weaponry was the next question and that would be difficult as anyone caught with a firearm in a country like Guyana would be dead meat immediately. Taking a firearm in the country would be impossible and he didn't trust himself with just a knife. His one knife experience was one night when his platoon was overrun in the bush and it sure wasn't a good one. The tit sling would work if he could get it into the country but a face-to-face cold-blooded kill, where he could smell the guy's breath, wasn't particularly appealing. It was probably the only viable option though and his experience on the practice ranges with the device were all good. The two things that were going to make the whole mission difficult were the same as always. Those were timing and logistics. It always required being in the right place at the right time with the right equipment. *This whole thing was going to take some thinking and a good amount of luck.*

*   *   *   *

Back at the office the weeks passed as the details of the assassination plan came together. He made the inquiries to line up the credentials and paperwork necessary to visit Guyana. He did some research on the country and found a big part of its economy were mining and mineral ores in the interior. The weather was tropical and hot with monsoon rains this time of year. He would enter the country under his false I.D with a cover story that he was a bauxite buyer from the states and was there to negotiate with the aluminum ore mines back in the jungles. Once he got in country, he could disappear without raising a lot of suspicion with the locals. Back in the states his cover would be a sailing trip with time at sea being the alibi for his absence and the fact he was totally out of touch for a period of time. Just in case someone questions why he didn't use the boat's radio he would disable it when he returned and claim it was broken all along. He'd get it fixed when he docked and acquire a simple receipt for a repair. The excuse would be a little thin but hopefully it would be good enough to stick. He would back everything up with proof so any questions could be answered quickly if the cops started snooping around. The key was to be out in front of any questions that might arise. As he entered the front door to the office he went over to the inboxes on the receptionist desk and retrieved his phone messages.

"What's in the machine shop right now Mary?" Chris asked the receptionist without looking up from the messages.

She checked the schedule on her desk and replied, "Nothing it appears."

"I'm staying late and using the shop tonight if anyone asks. Got a little car project that needs a custom-made part. I'll be using the equipment myself tonight. Put it on the schedule," he said.

The preoccupation with Braburn caused him to neglect his work the last few weeks so the work day was unpleasant with things in a state of confusion. As it approached quitting time, waiting for everyone to leave seemed to take forever. The nervousness of needing privacy in the shop made him somewhat antsy. His machining skills were slightly limited and running the shop's milling machine was something he hadn't done for a while. If someone walked in and saw him cutting the bottom off a scuba tank it would be hard to explain. The process would take a while so he needed to let the offices empty out. After everyone was gone Jim stuck his head in the office door on his way out and noticed the scuba bottle sitting on his office floor.

"What's with the tank Captain?" Jim asked.

"Oh, just checking the J-valve, think the sucker is leaking some. Gonna' draw some water in the utility room sink and bubble test it," he answered.

"Throw it in the junk if you even suspect it. Don't want you down in a hundred and fifty feet of water with a dicey bottle. Ain't worth the risk," Jim replied.

"If everyone is gone lock the front door and kill the lights in the lobby when you leave. I'm going to stay a while. Oh, by the way, what's the boat schedule the next few weeks?" he asked.

"I'm flying out the end of the week and taking it to the islands with that chick from NASA. Have to admit I have some ulterior motives on this one buddy. I could marry this girl. Don't know how long we can stay out though. That nozzle project at NASA is kind of a mess. Bureaucrats are all running for cover cause the thing doesn't work very well," Jim groaned.

"I told you that slot injection stuff wouldn't work. Glad I'm not part of that cluster-fuck," he replied.

"I should have listened to you. It sounded good on paper though and the big money sucked me in," Jim answered.

"Why don't you take the boat way down into the lesser Antilles near the equator? Fly back, and Jeannie and I will go get it. I'm dying to go down into the islands that far, maybe St Kitz or Grenada. You sail it down, fly home and we'll sail it back," he said.

"Hell man that's the end of the islands. Next stop is South America. Don't know what we would be getting into. Guess it's civilized. That's a possible. Let me think about it," said Jim turning to leave.

The sound of the electric building door lock catching brought a sigh of relief. He picked the scuba bottle up off the floor, grabbed the old prototype tit sling from a bottom drawer of his desk and headed for the shop. After removing the tank's valve and securing the tank to the milling machine bed he started the process of cutting the bottom off the tank. As he watched the fly cutter separate the base he could see this was going to work. With the long thick rubber boot covering the bottom of the bottle no one would notice anything. He could stuff the sling into the empty bottle, bond the boot with some adhesive and carry it on his flight into Guyana claiming he was there to dive. He carried scuba bottles on flights before without question. If customs stopped him they would just check to insure the bottle wasn't pressurized by cracking the valve and wave him through. This would get his weapon into the country. Heading for his apartment it seemed darker than usual that night and it reminded him to check the moonlight and tides when he finally set a time to leave.

*   *   *   *

Retrieving his dope stash from under the counter Odwalla was looking forward to taking the edge off by blowing himself a little tune. The surroundings of his shop and the noise of the merchants

173

hassling on the street outside, for some reason agitated him more than usual. That shouldn't have been the case because there was good news the last few weeks regarding the killings at the airport. He was about convinced there was more than a good chance the shooting of the Americans at the airport was going to pass. Durnham swung a bigger stick than he thought. The FBI was stopped in their tracks. It was just that everything made him nervous anymore it seemed. The whole reaction was a return of the old "watch your back" sense that developed during his prison days. There was just a feeling things were not right or there was danger around. The last time he felt this way was in Boston just before the Feds showed up to arrest him. He felt the same way the last few weeks. The worst part was not knowing who to trust. Also the fact he was ordered to leave his side arm in the barracks when in public seemed odd. Prison taught him two things for sure. One, never let your guard down and two, the person that kills you is the one you least expect. Davis was his closest brother here in Guyana but that only meant he would be the one they would pick to take him down. He decided he wasn't going to turn his back on anyone from now on, not even friends. As he tried to relax he rocked back in his chair, inhaled the marijuana smoke and observed the nearly finished painting on the easel.

The overall scene on the canvas was an abstract of the turmoil at the art store in St Louis years ago. For some reason that was bubbling up in his mind more frequently the last few months and he was looking to the paint brush to be an outlet for the stress. The painting didn't seem to be working though. He couldn't help but wonder about the white woman that caused it all. *She will think twice next time about hiking her skirt to tease some poor little nigger boy.* He couldn't suppress the smile that came to his face when he remembered her praying to Jesus as he dragged her back behind the counter. *Sure shut her ass up when I pulled the sweater off and stuffed it in her mouth but the look in those eyes is still haunting me.* She seemed to be looking clear through him all through the event. He awakened some nights with those eyes in a dream. There was no way to understand how she was still alive because he sure intended to leave her dead. *She was as fucked-up as anyone I ever saw in my life when I left that store. The fact that she lived is the source of all my trouble.* As he mellowed out, the vision in his mind of the scene melded into the painting as he stared at it and he dozed off with his back to the wall.

* * * *

"Hey baby, how about two weeks from today, you and me, boat trip, sun, blue water, exotic islands," he blurted out when Jeannie answered her phone.

"What are you talking about? she said

"Sailing trip down near the equator, that's what," he responded.

"It's kind of short notice but mom left for Michigan with my sister yesterday so I probably can do it. It will depend on work," she said

"Hey, don't give me the job thing. Quit the damn job, this will be worth it. Besides, I've always wanted to make you a kept woman. Your new job description can be worshiping me. You're gonna' love where this trip takes us. South America almost. See if you can arrange it. I'll get the tickets on this end when I find out where the boat is going to be and call you in a couple of days," he replied

As he laid the plan for the sailing trip out on the phone to Jeannie, he felt a little guilty about deceiving her. He intentionally called her from the receptionist desk so Mary would overhear the plan in case he needed a witness after this was over. It seemed that at this point every thought that passed through his mind keyed on his mission. The basic plan was that when he came out of Guyana they would hook up at the boat and sail north. Lay around the islands for a week or so completely out of touch and then just end the trip together back at Charlotte Harbor with a dead radio.

That evening lying in bed he paged through old newspaper clippings of stories regarding his sister's assault. There was some good information between the St Louis and Boston articles he rounded up the last few years. He made it a point to save them for just this moment. The Boston stories of course were sympathetic to Braburn and referred to him using his Nation name Malik Jakim. One of them even contained an exceptionally good photograph of Braburn. He studied it closely and tried to catalogue the facial features in his mind. Recognizing the guy on sight was going to be a must. He particularly studied the nose and eyes as those couldn't be covered by facial hair. In addition, since the photo was a partial profile shot, some of the features of the left ear were very clear.

As he rolled different possible scenarios over in his mind of just how this thing might come down, he realized there wasn't any way to plan the actual sequence of events. It would all have to be played-out on site with instant decisions. He trusted his ability to make the right decisions at the right time plus his military instincts were returning the last few weeks. There was a certainty, almost a cockiness that went with the confidence he felt. The whole thing seemed to tie in to the feelings he recalled having before some of his missions in the bush. A person just knew he was going to succeed before it ever even happened. It was hard to explain but it manifested itself as an anxious feeling. It made him want to get started right now. The mind was ready and thanks to the swimming on the boat trips the last few months so was the body.

He continued to focus on the newspaper clippings especially the picture of Braburn with a small goatee and a short afro hairstyle.

Looking the photo in the eyes, the smile on Braburn's face sored him to the core. *Look at the son-of-a-bitch. He really believes he has beaten the system. It's time to educate this vicious animal.* He tried to visualize the man with a clean-shaven face. There was a very good possibility Braburn would have modified his appearance. Thinking about it though he concluded with an ego like this one, the man probably was not even trying to hide. Braburn would probably be trying to flaunt it to the rest of the world, but for the sake of certainty, he was going to have to find a way to completely confirm the man's identity before acting. That probably meant more than just sight as the photos were a few years old. The thought of a conversation with the guy was not appealing but would probably be required. This introduced an unknown because none of his Viet Nam experiences ever involved a personal exchange with an enemy. His only really cold-blooded experience was with the kid in the village and that vision kept coming back in his dreams. The thought of talking to this person made him somewhat nervous. He decided to crop the ear from the photo and make a copy of it to carry with him. He would make a visit to Braburn's shop and get a look at the man's left ear for a positive I.D.

The general plan was simple. The whole thing would be based on the element of surprise, hit and run. If he could catch him at his art store, his guard would be down. There he would just jockey for position and fire the sling to put one through the man's heart. A one shot kill, that was the key. Then make a run for it inland to the mine area's and find a way back to the coast from the interior of the country avoiding the cities. As he drifted off to sleep, he catalogued the items he would need to have with him. The fact the country's currency was the American dollar was a real plus because he could carry cash in and use it to bribe his way out. Covering his trail was going to be the key to success. As he reached for the light on the nightstand the phone rang. A familiar voice rang out sounding somewhat excited.

"Hey Captain, the boat's in place," said Jim.

"How far did you get," he replied.

"Clear down to Grenada, man. End of the goddamn world seems like. You're going to like this one. Different breed of cat from the Bahamas. Put the boat up at Diaggo's Marina Grand Anse Beach just south of St George. Right at the bottom of the island. Airport is within a stone's throw. Paid a kid at the marina desk to watch the boat till you get here. He has the keys. I'm headed for Houston. Meeting with NASA big guns," said Jim

"Yea last I heard the NASA boys are wanting blood. Good luck man," he replied.

"They want me to reassign you to the slot injection engine cooling design project. Threatening to pull the money if I don't," Jim said.

"Better learn to tap dance my friend because I need some time. Smooze the old section chief. I won't be back for at least two weeks. Buy him a date or something. Maybe that will help," Chris joked.

"This ain't funny man. It's big bucks on the line. I saw your report with the suggestions for the fix. They like it too. I can get us some time but you gotta get us out of this one when you get back," said Jim.

"I'll think about it when I'm out there riding the blue water. Being with Jeannie takes the pressure off my brain, if you get my drift. I'll be a new man when I get home," he replied.

"Hey tip that kid another ten if the boats alright whenever you get here. This Marina is top drawer. There is a phone at the slip. Don't have to leave the pier to talk. Write this number down," Jim said.

The call pulled the trigger. This was the opportunity to slip into Guyana and even the score for his sister. The general plan was all laid out and it was time to set the dates and get the tickets. As he hung up his heart began to race as he decided to call Jeannie and set a rendezvous with her at the boat.

*   *   *   *

As dawn broke on the morning of departure Chris awoke having rested well through the night. He was amazed how good he slept and how calm and rested he felt. His mental state was a throwback to the combat days where the human body controls the nervousness and forces itself to get the rest it knows it might need. The morning felt good and he decided to take a walk in the cool Tennessee air to stretch his legs. The jogging trail in the woods behind the apartment complex was deserted at this time of day and the solace and down time to think fit the seriousness of his mood. The morning haze hung over the woods just enough to give the moments a spiritual feeling. As he walked along he pushed back on the thoughts of what he was about to do. There was still a twinge of moral remorse with killing that was a holdover from his religious upbringing. In the low light the look on the face of the kid he killed in the village in Nam appeared in his mind's eye. All his other kills were in heavy action and were faceless. Most of them an absolute blur. The thing with Braburn would be the first hate based kill of his life. This would be different. Knowing and studying the man for so many years made the thought of killing him in cold blood a haunt. He was almost like an acquaintance. *What if I can't drop the hammer when the time comes. Hesitation could be a death sentence or cause a miss. If I don't surprise this son-of-a-bitch I could end up in jail in Guyana. No one will even know I'm there and there will not be a chance of surviving. The truth is I won't know until it's time to push*

179

the button and I will just have to risk it. There is no turning back now. Keep telling yourself it is for the family.

As the day passed he watched the time to make sure the two capsules with the bullets sealed in them could be swallowed at the right time. He fasted the previous twenty-four hours to insure his gut was empty. The medical encyclopedia gave eight hours as the time needed to pass the objects. He figured about two hours before his flight from Nashville to his connection in Miami, he would need to swallow them. That timing should put him in private in a hotel in Guyana to retrieve the bullets when they reached the end of his system. He sealed two regular thirty-two caliper bullets in the plastic capsules he kept in his desk at work. Gluing the sections of each capsule together with acetone he was assured the bullets would not be exposed to digestive fluids. Now he was simply faced with swallowing two objects that looked like oversized white jellybeans. As he sat and looked at the objects the reality that he couldn't put it off much longer loomed. *It's now or never if I'm going to have ammo for the sling.* With an eight-ounce glass of water for a chaser he choked them down. It was painless to his surprise.

CHAPTER 12

THE KILL

The low approach to Georgetown gave a clear view of the lights of the city and the layout of the community. It was dawn when the flight left Miami and the view of the clear gulf waters rather whispered something holy on the climb out. The whole scene certainly did not fit a man on a mission to administer death. During the flight, passing over the islands, there were scenes like something from a travel brochure but the descent to earth brought it all back to reality. Chris was suddenly filled with the harsh realization his mission here and now was to kill a man.

With the flaps down the 727 kind of floated and drifted wistfully over the outer markers of what was obviously at best a marginal airport. This was a slow approach and the high engine power settings indicated the length of the runway was probably equally marginal. His years in the aircraft industry always made him cognizant of all the sounds and motions of any airliner he was flying. As he gazed out the window and felt the tension rising in his body he noticed, like in all cities, the houses that littered the noise-ridden runway approach were the low end of the community. It was obvious this neighborhood was a cut below the worst he'd seen even in Viet Nam. It screamed of horrible poverty and a less than third world lifestyle. The scene caused the thought of the money he was carrying to pass through his mind. He definitely needed to keep the "watch your back instincts" turned on at all time when in these streets.

He figured he would catch a cab over to a more prosperous part of the city and check into a hotel for the night. That would give him a chance to get everything prepared for the hunt tomorrow in a private and relaxed atmosphere. In addition, he needed to hook up with some locals that wanted to talk and get the scoop on things around the city. A hotel lobby was a good place to find that kind of conversation. Locating Braburn's art store as soon as possible was critical. That connection was really all he had to go on to find the man. At this point he did not even know where to locate his mark. He figured there couldn't be too many places that fit the description Sergeant Rush gave him. Rush described it as small and off the beaten path and dealing in both art and music. The bottom line was from this point forward every song in this unfolding opera would have to be played out by ear. Time was of the essence as he needed to get back to the marina in Morne Rouge, the sooner the better. Jeannie would be arriving to meet him at the boat in less than thirty-six hours and as far as she knew he was already there at that very moment waiting for her. He totally deceived regarding the real reason for the trip for her own good and hopefully things would remain that way.

He studied the maps of local roads and made a basic plan for getting out of Guyana but everything was going to have to happen just right. After the confrontation with Braburn he would catch a bus into the jungle toward the Bauxite mines. The area was laced with streams that lead back to the coast and he could hire a boat to bring him back out. Once on the coast, if he could get out to one of the close islands, there were private carriers for hire and he would get one of them to fly him up to Grenada.

As the plane rolled to a stop and the attendants lowered the stairs at the rear of the 727, he pulled the small brown grip from under the seat in front of him. The scuba bottle with the sling hidden in it was on the floor in the front coat closet of the plane. Considering the risk with taking the modified scuba bottle through customs, he decided to push out into the isle, snag the bottle and stay in the crowd as they exited. That way the customs inspectors would be pressed by a crowd and be more likely to wave him and the bottle through. Moving up through the line one passenger at a time he could feel the tension building as he observed the agent he would have to confront. The agent was a large black man and his demeanor was typical third world. He was obviously looking for any kind of score his uniform and badge could force on a naive tourist. Chris reached inside his light weight seer-sucker coat pocket and retrieved one of the twenty dollar bills he stashed there for bribes. As he approached the agent he rolled the bill into a small wad. With a slight grunt, he hefted the scuba tank up in the air and set it and the small grip on the table next to the agent in one move. Retrieving his passport, he handed it over with a smile and began to speak before the agent could.

"Can you recommend a good hotel?" he asked while quickly tucking the wad into the agent's free hand.

"Many excellent hotels in Georgetown Mister (uhh) Stevens," the agent replied glancing at the passport and simultaneously shifting his eyes to his other hand to size up the bribe.

The best is "The Masters". It's up by the Government complex. Very expensive but I can see that won't bother you. Here on Bauxite business? I'm guessing by the scuba tank you also plan to visit our famous sea turtles," he said smiling.

"Yes, to both," Chris replied. "Where's the best place to see the turtles?

"Down the coast almost to Suriname. You are in luck. The mines are in the right direction for you. It will be easy to find. Just straight out to the coast along the Ramshu River from the mines. Anyone could find it even a tourist," the agent replied.

Stamping the entry page of the passport the customs agent waved his hand in the direction of the main entrance. Chris breathed a sigh of relief at the realization he just made the first hurdle by passing customs. Mr. Stevens and his weapon just found their way into Guyana. Snagging his gear, he headed for the taxi curb. The cabs all looked ratty so he just chose the first one in line. As he settled in the back seat he felt a slight cramp in his lower gut and realized he probably needed to get to a hotel as soon as possible. The plastic capsules he swallowed before leaving Miami were obviously in his lower colon. He needed a private place to dump them and a public restroom in a third world country was not going to be a good choice.

*   *   *   *

Odwalla's day was a total bitch so he closed the shop early and headed to the apartment to get high. Nothing seemed right at the shop and his free time to paint was being limited. He needed some relief for his tension and it was his woman's time of the month to top it all off. He was so jumpy lately he was even afraid to let his guard down long enough to get high. As he mulled a trip to the whore district over in his mind, Davis came through the door.

"You look like shit man, what to hell's wrong?" Davis asked.

"Got a bad mojo feeling man. Don't like what's been going on around this motherfucker. I don't like they ain't ask us to do nothing since the shit went down at the airport. Maybe they done with us man and you know this kind of job you don't get fired off of. Man leaves this kind of job in a box or dumped into the ocean. I'm real tight man, real tight," he answered.

"Yea, something ain't right," Davis replied.

"Heard today that white cat from the CIA been sniffin' around. Afraid them dogs don't get called off. They get even if you know what I'm sayin'. They don't like people killin' their friends. They ghosts, come and go without any tracks. Leave dead men in their paths. I'm lookin' hard at any cat that seems to be from somewhere else right now. I'll tell you that. Specially white ones," Davis said.

Davis went out the door in a huff. Odwalla decided to relax so he would chance a little dope. As he lit up he immediately felt the smoke temper his emotional edge. He figured the whole situation the same way Davis did. The authorities in the states were not going to let the murders at the airport go even if they said they were. Someone was going to pay with their ass. This probably meant him for sure since he was the leader. He dozed off slightly from the smoke as it dulled his thoughts. *Stay on top of everyone, especially strange white people. I've got to figure a way to get out of this shithole of a country if I'm going to survive.*

*   *   *   *

While checking in to the hotel the cramps in Chris's gut got worse. There was some concern the desk clerk would notice his fidgeting and impatience to get to his room, so he tried to hold his cool while registering. The room turned out to be modern and comfortable but most important it was very private. As he latched the door he dropped his luggage and staggered over to the bed to sit down to try to collect his thoughts. The cramps were about to overwhelm him. He realized he needed to pass the two plastic capsules that contained the bullets as soon as possible. This digestion thing was a more miserable experience than expected. It was becoming debilitating. Spreading a towel on the bathroom floor, he decided to force the issue and get the cartridges out of his gut. This pain needed to pass the sooner the better as it was affecting his thinking. As he squatted over the towel he could feel the plastic capsules move inside him and finally there was the sound of them hitting the floor. He was slightly dizzy from the whole thing but he already felt better.

The ammo thing was a compromise as the cyanide-laced stuff was not available without creating a trail that anyone could follow. That ammo was something the Feds were already tracking. Using it would raise an immediate red flag that pointed directly at him. In addition, to smuggle it into Guyana the only way would be to swallow it and there was no way he was going to risk putting cyanide inside his body even if it were in a container. The compromise was to use the sling with regular thirty-two caliper ammo. The bottom line appeared to be simply, for the sake of keeping things untraceable, he would have to make the first shot almost perfect. Reloading would probably not be an option even though he brought two bullets. This would put a little more pressure on him to exercise extreme care with taking aim and pulling the trigger when he went to take the shot.

He stretched out on the bed and laid a cool damp cloth across his brow. It was a relief to feel a sense of control being restored. Finally relieved he decided to try to eat something to completely settle his stomach. The tension of the whole situation and his body's reactions suppressed his appetite but he figured he'd better force something down. Latching the hotel room door, he remembered the scuba bottle was inside in plain sight. Places like this were notorious for theft and all he needed was to return and find the scuba bottle gone. He decided to retrieve it from inside the room and carry it with him to the restaurant just to be safe.

The hotel restaurant was just off the main lobby. It was small but well-appointed with a hint of East Indian décor and the low plinking sound of sitar music in the background. As he took a table and set the scuba tank in the chair next to him, he could see the Indian desk clerk who checked him in was homing-in from the lobby. He watched the man approach his table. *This is a piece of luck. This old boy will know the city like the back of his hand.*

"How did you find the room Mr. Stevens?" asked the clerk with a slight accent.

"Fine, actually very nice," Chris answered.

"Let me introduce myself, Baldev Patel at your service. I could have arranged a much more attractive dinner date than your friend there. I have some very good connections with local ladies. Guyana's Indian women are the most beautiful you know," said the clerk glancing at the scuba bottle in the chair with a smile.

"I brought the bottle to make sure it doesn't disappear in my absence. Have a seat I could use the company," he answered smiling back.

"I can see you don't trust our local people. That shows you are a wise man," Baldev replied with a chuckle.

It was obvious Baldev was an intelligent man who was thirsty for some challenging conversation to relieve the boredom of his mundane desk job. He settled into a chair and after a few casual courtesy questions about business and other small talk, the man seemed to quickly become comfortable. As things progressed, Chris learned more about Georgetown in a few minutes than he could have from studying all the travel brochures ever printed. Baldev lived in Georgetown all his life and he knew the history of the country plus every nook and cranny of the city streets. The ethnic issues between the races were obviously a big part of life in the city. The Indian clerk filled Chris in on the political and social make-up of the place. He pointed out where in the city to be careful and who to avoid. The man never tried to cover the fact he was extremely racist and his years of dealing with the Africans had not endeared them to him. The city was heavily segregated with the Asians living separate from the Africans. From the fear on the man's face when he discussed the government, it was obvious the military defense force ruled the country with terror tactics and autonomy. It was also clear the force consisted of mostly Africans. Casually asking about souvenirs to take back to the states, Chris managed to delicately move the conversation to the subject of local African art. He was specifically seeking shop locations. Some gold nuggets of information fell from Baldev's mouth as he reeled off shop after shop. Mentally culling the list there were three locations that fit the bill of Braburn's art shop. The one thing that stood out in officer Rush's description was the shop was on a side street that was only wide enough for pedestrian traffic. Two of the places fit that description.

Chris knew better than to show much interest, as this man was bright enough to pick up on things. If suddenly a murder occurred at one of the places he pointed out, he might remember this conversation. He definitely came across as a person who would be willing to blow the whistle if he sensed a profit in it. Changing the subject to diving, Chris intentionally diverted the conversation to the coast and started asking questions about where to get diving gear, rent boats and such. This led to information on buses to the mine area and possible transportation back out to the coast. With the conversation winding down he paid the tab and left an extra good tip, then thanked Baldev and excused himself. He was beaming from what he just learned. He couldn't believe his luck and he decided to take a walk to relieve his tension and do some thinking. Baldev was back at the front desk, so as he walked by Chris asked Baldev to watch the scuba tank and exited the hotel.

The city streets were dark even though it was still early and the clamor of the street noise was an immediate unpleasant distraction. The smells of pollution and ethnic foods cooking reminded him of his R & R in the Philippines during the Viet Nam days. That trip was a mess and thinking about it made him a little nauseous. His feelings now were the same as on that day. The feeling that everyone around him saw him as a profit target. The feeling was irritating unto itself and he assumed it was partially due to the fact there seemed to be overwhelming chaos all around him. He suddenly felt he stuck out like a sore thumb in the crowd and everyone was looking at him. The ringing returned to his ears. The fact the one thing he wanted most on this trip was to not be noticed, prompted him to turn around and go back to his room. Heading back, there was a sudden moment of heightened insecurity and doubt that gave him a start. *Maybe this whole decision is a mistake. I'm certainly going to have to shake this feeling to proceed.* He headed to his room for a couple of shots of scotch to dull the emotion a little. The fact alcohol entered his mind so quickly disturbed him because tomorrow he needed to be sober as a judge. As he walked along the memory of the kid in Viet Nam entered his mind and the haunt of committing cold-blooded murder shook his psyche.

*   *   *   *

As daylight broke over the city Odwalla awoke with a start. He thought something moved in his room but it was just his woman rolling over. Sangeeta mumbled something and turned on her side. He needed sex but his woman was fouled this time of the month under his religion's law. Tight as he was he needed something though. He grabbed her head and forced it under the covers. As he forced her to satisfy him he mumbled profanities at her while enjoying her squirming and trying to fight back. She kept resisting so to stop her he twisted her hair until she broke into tears. When he finished and was relieved he needed something to eat. The heavy dose of marijuana he smoked last night combined with the violent sex brought his hunger to the surface. He smiled to himself as he thought about how women love some pain with their sex. That was something he learned from his mother as a child.

"Get up bitch and do some food. You need to get your ass down and open the shop this morning. I meetin' with Davis early," he said.

"What do you want to eat? "she asked.

"Anything but those god-damned bananas chips. That's all this place is, one big banana. I been eatin' that shit every day since I got here. Cook something you lazy bitch. Do some eggs. Get off your ass. I need to move," he answered jerking her out of bed by the arm.

As she walked across the room gently crying, her naked black body glistened in the low morning sun's rays that were passing through the gap in the shabby window curtains. At only sixteen she was enslaved through a family debt to Durham. The government offered for her to work it off as Odwalla's house woman but the whole thing was getting unbearable. She endured his physical and sexual abuse time after time. She hated him so much that the last time he was out on a job she was praying someone would kill him. She knew she could not get away with it herself. All the women who served the defense force knew the price for disobedience. Time and again she heard of women being taken out to sea in a government helicopter and tossed out to the sharks. She seethed at the hopelessness of her situation and did as she was ordered.

"Let me ask you something bitch. You ain't seen any strange white men around my place have you? Or maybe heard about it?" he said.

"No," she answered.

"You do, you come to me right now. I mean don't wait to tell me. I want it right then," he said.

The overwhelming paranoia seemed to be getting worse the more dope he smoked. It was getting to the point where he saw a white spook in every doorway. The one thing he felt certain about though was, if the CIA sent somebody, it would be a white man.

That helped a little as whites were pretty scarce around Guyana and the assassin would be easy to spot.

* * * *

The morning brought little relief from the tension Chris was feeling. It was a fitful night with little sleep but that was not a surprise. He never figured he would. It was a familiar feeling just like what seemed a million times before when leaving safety for a mission in the bush in Nam. It was odd in that he seemed almost paralyzed and there was a reluctance to take those first few steps to leave. He went through the things in his grip and smiled slightly when the wire cutters he used on the boat to fix the rigging were in the bottom of the bag. *How did those get in there?* Then he remembered he included them so he would have the tools to remove the base from the scuba bottle and cut open the plastic bullet capsules. He was traveling light intentionally. He didn't want to carry anything he wouldn't need but the dikes might come in handy. The suit he wore on the plane was not going to be practical when he was on the run in the bush. He needed to get rid of it completely somewhere on the street. He pulled the old pair of fatigues from the bag along with a pair of sneakers. He wanted a casual look to blend in to the street people as much as possible. A man in a suit in a place like this attracts attention. That he wanted to avoid. With his fatigues and shoes on and shirtless, he hefted the scuba tank to the table and cut the rubber boot with the dikes. As he pried it loose the sling dropped out the bottom of the tank. Then he clipped the plastic capsules in half and set the two bullets on the night stand. Retrieving one of the bullets from the nightstand, he loaded the sling, slipped it on and laced it up tight. The dress shirt he wore on the plane would have to do so he slipped it on and buttoned it as high as the cartridge that was now affixed to his chest. Quickly picking things up he dropped the extra bullet and the dykes in his left front fatigue pocket and the slings firing remote in the right. Everything else he dropped in the grip and zipped it up. He was now focused on getting rid of the grip and scuba bottle without leaving a trail that would lead back to the hotel and the stranger who stayed there last night.

Slipping through the lobby and exiting through the side door of the hotel, he was suddenly flushed with a familiar feeling. He immediately recognized it as the pre-combat rush he felt in Viet Nam when he crossed a basecamp threshold headed into the bush. It was always the same and oddly enough it felt good. His nerves settled down and his focus sharpened. He successfully dodged Baldev and any questions from him as he slipped out a side door of the hotel. Behind the hotel in the alley he spotted a smoking trash barrel where the kitchen help just disposed and lit off some trash. As he past he quickly tossed the gripe in the can and it disappeared into the flames. The next issue was finding a place to dump the empty scuba bottle. It felt good making it to the street clean and ready to hunt. The streets were uncrowded unlike the night before. People were reluctant to make eye contact and he realized changing to casual dress was allowing him to blend in even though he was the only white person in sight. That was good. He now felt secure walking the street. It was obvious these people were only looking for a white man to be a money mark. The next problem was dumping the scuba bottle. He needed to dump it away from the hotel to insure there would be no feedback, if someone noticed it. The hotel staff, particularly Baldev, could tie it to him.

He swung up on a ratty old streetcar as it passed and headed for the African section of town and his first address. The streets were rough so he held on as he bounced around on the bus seat. The fact it wasn't crowded was a relief. He cleared his mind and refocused. Rolling his checklist over in his mind, he made a mental note to be sure to cock the sling before approaching his mark. He smiled as he recalled the last time he made that kind of mistake. The first week in Nam during one of his first firefights he tossed a grenade without pulling the pen. Luckily no one saw it or he would have earned a nickname for sure.

The surroundings deteriorated quickly as the bus rolled deeper into the African area of the city. The whole place was laced with drainage ditches that ran along the side of the streets to allow for the monsoon run off. This time of year they all seemed to be full of rancid water and malaria mosquitos. The shanties and businesses along the street were all painted in bright pastel colors and it rather reminded him of a ghetto Miami Beach. There was a gayness to the scene. It conveyed a message about the instincts of humanity to overcome the misery of it all. People were going about the day's business of survival and paying little attention to each other. The street vendors were setting up for business but the pedestrian traffic was still light. As the bus approached his first target location he decided to drop off and walk in. The stop was deserted. There was still the bottle to deal with and directly behind the sidewalk at the bus stop the ditch was slightly below street level with foliage blocking the view. As the bus pulled away, he found himself alone so he hefted the aluminum scuba bottle up over the bank and heard it hit the water in the ditch. With the bottom open it would sink so his last baggage was now gone and he could focus purely on his mission.

When Sangeeta arrived at the shop she unlocked the door and felt the dread of another day of smelling oil paint overwhelm her. The hopelessness of her life and the continual torment by the most abusive man she ever knew made her almost wish the GDF would go ahead and throw her to the sharks. Waiting for Odwalla to arrive she decided she would make an excuse to get out of the dreary place for the rest of the day. It seemed the only thing she hated worse than Odwalla was the shop where he smoked dope and painted. The place just stunk like the man. She picked up the mess Odwalla left the day before and carried out the trash, then sat down at the rear of the shop. The street out front was mostly deserted at this time of day and she really did not understand why they even opened until afternoon. Then suddenly she received a start when a rattle at the front door revealed a large white man in fatigues and a white shirt. He stepped inside and slightly smiled. He surveyed the place rather thoroughly and spent some time before speaking.

"I'm looking for local original art to take back to the states," he said.

She noticed him looking around rather nervously.

"Need something to remember my trip by."

Silently she waved her hand waist high and palm up across in front of her to gesture, "help yourself". Chris began looking intently at various things particularly the sculptures as if he knew what he was doing. As he circled the paintings he noticed one on an easel that appeared just recently finished.

"What is this," he asked.

"Who is the artist?"

Sangeeta answered in a low voice,

" Man named Odwalla".

The name rang in his head like a bell and his heart began to pound. He looked away immediately hoping there wouldn't be any reaction from the woman.

"Is it for sale?" he asked avoiding eye contact.

"Don't know. You have to talk to the man," she replied.

"Is he here," he asked.

"No, probably be here soon," she replied.

"Guess I'll be back then," he said.

There was an urgent feeling he must get outside to catch his breath. Entering the street, he was a little disturbed that he felt slightly weak kneed. The feeling scared him some. He came all this way and put everything in place. He couldn't lose it now. Maybe he thought, it would be better to shoot the man in the street and avoid the store. The woman was going to be a major complication. If he took the time to wait for her to leave to catch Braburn alone, someone could notice him milling around these narrow streets. If he shot him on the street, he would have to stalk him some and probably not have a choice as to a location to pull the trigger. With the doubt bouncing around in his head his luck held and the choice was made for him.

Just then, a black man appeared headed up the street in his direction. Chris ducked into a side alley. A strange dose of fear suddenly gripped him and he felt if he made eye contact with the man he would give himself away. He felt his natural instincts involuntarily draw his vision to the man's left ear. Before leaving the hotel he again reviewed the ear photo from his wallet but he was going to have to get a closer look to make a positive I.D. All the man's features looked like Braburn's newspaper photo but just a little older. One odd thing was the man appeared to be agitated and moving very quickly. He was visibly a hate-filled man and seemed to be mumbling to himself. Stepping back into the alley as the man passed, the certainty built that this was Braburn and it was confirmed as he turned to survey the street before entering the art store. The shape of the ear matched the indelible image in Chris's mind.

"I'm going to be out most of the day," said Sangeeta as Odwalla stepped inside.

"Man was here earlier, looking for a souvenir. Asked about the new painting you're doing. Wanted to know if it was finished yet," she added.

"What man? What did you tell him?" he said looking concerned.

"Was it a white man?" he asked.

"Yea, looks like he might be some of the American mine people. Said he will be back to talk to you about it," she said.

She could sense he was thinking about the white man and was preoccupied with his thoughts, so she grabbed her bag and headed for the door before he could settle down and start in on her. As the door closed Odwalla was not thinking of her at all. The strange white man was all that was on his mind. *Funny I haven't seen or even heard about this man on the streets.* He went straight to the rear of the shop, retrieved the homemade garrote from the desk drawer and hung it over the drawer pull by the wire. If this white man was who he thought he was, he was going to need it. Not being armed was a real issue because he always figured a hit at his shop would probably involve a knife. He heard about a couple of probable CIA hits in Georgetown and both involved knives. *There is nothing more deadly than a blade man. Watch this motherfucker's hands.* That was something he learned in knife fights in prison.

Standing almost frozen in his tracks watching the shop's door Chris surveyed the surroundings. The street was mostly deserted and the potential to pull this off and make a clean run for it looked good. The problem was the woman in the shop, but just then the problem was solved. She burst out the front door and headed up the street in what seemed to be a big hurry. Suddenly his mind went clear and his objective was right in front of him. A vision of his beaten sister entered his mind and her hallowed face from years of torment was as clear as day. With a rush of adrenalin, he reached inside his shirt and pulled the lever to cock the sling. With clear focus he crossed the street, grasped the door handle to the shop and stepped inside.

A feeling like electricity filled the air in the room and it escalated immediately like the crescendo of a musical score. Both men were aware of the other and both knew something was about to happen. Chris could feel Odwalla's eyes burning a hole in him. Trying to mask his emotions Chris looked down at a sculpture and tried to appear calm. Chris's state of mind was right for the moment at this point. It instantly inflated to total hatred. At the same instant the fear in Odwalla spiked as he immediately concluded this was the hitman he was expecting. Trying to look casual and jockey for position Chris moved closer to the rear of the shop as Odwalla got up from his chair and bent over the desk. With his back half turned and about two steps from Odwalla, Chris caught arm motion out of the corner of his eye. As he instinctively raised his right arm to deflect the motion he was caught by the guitar string garrote that Odwalla retrieved from the desk drawer handle. Chris found himself with Odwalla behind him and the garrote wrapped around his face. He intercepted it when it was looping over his head such that the string was hung on the center of his forearm. It missed the neck and was being held by his right forearm that was being mercilessly pulled against his right cheek. The cable immediately cut into the tissue of his arm muscle and was severing it to the bone. The two men were locked in a struggle of pure strength, Odwalla behind Chris, both bent at the waist. The pair were writhing around the shop knocking things over. With his free hand Chris reached down as low as he could, caught the back of Odwalla's knee and attempted to up-end him. He didn't have the strength with one arm and as his hand slipped from Odwalla's leg it brushed against his left pocket. He felt the wire dikes inside and with nothing but reflex retrieved them and raised them to his neck. With one motion he clipped the guitar string.

Odwalla's full weight was pulling the string and as it separated he fell on his back pulling Chris to the floor with him. With instant response Odwalla rolled over on top of Chris and grabbed his throat in a chokehold. Odwalla was straddling him hell bent on choking Chris to death. Fighting unconsciousness Chris shoved his left hand between the two bodies and tripped the firing pin inside his shirt. The thirty-two cartridge went off and as if in slow motion Odwalla's upper body reeled backward at the waist. His eyes opened wide and rolled upward as if looking at the ceiling. He then let out his breath and fell limp on Chris's chest. Lying there under his nemesis's limp body, he caught his breath and of all things, an odd memory entered his mind. The word "bullseye" rang in his ears. It was from the days at the lab testing the sling and was what the technician yelled the first time he test-fired the device. An odd smile came across his lips as he absorbed the relief and gathered his thoughts.

Immediately reality set in and the flight reflex took over. His arm was bleeding badly and he needed to deal with that before entering the streets. As he rose from the floor he picked-up what appeared to be a dust cloth from the desk and wrapped it around the wounded arm as a tourniquet to control the bleeding. Even though the whole thing only took seconds, the pressure of time bore down on his mind. As he exited the shop he stepped over his dead adversary and could see the man's open-eyed stare with dilated pupils. Braburn was dead. He simultaneously reached over and snagged Odwalla's painting off the floor to use as cover for his wound. He figured he could carry it in public and cover his arm wound to get out of the street unnoticed.

The street looked almost deserted when he surveyed it through the front windows of the shop and picking his time he stepped out to head down the street toward the edge of town. He quick stepped just under a run being driven by pure adrenaline. The key now was to get out of town and over to the bauxite mine region of the country as soon as possible. The question was could he make the bus stop without attracting any attention. His head swirled from the whole event as he was running on survival instincts. His biggest concern now was to avoid passing out from the arm wound.

He felt some of the symptoms of shock setting in but the pain was subsiding as the arm was getting totally numb. Passing the people in the streets and searching for the bus stop was a complete blur. He had no idea where he was. What few people he met still seemed to avoid eye contact even though it was obvious something was wrong. Memories of running to escape from fire-fights during combat vividly appeared in full color in his mind. All the sounds around him were amplified. A vision of the two boys he lost in an ambush hole one night near La Trang was as clear as day. Their heads were practically severed with piano wire garrotes by sappers who crawled up behind them in the dark while they dozed on watch. The dinks penetrated the perimeter and ran through the camp firing and setting off grenades at will. The whole event was total chaos and confusion. For some reason that same feeling of not knowing which way to run was coming through now. He never thought that night that one day he would face the possibility of a fate similar to those two kids. In his mind's eye he could see the look on their dead faces when he packed them in body bags the next day.

It was a miracle he was able to find the bus stop he scoped-out prior to going to the shop. He never considered an injury coming into the mix. As he approached the small group waiting at the stop he stood in the rear to avoid attention. The wait seemed to be an eternity when finally, the bus came into view. He held the painting over his wound and boarded the bus last, quickly handing the driver a twenty-dollar bill. He didn't wait for the change and just staggered to the rear. His hope was a little grease would shut the driver up. It seemed to work as the driver just glanced back over his shoulder and pulled the doors closed.

CHAPTER 13

RUNNING FOR IT

The bus ride from Georgetown with the wounded arm only increased Chris' delirious state. Ever since the event, he was running on pure body chemistry. Scurrying through the streets to escape was a complete blur but it appeared he succeeded in limiting undue attention. The locals wanted to stay obscure so they avoided eye contact but with the delirium, he couldn't be completely sure he wasn't noticed. There was only a vague memory of finding the bus at the edge of town. He really couldn't remember the details of how he managed to find it but his feelings were it was a clean getaway. The painting he snagged on his way out of the shop worked as a cover to hide his wound. At least enough to slip through the empty streets and end up in the last row of seats on a bus headed for the mine area. He lost some blood but the crude tourniquet he grabbed when he left the shop did its job. The wire missed any main blood vessels so the bleeding was not profuse. He finally stopped it with some clean bandages he bought when the bus made its first rural stop. He knew the cut was deep but was reluctant to examine it closely for fear of what he might find. He was praying the tendons and ligaments in the arm were still intact. There was no telling at this point but he was disturbed he couldn't move his fingers. The pain was almost overwhelming and his only relief was a bottle of cheap rum he picked up when he got the bandages. He faced the choice of having a clear head or dulling the pain with the alcohol and he chose the alcohol.

A delay due to the mid-day monsoon held the bus in the middle of nowhere for several hours while they sat it out in the blinding rain. The stench in the dilapidated old bus upholstery permeated the air in the closed space and exacerbated the nausea the rum was causing. There was no choice but to tolerate it. The rum was a lifesaver. He would never have survived sitting stopped in the rainstorm without it. Time was the issue with the bus stalled. Since leaving Georgetown the delay cost a half a day's time. He was going to need the time to make the rendezvous at the boat in Grenada to get in ahead of Jeannie. The day on the bus passed at a snail's pace and as darkness fell his condition continued to deteriorate. He now couldn't think straight or make decisions.

In his delirium, he dozed to the hum of the old bus engine laboring down the deserted jungle road. He knew he needed to reserve his strength. The truth was he was as alone as much as ever in his life and everything at this point was in the hands of pure fate. His mind rolled over and over attempting to put the confrontation with Braburn into prospective.

Where did the unprovoked attack come from? There is no way the man could have been expecting me. It almost seemed that Braburn knew exactly who I was when I walked in the store. I knew something wasn't right when we made eye contact. Lucky thing was I didn't turn my back completely. It is an absolute certainty no one else in the world knew I would be there to kill Braburn. I didn't tell a soul, not even my brother. Where did the attack come from? Never expected it to get physical with Braburn. The man was strong as a bull. The whole thing is absolutely baffling. The fact that my sail rigging needed repair before I left the boat put the wire cutters on the table in front of me when I was looking for a tool to take with me to cut the boot off the scuba bottle. They just happened to be there. Even the fact I left them in my pocket was a pure absent minded mistake.

The bus driver seemed to want to mind his own business. He only glanced to the rear occasionally all through the day as the bus made its normal stops. It was good the bus wasn't crowded and the passengers that came and went really didn't notice him way in the back. There weren't very many and luckily they stayed near the front of the bus. As darkness fell with the cloud cover there wasn't a shred of light in the jungle. The darkness was now total with the only light being the shivering sealed beams of the old bus's headlights as it bounced along the dirt trail that weaved through the jungle. The road was so rough and rutted the speed as a mere crawl. For the last few hours there was a sensation of swimming in black ink. Between the pain and the closeness of the environment Chris was on the edge of an unfamiliar panic feeling.

Suddenly the driver seemed to take interest. Unable to answer his questions Chris sensed the man was losing patience. Finally, the bus lurched to a stop and he realized he was the only passenger left aboard. The aggravated driver pointed to the door.

"End of the line my friend," he said smiling slightly.

"Where are we?" Chris asked.

"Ramshu mining camp," he answered.

The driver retrieved a bundle of clean shop rags from under the dash of the bus and handed them over as Chris passed his seat on the way out.

"Bind that wound with these. They are a lot cleaner than the jungle. I mean bind it so tight it hurts. In this place it can get worse quick. Don't make it worse," said the driver.

"Don't know what your deal is my friend and I don't want to know but this is as far as passengers go. Take my advice get out here and avoid the village. Don't run into the GDF. Everyone else will be O K. People here don't want any part of trouble so they keep their mouths shut. There are people here who will take you out to the coast but don't trust them. Most of these river people would steal the pennies off a dead man's eyes."

Chris retrieved three more twenty-dollar bills from of his pants pocket and handed them to the driver.

"You never saw me. Right my friend?" he said.

The driver tipped his hat and closed the door.

As he stepped off he noticed there were some lights over the hill and he assumed the path where the bus stopped lead to a town. As the bus disappeared into the dark and the smell of diesel exhaust dissipated, he realized he was alone in the middle of nowhere. He needed to rest because he was too far out of it to think at all. He just knew two things for sure, he needed water and sleep. He was confused so he stumbled along the path that led up a hill. The silence was almost deafening but he was looking for a spot to rest without being disturbed. The rains deposited puddles of fresh water in the bases of the large leaves of the elephant ear plants. As he passed them on the path he licked off at least enough water to survive until daylight. Exhausted and faint he could go no further so he just stumbled over to some tall grass and lay down.

His head swirled as he recalled the events of the day. He again mulled over the events of the day. He still couldn't figure Braburn's unprovoked attack. *Where in the hell did that come from? But then again how could I have been so lucky to be carrying those dikes.* Confused and delirious he mumbled for someone to call the choppers to get a ride out of this bush. He wondered aloud what time it was and guessed it to be about ten o'clock. At least his arm was numb enough to lose some of the throbbing. He bound his wound tighter and drifted off in the dark to a restless sleep, alone and completely lost. He would need rest and daylight to figure the next moves.

*   *   *   *

204

Sangeeta's dread was to the core as she returned to the shop around noon to check-in just so she wouldn't be punished. *Better to appease the mean bastard than to confront him.* She couldn't help but notice from a distance the shop door was ajar which probably meant he was smoking dope and would be in a foul mood. As she gritted her teeth and stepped inside it was immediately obvious that wasn't the case. Everything on one side of the shop was in the floor and there in the isle lay Odwalla on his side with his eyes wide open staring at the wall in a puddle of blood. The scene brought her first smile of the day. *Somebody finally killed the miserable bastard.* She rotated and went to the door yelling for the neighbors to call the constable. As she waited outside the door the other shopkeepers congregated and the buzz was uncontrollable. When she asked if anyone saw or heard anything. Two people confirmed that two different black men enter the shop in the morning and both left very quickly. Everyone figured it must have been a robbery. The constable made the call to the GDF and told everyone to stay outside until the authorities showed up. As she expected the one on the scene to take charge was Davis and as he questioned her in the street she could feel his sexual interest in her. He was asking her about Odwalla's apartment and the things he owned never showing any interest in the fact his so-called friend was just killed.

Davis ordered the other officers to stay put and entered the shop alone. He was convinced this was the CIA hit they were expecting. If it were, that was good for him. This killing would probably satisfy the man. One dead body would pay the debt and get him off the hook. The scene with Odwalla on his side with the staring eyes reminded Davis of the look the man would get when he killed someone and was recalling it. Rolling the body over revealed a single shot straight to the heart. *Definitely a professional hit, dead center.* Probably a thirty-two caliper as it was too small for a forty-five. He noticed the painting that was on the easel when he visited the last time was gone but it appeared to be the only thing missing. Checking Odwalla's pockets yielded five hundred cash and the man's African passport. He stuffed the cash in his pocket, threw the passport on the man's body and stepped over it moving to the back of the shop. Wheels were turning in his head as he mentally marked the scorecard of his luck. First, they picked Odwalla as the hit and he was no longer on their short list. Second, he was five hundred dollars richer. Third, he would get Odwalla's apartment and job, plus best of all his woman. For it to work for him this whole thing needed to just go away as soon as possible. As he stepped back outside he barked to the crowd.

"This is a crime scene, everyone stay out. Definitely a robbery. Pockets are empty. Money's all missing," he emphasized.

He waved two of his uniformed men over in the direction of the shop and ordered them to take the body back to the barracks. As they carried the body past the crowd he said softly to them, "Call the chopper crew". This was going to be easy to clear up quickly. Tomorrow Braburn will have never existed. He did dread having to talk to Boston and inform the Nation's leaders that their so-called jesus was dead, but then again it was probably going to feel good. From here on, he was the man in Guyana. With Davis shouting orders to disperse the crowd, Sangeeta stepped forward.

"Tell me bitch were you around this place early today?" he asked.

"Yea, I opened the shop this morning. Only saw a white man who came in early looking for a souvenir," she answered.

"You keep your mouth shut about that, understand? No white man, understand," he barked at her.

"One of those black mothers that the witnesses saw killed the man to rob him. That's the story," he replied angerly.

206

As she started to speak he glared at her so she just nodded. He ordered her to clean up the blood and go pack Odwalla's stuff at the apartment. Then he looked her up and down, smiled and added, "Be there to fix my supper". She felt her joy of the day melt away because it was obvious her life was not going to change.

*   *   *   *

For a little boy of twelve the Ramshu was a playground instead of a stream of horrors like most South American rivers. Vipol lived on the river and worked on it long enough to know the dangers. By living among the miners with no schooling all his knowledge was acquired hands-on. He ran in the jungles since he was eight and the signs of danger were as familiar as the back of his hand. He knew how to avoid or scare off the deadly animals. The caymans and the big constrictor snakes like the Anaconda never stopped him from having his way in the jungle. It was the insects that posed the real threat but he learned from the old black boatman all the African ways and natural medicines. Most of the insect venoms could be treated with plants that grew in the jungle if one knew how to prepare them. The river piranha could be avoided by spotting the signs of where they schooled. The old boatman taught him well and he would swim in the river at will. The local miners had some books and with the help of the old woman at the mine company store he learned to read a little English and use his numbers. Although his formal education was sparse, his street knowledge was superb and he could read people on sight. Being on his own honed his primitive life skills to a fine edge for a child of twelve.

As a special treat he decided to take the day off and relax in a little boy's world. The week was lucrative for earning money and he accumulated a little extra so, all in all he was feeling kind of smug. He dreamt of the day when he would be old enough to run the monster power diggers at the bauxite pits. Even just watching them work from afar made him happy. He figured out the process by just watching the operators and would spend his spare time sitting on the hill overlooking the mine, just studying it all. As he sat on the ground he would pile up the dust with his hands and move the piles mimicking the diggers all the while challenging himself to second-guess their next moves. Wishing his time as a child would pass all he wanted was to be a grown-up and work at the mines. Today was going to be a day of rest so he hummed to himself as he climbed the hill to his vantage point overlooking the pits to spend the day learning.

About halfway up the path to his favorite spot, something lying in the grass on the right side caught his eye. One close look and he realized it was apparently a dead man lying on his side. Gingerly pushing through the tall grass he quickly realized the man wasn't dead at all. He was moving slightly. There was a bound wound on the man's right arm and a bloody bandage hanging loosely near his wrist. The man jerked when he sensed a presence and quickly sat up wincing from the pain.

"Are you alright mister," asked Vipol stepping back slightly.

"Who are you? Where am I?" was the reply.

"You are at the Ramshu bauxite dig site just off the river. Is your arm alright?" said the kid.

"Yea it's fine. How far from here to the coast? Are there any people around?"

"Village on the other side of the hill. No doctor though only miners," answered Vipol.

"How far to the coast?" he asked

"Depends, by bus six hours, by river ten. Your arm needs barot plant poultice, right away. Skin color says it's starting to foul. How long you been out here in the jungle? Bad stuff for cuts in the jungle during the monsoon time. Good you covered the sore," said Vipol.

The kid seemed sincere and the bottom line was Chris was going to have to trust the little boy. He could see the kid was not stupid but sensed that there was something fishy about a wounded man suddenly appearing alone beside the road. Trying to think straight was difficult as his arm pain and thirst was completely consuming him.

"You don't have any water with you do you?" he asked.

"No, I can go over the hill and get some from the village," answered Vipol.

"Is your mom at home?" he replied.

"No mom, just Vipol. My mother is dead and never had a father. Live on the river alone with my cat. Fishing man and river man, that's me. I can get water at the mine shack and bandages from the store lady. Do you want me to go?" said Vipol.

"Is the GDF in the village?" he asked.

"No, but some of the miners are their friends. Mostly people just stay shut up around here and just be quite. I will just go and come, no one will know. GDF is looking for Vipol too. Want me back in Georgetown with the orphans. I'm a runaway. I will just be a ghost and return with your needs," said the little boy.

Chris retrieved a twenty from his pocket and nodded to the kid to proceed. It was obvious the bill was the first twenty the kid ever saw in his life. He ran his fingers over it to see if it was real. The thought crossed Chris's mind that maybe he was in luck again. If the kid was dodging the law, it meant he was also fugitive. *What could be more perfect?* As he watched the kid disappear over the hill he decided to find some cover in case the kid was lying and brought company back with him. At this point there was no choice as the nausea was returning with the numbness wearing off in his arm. The whole thing got down to the fact he must keep it together and get out to the coast. He wasn't sure if he could the way he was feeling, but he couldn't let up until he got offshore.

I have to give it to Braburn. The no good son-of-a-bitch banged me up pretty bad. He was a strong son-of-a-bitch but not strong enough. A picture of the surprise on the man's face with the eyes rolled back entered his mind and at that moment, he thought of his sister Jody. It brought a slight smile and he felt the grit rise up in his gut. *If she can get through the things she's endured I can get through this.*

"What do you need with bandage gauze and a gallon jar?" the old woman in the store asked.

"Playing on the hill today. They will be my toys," Vipol replied.

"Funny toys for a boy," she chuckled and brushed him off.

He knew the old woman was soft on him and would let it go. As he started to retrieve the twenty-dollar bill from his pants he realized his having that much money would start the old woman's tongue wagging. There was no way an orphan would ever have that much money at one time so he just made an excuse and told her he would pay her later. Heading off in a dead run the excitement nearly exploded inside him. He knew something no one else did for the first time in his life. For a twelve-year-old boy having this big of a secret was the best day's play of them all.

After downing half of the gallon jug of water in what seemed to be one drink, Chris set down the jar and studied the little boys face. He saw sincerity and deep sadness that transcended the age of the kid. Little Vipol was twelve going on twenty-five. Bottom line was there was no choice but to trust the kid. His arm wound was debilitating and his stamina was totally sapped. He wasn't sure if he could even walk. What he really needed was to not be on the run at all and instead, to just lay up somewhere for about twenty-four hours. If he could get a boat, there was the possibility he could sleep and just drift to the coast. By the time he got there he might have some of his strength back. The real attraction of traveling by boat was the privacy. He wouldn't have to deal with any people or questions yet he would still get to the coast.

"This old black boatman you mentioned, does he go out to the coast. I mean for money. Does he hire out," asked Chris.

"Yes, but you don't want him. He would do anything for money and tell the GDF," answered Vipol.

"Why doesn't he turn you in?" asked Chris.

"I can make the motors work on his boats. He is a stupid one. Needs me for the river runs. I can get a boat and take you out to Camroon on the coast. The old man will let me use one to fish," said Vipol.

"You mean he will let you use it over night?" asked Chris.

"No, but when I return I will just give him this money and he will say nothing. This is big money to him," said Vipol.

"How far is it to this boat?" he asked dreading the thought of having to walk.

"It's behind the mine. You don't want to go to the dock. I'll go get it and pick you up. Go back to the road, walk to the big Mahogany tree on this side, then straight through the jungle to the river and wait. When you leave the road watch very closely where you step. It's not far but there will be snakes."

As Vipol skipped off to the boat dock, the visions of this great adventure that was unfolding danced in his head. This white man was the first person he ever met who seemed to be as outcast as he was in this country. He knew down deep there was something unspeakable about this wounded man but there was a certain satisfaction in helping him. As he passed through the village he stopped at his sleeping spot and retrieved his cat. The old tabby was his good luck charm and he never went out on the river without her.

As Chris sat on the bank watching the river he couldn't help but compare this place to the Nam. Over there snakes were a common site but the real fear was running into a tiger. It was always rumored that was the only thing the V.C. feared. This place put the Viet Nam bush to shame. All he could hope was this kid could get him down the river without being stopped or something eating both of them. Every sense in his body said this was going to be a long painful trip but at least there was some light at the end of the tunnel. *It's not like I have a hell of a lot of choices.*

The boat was better than expected and the kid placed a pad in the front end as a pallet for him. The gunnels were high enough to conceal a person. As they settled in and shoved off there was a feeling of relief but he noticed the kid was still a little tense. The whole scene brought a smile to his lips. *My own private ambulance. This must be medivac Guyana style.* The kid fired the old outboard and headed down river. After a few minutes he cut the engine and turned into the bank beaching the nose of the boat with a jolt. He scrambled over his passenger, jumped off and ran into the jungle. The whole scene suddenly hit Chris. *The little bastard has sold me out.* He got set to see the police appear at any time when to his surprise the kid suddenly reappeared with both hands full of jungle plants and leaped back in the boat. He handed a round stalk about the size of asparagus to him and said, "chew this". The other plants he mashed on the sheet metal engine cover to form a paste. Then he opened the bandages and began spreading the paste on the arm wound.

"These are grabo and jemo plants. Will help the pain and keep the bugs off," said Vipol.

The sound of the old engine reigniting was a relief and he could feel himself starting to relax. The throbbing in his arm subsided it seemed almost instantly after swallowing the juice from the plant. He dozed off noticing the kid also settled back and relaxed. The medicine was working and they were on their way. Even the old cat crawled over on the pallet and curled up next to his leg. He couldn't help but wonder about the old cat and before sleeping he ask about it.

"What is the deal with the cat? Is she fish bait?" Chris joked.

"Take her always on the river. She can smell the animals and will tell me if there is danger," answered Vipol.

The hum of the outboard and the wash of the river against the hull began to lull him to sleep. The wonder of it all and the ingenuity of the human species amazed him. The cat was this kid's burglar alarm. In Viet Nam the ARVN used flocks of ducks the same way. *When there is a need the survival instincts will always prevail.* Suddenly he completely trusted the kid and realized he was going to be able to doze off.

*　　　*　　　*　　　*

Jeannie's flight to Miami was delayed leaving Phoenix so she was pressed for time to make her connection. Hustling through the Miami airport to connect with the island hopper she grumbled under her breath, "Why do they put these damn commuters at the end of the furthest concourse?" If she missed this thing there would not be another flight until tomorrow. As she neared the gate the attendants were looking in her direction so she flagged them. They smiled knowingly and reopened the door to the tarmac. In spite of a rough start to the trip she was on her way to Grenada. Letting down and settling in for the flight, she reviewed the notes she made regarding the location of the boat. Chris's call earlier in the week made it all sound simple but these foreign islands seemed to make everything a hassle.

After the trip over the islands she was feeling excited as the plane landed at the Grenada airport. The marina was within walking distance. Her luck didn't hold though as things were to turn sour quickly. When she checked in at the dock office the attendants were a little reluctant to give her the boat keys. They informed her that Chris wasn't there and that he walked off three days ago and left no instructions. That news startled her and she was taken back. *What is going on? This doesn't sound like Chris.* It wasn't typical of his behavior and the whole thing made her take a moment and clear her thoughts. She knew he wasn't afraid of diving alone or stopping in some roadside tavern for a drink. All kinds of thoughts swirled in her mind of bad things that could have happened to him from drowning to abduction.

After finally convincing the dock crew she was supposed to be there, they finally unlocked the boat and powered it up with the dock electricity. Chris informed her there would be a phone at the boat so she only knew to wait for a call. Before settling she stepped over on the dock, found the phone box and checked for a dial tone. Everything was working and she decided she was close enough to hear it ring. The galley was stocked and she was hungry so she fixed a bowl of breakfast food mostly to just have something to do. Rolling it all over and over in her mind her fear built and she felt panic setting in. Her dilemma was the amount of time to wait before sounding any alarms. She knew if she did that, and it was a false alarm, he would have a fit and she would never hear the end of it. As she curled up on the galley sofa, she decided to just give it until noon tomorrow. After all this wasn't normal behavior. She was worried about his diving alone but the fact the dock boy said he was wearing a seersucker suit and carrying a scuba tank didn't fit together. *A seersucker suit? He has to be kidding.*

Midday monsoon rains are merciless at best and they always arrived right on time in Guyana but little Vipol was prepared. Before the skiffs floor even got wet he had a tarp up with some cane poles for shelter. As it bore down and obscured vison there was never any doubt the little guy would get them through it. This kid was smart there was no doubting that and he obviously knew the river like the back of his hand. As he thought about the whole situation a light smile crossed Chris' lips for the first time since the shooting. *This whole scenario boils down to one survivor helping another survivor, survive.*

The rainwater was pure so he set the gallon jug out from under the tarp to collect the run off and repeatedly drank what he could collect with his hands. The rest helped and he was feeling a little stronger, but still really punk. At this point the worry was getting infection in his arm from the jungle environment. Even little Vipol kept looking at the wound as if concerned about the same thing.

The river trip went smooth. He was able to sleep in the floor of the boat and stay out of site to passers-by. Other boats just saw the scene of a kid out for a day of fishing. It was a familiar sight all along the river. It would soon be dark and from the brackish smell he guessed they were approaching the sea. Soon civilization would set back in and getting past the city without attracting any attention would be the concern. Trying to sort out his confusion on the time of day, the realization Jeannie was probably in Grenada hit him. His absence would scare her and she might hit the panic button. He decided to find a phone when they got in town and call the number at the dock. This was a glitch he never considered and revaluating, he probably should have worked it differently. Settling her down would be worth the risk of a phone call. Hopefully, he could concoct a story to appease her. The worst part was right now he was starting to feel really bad and wasn't sure he could even get on his feet.

CHAPTER 14

THE LITTLE HERO

Little Vipol came through. He managed to make the river trip and avoid the other river traffic. The kid was smart enough to make a comment and a joke with passing boats so as to not raise suspicion. The way he handled things showed he understood people and knew his personality was a survival skill. He was exceptionally bright and way beyond his years mentally. The old cat sounded the alarm on two occasions, rising up when she heard something in the distance. Chris fitfully slept most of the trip down river nursing his wound as best he could. As he raised up to look over the gunnel of the boat the outskirts of Camroon were coming into view. All signs indicated they were nearing the sea and leaving the jungle. Luckily, the town was not a big place and not very busy. It looked like they could dodge most of the populated areas with dark setting in. One positive was the weather. It was clearing and the wind was low so the sea would not be too rough. Chris's luck seemed to be holding. The priority now was finding a phone to call Jeannie before she panicked and set some negative things in motion. That could be a challenge without actually having to go into the town. The little fellow had never made a phone call so the whole concept was foreign to him. He was only familiar with a stop along the river that the old black boatman used the one time he traveled this far out. He remembered there was a pier and a shack where they bought gas and it was remotely located before they reached the city. Vipol informed Chris he thought there might be a phone there because there was electricity. Regardless they definitely needed to stop to get some gas. Food was another issue that needed to be addressed and the pier shack's kitchen sold some staples.

217

The last half of the river trip was not kind to Chris and it appeared infection was setting into the wounded arm. It was horribly discolored and swollen almost double. The jungle atmosphere proved to be impossible to keep out of the wound. Making this run produced hours of exposure of the wound in addition to all the other filth along the way. Vipol was familiar with the condition and there was an African name for it Chris didn't recognize. He kept the homemade plant salve on the cut the whole trip but it was still getting worse. The kid demeanor was that of concern as he was nervously checking the wound every few minutes. Seeking a doctor was out of the question at least until they got to one of the offshore islands that were not part of Guyana. The harsh truth was Chris was sinking very fast and it would not be long until he was too sick to be mobile. Sickness wasn't something he factored into the equation and there was no contingency plan for dealing with it. He could not end up in a local medical facility without setting off bells. The truth was he was going to have to bear the torture and try to stay conscious until they were in a safer place.

One piece of luck did evolve when they stopped at the pier for gas. There was a phone available but getting Chris out of the boat to access it was going to be the problem. Vipol made the arrangements like a man and fetched the dockhand for help. Between the three of them Chris was able to stagger into the shack were the phone was located. As they struggled up the pier, a sense of doom set in but it was offset by overwhelming relief when Jeannie answered the phone on the other end. She could tell something was bad wrong and was on the verge of tears but the relief of knowing he was all right made it tolerable.

"Chris, what's going on? I am about to lose it here. Where are you?" she asked anxiously.

"I've got to level with you baby. I'm in Guyana. I've hurt my arm. Got a wound that is bad infected. Been three days now. Gotta figure out how to get back to my unit and call medivac," he said hallucinating.

As the phone fell to the floor little Vipol picked it up gingerly and said hello. Jeannie quizzed him and he filled her in on many of the details. The first thing she asked him to do were some medical field test of pinching the cut and describing the fluids it produced. Her conclusion was the arms condition was approaching gangrene and he needed help at that very moment. Jeannie knew something was going to have to be done right then. Within twenty-four hours it would be life threatening. Mentally sorting through the alternatives, she could see there weren't very many, and there were no really good ones. What he needed right now was the penicillin she carried in her nurse's survival bag. Getting it to him was the hitch. Little Vipol warned her that they were fugitives. He didn't explain exactly why because he really did not know, but she had her suspicions. If Chris ended up in some third world hospital at best he would lose his arm and at worst his life. Saving him was going to require effort to deal with this situation without any outside help. She was terrified by the thought that trying to actually retrieve him meant sailing the boat alone and finding a rendezvous point. The sailing lessons were play-time together and she wasn't sure enough of it stuck to enable her to take the boat out alone. Let alone find some spec of land in the open sea. She did not exactly understand the wind issues with the sails and if things were not exactly right, it could put her in big trouble. There was some confidence with setting and holding a compass heading because her map skills were good from her days in girl scouts. She could manage the sails alone with the power wenches and the advanced features on the boat but there was a nagging doubt about the winds. If it blew from the stern like

219

during the lessons, things would be fine. If it changed she would be in big trouble, but the fact the boat engine was a backup would be the saving grace as long as the sea was not too rough.

Little Vipol informed her of a tiny island called Vespu Chris mentioned as their destination. It was not too far out to sea from the mouth of the Ramshu and was remote and uninhabited. Chris figured they could make it in the shallow riverboat, if the sea wasn't too rough. She told him to hold the phone while she checked the charts to see where it was located. While he held the line, she ducked into the Bright Star's cabin and rolled out the navigation charts on the galley table. Hurriedly shuffling through the maps she fumbled with the sheer quantity and was approaching tears when the right one miraculously came to the top. She was pushing herself and knew there was a danger of getting something wrong. She knew her and the kid both must get this thing right if they were going to find each other since the riverboat did not have a radio. According to the chart the island was a few degrees west of straight south from her location and looked fairly easy to find. The distance scale Chris taught her to use said the estimated trip time was about six hours if she could average eight knots. As she ran back to the phone she glanced at the weather vane and confirmed the wind was just about right. The decision was made.

"O k, I'm coming to get him," she said excitedly to Vipol.

"You take the boat out to Vespu and go around to the north side of the island and wait on an empty beach. Be watching and make sure you stay where I can see you. I will meet you there with a sailboat in about eight hours. You can identify this boat by its colors. It is white over black and has a gray canvas hood over the back end. I'll motor along the beach until I find you," she said.

"How long is eight hours?" asked Vipol.

"One night, I should be there at about daylight," she replied.

The whole plan was as complete as it could be so she hung up the phone and returned to the boat. There was a certain safe feeling when she settled in the cabin to chart her course. One good thing was she was leaving from a physical location at the south end of Grenada, but then again it was open sea all the way with no place to get in if an emergency arose. When she hit the open sea there was no significant land between her and the destination. With her pencil in hand she marked her course on the map and lay on the protractor. The course was due south by ten degrees southwest. All she needed to remember was the ten degrees.

Returning to the cockpit to cast off she repeated aloud to herself over and over, "It's just like a car, it's just like a car." When she hit the main power switch, it brought the instrument console to life. Things were coming back to her automatically. She started and then killed the engine just to be sure it ran and checked the fuel. Chris left the boat fully stocked and ready to go. The fresh water tanks were full and the galley contained plenty of food. With one swift move she traversed the deck and tossed off the dock lines. As the boat drifted slowly away from the pier, she hit the engine to motor out of the harbor. She spun the wheel to turn to the open sea and was suddenly overcome with a rush of confidence. At that moment she realized she was facing a night at sea alone. That realization combined with the emptiness of the dark horizon changed the feeling to overwhelming loneliness. As she hit the electric wench switches to hoist the sails and to come to her compass heading, she took a deep breath. She cast off into the abyss all alone.

*   *   *   *

Jody's morning started with a different feeling than usual. The golden glow of the low fall sunrise combined with the dark blue clear Missouri skies seemed to relieve the gnawing in her guts that was her normal day. As she looked out the bedroom window she realized her mind was clear as if a haze was gone. It was startling at first because in the last few years her reaction to waking up each morning was total dread. Suddenly it felt like it was going to be a good day for the first time in years. With her coffee and cigarette in hand, she settled at the dining table. She watched her kids dress and get their things together for school. She marveled at how beautiful they were. The realization she had not even noticed them for a long time hit her. It was as if since the attack the world was in black and white and now someone instantly switched on the color. Enjoying the jabber and confusion of kids trying to get off to school, she picked up their cereal bowls and cleared the table. She decided to go shopping later to get a roast to prepare a family meal for the evening. She could not remember the last time they sat down together. A flash of guilt enveloped her as she thought about the burden she has been on her husband, Tom since the assault. He quietly did double duty with his work and the children and rarely grumbled about it. As she wiped the counters the phone rang.

"Jody this is Westburg, Saint Louis County P D. Are you sitting down?" he asked.

There was a sudden jolt of fear that coursed through her body at just the sound of his voice. For a moment her euphoria was bumped to the side.

"What is it?" she asked.

"Someone got our boy three days ago. Just came across the FBI wire last night. Shot to death in his shop in Guyana. The bozos down there are ruling it a robbery but it looks like a professional hit to me. One shot, dead center, at work, early in the day," he said.

"So that's it. I knew something was different this morning when I woke up. Do you believe in God?" she said.

"Yea, I do but I'm not sure he had that much to do with it. Where is that brother of yours? Called his office and they just said he was out for a few days," he said sarcastically.

"I haven't talked to him for a while. Probably sailing. My brother John will know," she answered.

"Tell him we need to close this thing out on our end so we need a sit down with your whole bunch. See if you can circle the wagons and Sergeant Rush and I will come up. Needless to say, there is no big hurray though. At least not now," he chuckled.

"I'll call you back," she replied.

She wondered the last few days about Chris because he usually called to check on her. That wasn't normal. *Oh well, he's probably fooling with that damn boat again. Ten to one there will be a girl involved.* It was funny that the news didn't affected her. The adjustment of her feelings was already there when she woke up from sleeping. It was as if she already knew the trauma was over and her family was safe again. She would call John and let him run Chris down because he knew more about her bachelor brother's antics.

*   *   *   *

The compass heading held solid as Jeannie tied the tiller wheel to go below and make some coffee. She needed the caffeine to fight off sleep and as she returned to the helm the smell of the coffee in the night salt air comforted her. The prevailing westerlies offered up wind that was from the stern and slightly off the port side. They were very favorable and she commented to herself on her luck. The engulfing darkness was swallowing up the boat with the only light being the glowing plankton in the wakes and the lights of an occasional cargo ship off on the horizon. The binoculars from the cabin gave a view of the distant ships as Chris taught her to watch their lights and project their path. The biggest fear of night sailing

223

was being run over. The glowing plankton phenomena was mesmerizing, as it seemed to light the clear water in the wake of the boat like a green neon sign, as if to present the hull of the boat to the sea. She watched the glow in a half daze as the time passed. It would be light soon she thought and she was still making good time. She adjusted the sail with a small shift in the wind and her speed was falling back. If it got much lower she would fire the engine and motor sail to add some speed. The island was to be on her course and should be getting close.

Dozing some, the fatigue was taking its toll. As her head bobbed, she snapped awake and realized it was breaking dawn. *How long have I been asleep?* The eastern light barely revealed a land spec on the horizon off to the right dead ahead. "That's got to be it," she said to herself verifying the compass heading. The wind dropped even more so she hit the engine start and fired the small inboard diesel to give the boat a boost. She felt it take and released the tiller ties to control the wheel herself so she could make a heading adjustment. This far out she just centered the nose of the boat on the spec of an island and headed straight for its center.

The approach seemed to take forever as the anticipation built accompanied by the fear of what she might find. It was similar to the feeling she experienced when working the emergency room waiting for a gurney from an ambulance. One never knew what to expect. In this case Chris could be unconscious or past the point of saving the arm. Worse yet she might not even find him. As the island slowly approached, there was a flicker of a red light on the left side. Maybe it was a boat then again maybe a beach fire. She headed straight for it. With full daylight breaking now she could see so she winched in the sails to motor closer. It was a beach fire and a big one. Little Vipol figured it out and built a signal fire. Running along the beach waving his arms the joy in the kid was site to behold. The little fellow was celebrating his success. She saw him pick something gray up off the beach and shove the riverboat from the sand, so she cut her engine and released the anchor. The next challenge was going to be getting this mostly unconscious two-hundred-pound limp man onto the sailboat.

The little fellow knew to waste no time. The sound of his dilapidated old engine straining to get out to the sailboat was music to all ears. As he pulled alongside, with a grin from ear to ear he yelled, "I am Vipol". He stood up in the riverboat and grabbed the Bright Star's lower deck rail holding on for dear life. As she looked over the side it was apparent Chris was teetering on unconsciousness. Lifting him over on the deck was going to be a problem. Then it hit her. *Of course the electric mast wench.* Unclipping the mainsail tailing cable she hit the wench switch to let out some slack and threw the cable end over the stern. Motioning for Vipol to bring his boat to the transom she directed him to wrap the cable around Chris' chest under his arms and clip the latch on the end. When she hit the switch to tighten the cable his body rose and with both her and Vipol helping, the dead weight was lifted from the skiff and pulled over the rail. Oddly enough the thud of his body hitting the cockpit floor was a pleasant sound. With bench pillows and her blanket from last night she made a bed then adjusted his position so he could lie with his wounded arm up.

Escape was the primary thing on her mind so she immediately fired the engine and spun the tiller wheel to turn the boat out to sea. As she looked back over her shoulder the little riverboat was moving away and Vipol standing in the boat was smiling and waving. At that point, she got the first indication the patient was still alive.

"What to hell are you doing," Chris said raising his head.

"Those people back there will eat him alive if he returns. Go get him."

She spun the wheel again and circled back. Vipol could not believe it when she yelled, "get on". His reflexes were instant. He grabbed his old cat and simultaneously pulled the plug in the riverboat's floor to sink it. As he jumped aboard the Bright Star he snagged the painting from the floor of the riverboat. It somehow successfully made the trip unscathed. One more steering adjustment and they were headed north. The look on the little boy's face as he watched the riverboat sink into oblivion was a lesson in life. He turned to her and commented, "The black boatman is going to be mad at me." He actually did not realize he had just stepped off into the rest of the world.

Before the island was even out of sight she was injecting the penicillin she always carried. The arm was bad but could have been worse. Vipol's swamp-doctoring had helped considerably. He bathed it with salt water once they reached the open sea and that seemed to have held the infection at bay the last few hours. Upon examining the arm closely, she could see it was a flesh wound and that the ligaments and tendons were not severely damaged. The key now was to get the fever to subside and get the man mobile. If they were stopped, he needed to do the talking to be convincing. She decided to leave him on the cockpit floor until he could manage to move himself.

The little boy looked at the boat's instrument console wide eyed as a barn owl on a summer night. She could see he was completely absorbed in what was happening and his mind was running a mile a minute. To free herself up she needed him to steer so she diverted her attention to hurriedly explaining how to hold the course and then she told him to take the wheel. Running under engine power was natural to the kid. He knew how the throttle worked without being told. With her mind at ease for the first time since she got the phone call she felt fatigue setting in. They all needed to sleep and just steadily head north and put distance between them and this part of the world. There was a long way to go but time was now on their side.

*   *   *   *

After three days Chris had come around and the arm had turned the corner. The mobility was back and the swelling was all but gone. He would have to favor it for a while but with a little finesse and a long sleeve shirt, no one would guess it ever been injured. They arrived in the Florida Keys and the pressure was off so they decided to anchor in a deserted cove on an unmarked Key to relax for a day or so. There were some issues to be considered with approaching home such as how to explain being gone so long. Most of all the question of "who is this new human being" would have to be dealt with. The immigration people were the biggest concern as Vipol was obviously from a foreign country. It was imperative to get ashore without him being detected. All they needed was a little more of that old Irish good luck.

As Jeannie soaked in the afternoon sun on the deck with the cat at her side, she planned a decent meal for a change. Dining was primitive the last few days so she figured it was time to get re-civilized. Chris and Vipol were in the water with the scuba gear. Chris was teaching him to buddy breath and clear his mask. The kid was in seventh heaven since he could swim with the fish and spear them at will, instead of just sitting and hoping they would grab a line. The clear gulfstream water was another new world for a boy of twelve who's only experience were the jungle rivers with their cloudy tannic acid waters. Watching Chris come up the swim ladder, Jeannie could see the joy he felt watching Vipol swim around under the boat with the tank. Observing the bubbles breaching the surface he said with a smile, "The kid's already got the air supply figured out. He's pacing his breaths".

Suddenly the radio came to life with a crackle breaking the peaceful silence and startling everyone. The voice on the other end said with authority. "This is the U S Coast Guard. Will the vessel off Shango Key at 42 degrees North and 21 degrees West please identify yourself"? Checking the compass, it was obvious it was the Bright Star they were referencing. Before he could answer a large Coast Guard Cutter broke over the horizon bearing down hell bent straight at them. Chris's mind went into overdrive. He couldn't answer the radio if he were going to plead it was broken so he just made himself visible on the foredeck. *This is going to take some finesse. I have an illegal on board and a 45 automatic in a drawer in the cabin. Cut in your head before you speak.* Both issues were big with the Guard. He dealt with them before and knew not to deny the gun. If he lied and they found it themselves, Bright Star would be impounded. Praying Vipol stayed under the water he searched for the bubbles and could see the kid was a long way out and headed around a small sand shoal. Praying for some luck the Cutter pulled alongside.

"Are there any weapons on board?" barked the Captain from the bridge using the intercom.

Chris shook his head yes.

"Are there only two of you on the boat?" he added.

Chris shook his head yes.

"You will both have to come aboard the cutter because if there are weapons we have to board you," the Captain said.

"Keep your hands in sight," he warned.

The full sized cutter alongside the little sailboat was an odd scene against the backdrop of the island. As the crew lowered a gang way the Captain descended from the bridge to meet them on deck.

When the gangway was in place Jeannie and Chris shuffled between the boats. The Officer was young and tan but appeared to be reasonable. The rest of the crew seemed to raise their rifles slightly when they heard the comment about weapons on the boat.

"This boat has been reported stolen from a marina in Mourne Rough Grenada. Are you aware of that?" said the Captain.

"Oh man, I didn't bother to check out because we left in the middle of the night. You have to be kidding me. Surely they didn't expect me to wake them up. Their payment comes from our company in the States. I don't owe them any money," answered Chris.

"They said there was only a woman and she was acting odd. Figured she stole the boat," added the Captain.

"I'll get a phone patch and you can talk to them and straighten it out. Where and what's the weapon that's on the boat?" he asked.

"Forty-five in the top drawer of the galley cabinets," he answered.

The two crewmembers that entered the cabin emerged from the Bright Star's cabin with the gun. They removed the clip and disabled the bolt. Finally, they both shook their heads with an all clear signal. The Captain seemed to relax. Scanning the horizon behind the Captain as they talked, Chris was praying the kid would not pop up out of the water before this ended.

After a conversation on the phone with the Marina owner he was handed his gun and clip with permission to re-board the Bright Star. There were instructions not to load the gun until they were completely clear. He and Jeannie both quickly stepped back on to the deck of the Bright Star thanking the Captain. As he turned to get underway he looked back and smiled.

"The gun's a good idea in these waters. I won't report it. The cat I didn't see needs immunizations. You are not supposed to bring pets home from the islands. Promise me you will take it in once you arrive. I have a cat of my own. Don't want her sick," he said with a smile as the cutter's diesel engines revved.

The cutter disappeared as quickly as it had appeared. The pressure was off and Jeannie was white as a sheet as she collapsed in a bridge chair. Chris made a mental note to disable the radio since he wanted to report it broken if needed. He hoped that was the only thing that slipped his mind in the confusion.

"Chris, you are going to be the death of me. What ever happened to that quiet nurse from Phoenix? I can't believe you lied to him when he asked if there was anyone else onboard," she said.

"I didn't lie. There was no one else onboard. He didn't ask me if there was someone else in the water," he answered with a smile.

Jeannie just shook her head and rocked back in her bridge chair to breathe deeply. Just then Vipol broke the surface off the transom with a big smile. Chris helped him breach the transom with the diving gear on and he settled on the deck to remove his flippers.

"Where were you?" Chris asked.

"Heard the boat coming and swam around the sand bar to hide. Did I do good?" he replied.

"Yea, you did really good," was the answer.

"Vipol didn't know how easy it is for a fish to hear a fisherman coming," said the smiling boy.

"I'm going to actually cook something so we can sit down to a supper. Do you think we can have some peace this evening?" Jeannie interrupted.

"You're lucky today babe," Chris replied.

"I guess you mean since I'm not in jail," she said sarcastically.

"No, since you are going to be cooking instead of doing laundry. If that kid's head popped up out of the water while the

Cutter was here, you would be laundering my underwear instead of cooking."

CHAPTER 15

SWEET RELIEF

Green turtle marina at Lake Barkley was a welcome site with the rows of boat moorings and the elevated glass enclosed high end restaurant overlooking the piers. Motoring through the channel across the "Land between the Lakes" the water was dead calm and the early morning dew glistened on the foliage. The world seemed at peace. There was a general air of relief permeating the sailboat crew and everyone could feel it, even the cat. All told the trip home was almost two weeks with the last few days being spent motoring up the river to Kentucky. For Jeannie it was two weeks of agonizing about the future. She finally completely resigned herself to leaving Phoenix and moving to Tennessee permanently. Chris healed and the only issues now were in his head. He didn't seem to have any remorse about all that happened. There were moments of reflection when he wished it could have been different. He realized just how luck was involved in the whole thing. He and Jeannie spent long hours on the trip home covering all of the events of the past few weeks. He completely leveled with her about everything. Right down to the details of the assassination. The emotional swings for her took a toll and she now knew more about herself than ever in her life. Considering, the experience was a good thing but she realized this whole event must stay their secret. In addition, it was the type of secret that was more than just buried. She hoped she would never face having to lie about any of it as that wasn't in her nature, but she made the decision she would if necessary. The stories and descriptions about the individuals involved left no doubt the world was a better place because of the events of the last few weeks.

Vipol made it ashore undetected. He wasn't sure what was happening to him as events and people swirled around him like a whirlwind. It was obvious though his new life was a godsend. He never lived a day since his mother's death that wasn't a struggle and now everything was handed to him. New clothing, a home and food without question were all there with no exchange expected. Incredible as it seemed there were suddenly people in his life who really cared for him. A feeling he never knew existed. Unlike his other dealings with people in his life this arrangement seemed to be permanent and genuine. Jeannie started reading lessons for him while they were still on the boat coming home and Chris started with the multiplication tables. He could soak knowledge up like a sponge as fast as they put it out. Both adults were amazed at the natural intelligence of the kid. His common sense and world experience saved the whole bunch on the way home more than once. Although Vipol did not exactly know what happened in Guyana he did know not to ask. Someday though he promised himself he would. He particularly wanted to know about the shirt Chris struggled to remove and sink in the Rhamshu as they left the bauxite mine area in the boat.

Jim left instructions for the Bright Star to be serviced and dry-docked to remove any barnacles accumulated on the hull from the salt-water exposure. The marina crew at the dock were waiting for them and Jeannie was packed several more than ready to abandon ship. Tying up and signing the marina paperwork, he instructed the dockhands to make a note on his report to have the radio repaired. As he staggered down the pier with a box of things from the galley Chris realized his arm was still not a hundred percent. Vipol would have to load the rest of the groceries from the galley into the car. They all still had their sea legs so everyone was a little shaky walking on dry land to the car. Jim made arrangement to have the car dropped at the marina and spotting it was a sight for sore eyes. The GTO fired on demand and he made a loop through the parking lot for one last look at the vessel. As they headed home no one spoke. There was really not much to say.

When they cracked the door to the apartment the old bachelor pad in Tennessee gave off a bit of a stale odor from being closed up for several weeks. Jeannie's first priority upon getting a whiff of the place immediately became getting it aired out and livable. She grumbled to herself something about filthy bachelors and how this cleaning job would take several days. Chris dropped his bag and headed straight to the office to check on the status of things at work. Vipol picked up some geometry texts when they passed through Mobile on the boat trip home and was sorting them out. There was a mysterious normalcy that quickly settled over the place as Jeannie decided to do some cleaning before bedtime.

Nothing worse than a moldy refrigerator. She pulled a wastebasket over and discarded outdated and moldy condiment bottles from the refrigerator door shelves. She would have to go shopping tomorrow. Vipol was working math problems at the dining table when the doorbell rang with a start. Her nerves took a quick hit and it made her realize she wasn't entirely settled yet. At the door was the apartment manager to inform her the complex was advertised as pet-free and the cat would have to go. She assured the manager Chris would be in touch to deal with it when he got home. She would call him and tell him to stop and talk. As the office manager shuffled off she dialed his office.

"Bad news lover boy. The cat isn't welcome here. The old biddy from the office just stopped by to inform you. Stop and see her when you come through the complex," she said authoritatively.

"I was afraid of that. What about our pet Indian boy are they going to let him stay?" he answered.

"Probably not. Guess it's moving time, but then again this place isn't big enough for the whole tribe so maybe it's no big deal," she said.

"I've been thinking about a house for a while. I'll give the old bag notice. You start looking for something to buy tomorrow," he replied.

"O K, stop and pick up some vitamins for Vipol at the pharmacy. I don't like the white spots on his fingernails. Cod liver oil, they are called Upjohn unicaps. Get a pound of bacon and a dozen eggs too. We'll need them for breakfast," she ordered.

The look on his face must have telegraphed his thoughts. Jim stepped through the office door and noticed the look.

"Hey Captain heard about your trip from the Coast Guard. They thought the boat was stolen. Called here to check on your story. What is it man you look like you have seen a ghost?" said Jim.

"I think I have," he answered.

"Left here a carefree bachelor and came back with a wife and kid," he replied.

"Have instructions to stop at the store on the way home. Can you believe it?" he asked.

They sat laughing together for some time. The conversation was natural as they talked about what transpired over the last few weeks with Chris carefully avoiding the events in Guyana. The boat was a new common denominator for the pair and the banter of comparing sailing notes added to the pleasure. For a change, it felt the same as when they were young men and didn't have a care in the world. Specifically, of interest was the situation with little Vipol and how to get him somewhat legal. Jim suggested he claim Vipol was Cuban and they retrieved him from a raft in the Florida Straits. That way he could apply for asylum under the wade ashore provision for Cuban refugees. It was a good suggestion and he decided to lay it out for the kid when he got home. The story would work and he was confident Vipol could keep it straight at least long enough for any heat regarding his identity to pass. Another big plus was the paperwork could be processed through company channels which would circumvent a lot of explaining. As Jim shuffled off Chris collected his thoughts and pulled the slot injection project file. *Time to get back to work. Going to have to wear a long sleeve shirt the rest of my life or come up with an excuse for the arm scar.*

*   *   *   *

The Nation received word from Davis about the death of Braburn. Davis called and talked to the attorney El Shabaz. He laid the whole thing out as Braburn being killed by CIA assassins in retaliation for what transpired at the airport in Guyana. It made total sense and besides Braburn long ago became a burden on the Nation. His standing with the top people had him throwing his weight around. He was calling the last several months demanding they bring him back to Boston. That was never possible with the heat he still drew from St Louis. Shabaz was quietly pleased the man would be out of their hair finally as he never liked or trusted him. There would be no conversation or exchange with the CIA people as the Nation was not in a position to question any of their actions. After a short conference the leadership of the Nation requested a plaque be placed in the community center to honor Malik Jakim and touting his work in the community. In addition, at evening prayer he would be acknowledged as a special servant of god. Other than that, as far as the Nation was concerned, he ceased to exist.

*   *   *   *

The St Louis County Police headquarters was alive with the news of Braburn's demise. They chased him for years always a step or two behind him. The FBI sent their report regarding what was known about the incident in Guyana. It was sketchy. There was no forensic evidence collected at the scene and it was obvious Guyana wanted it swept under the rug. The official report just simply said Braburn died from a bullet to the heart and the body was buried by official order. Westburg talked to Jody's family at first word and put off making the official "face to face" visit due to pressing issues in the office. He was not looking forward to driving to North Missouri one more time but bearing good news, for once, was going to make it a pleasure. As he worked his schedule he set aside the following Friday afternoon to finish things and make the trip. It would be imperative he take Sergeant Rush with him so after setting up a phone patch to a cruiser he finally reached Rush on the street.

"Hey Rush, what have you got on next Friday?" he asked.

"Nothing special. What's up?" Rush replied.

"Need to close out the Braburn case. Go meet with the family and get what we need for this final report," he answered.

"I'm good for Friday. Have you seen any of the loose stuff that's been trickling in from the Feds about Braburn's killing? Maybe none of our business but they are questioning some of the official stories," he replied.

"No, I haven't seen it but don't put a lot of stock in it. These people in Guyana don't really give a damn about anything relating to a justice system. What have you seen anyway?" he asked.

"We'll talk about it in the car on the way up. See if we can leave mid mourning. I want to get back for my son's football game Friday night. He's a halfback at Roosevelt high. Scouts from Mizzou will be there. Want him educated. No brain dead cop job for him," replied Rush laughing.

The last few weeks Jody's Fridays returned to be her favorite day. She was subbing down at the school and Father made her a better teaching offer for next year. The house was back in order and the kids and Tom where an entirely different bunch. Her weight was coming back up, she was sleeping nights, the circles under her eyes were gone and the world was again in technicolor. She tried not to dwell on what might have happened to her nemesis Braburn. She only knew knowing he was gone changed her whole world.

The kids left for school and as she started her housework, she hummed an old Rock and Roll tune from years ago. The phone broke the silence and she suddenly realized she forgot the St Louis County men were coming today for a final meeting.

"Jody, this is Buzz Westburg how are you today? We are leaving right now and should be at your place in about three hours. I wanted to confirm everyone will be there so we can close our file. I was particularly wondering if your brother is going to be there," he asked.

"As far as I know they will both be here. Chris has some pretty heavy work obligations but he said he would come for the day," she replied.

"Good, see you in a little bit," he answered hanging up.

She decided to vacuum the carpet in the den and with the noise she didn't hear Chris came in the back door. He walked in and quietly laid an oil painting on the table. Instead of interrupting her, he just stepped back in the kitchen, poured a cup of coffee and sat down to wait for her to finish. To observe her working was a delight. There was an incredible difference in her demeanor from the last time he saw her. She was back almost a hundred percent. Finally, she sensed someone, turned and smiled, turning off the machine with her foot.

"Let me put up the vacuum and I'll join you. What's with the painting?" she asked.

"Oh, just something I picked up down in the islands. Thought you might like it so I brought it up. Abstract of some kind. Don't know what it's supposed to be. Seems the artist said it was a clearing storm or some damn thing. Guess this type of painting is whatever you see in it," he replied faking a laugh.

"I see a calmness around the edges pervading the confusion and chaos in the center. To me it is a picture of my life today," she said.

"Whatever, don't put it anywhere too prominent," he replied.

As the crowd arrived the meeting was taking on more of a carnival atmosphere than a police investigation. As the brothers bantered back and forth the police officers seemed to enjoy the family antics. After some good laughs with some coffee and finger sandwiches they got down to filling out the report forms. Once they were complete and signed Buzz taped the stack of paper on the table to square it up, fastened them with a paperclip and dropped them in his briefcase. Snapping the latches to the case, he looked directly over at Chris with an eye to eye contact that was chilling.

"Jody tells me you have been gone on an extended sailing vacation," he said.

The words and the look went through Chris like a knife. His eyes cut quickly over to the painting leaning against the sofa as he suddenly realized it could tie him directly to the art store in Guyana. His arm began to ache and he was overwhelmed by feelings of self-doubt. *The son-of-a-bitch knows. He's got something. Don't favor the arm. If he keys on that painting I'm dead meat. Why in the hell didn't I leave that in the car?* Sucking it up and holding eye contact with the policeman he answered. "Went down and brought a company owned boat back from the Antilles with my main squeeze," he coldly replied with a slight smile.

240

"Does that trip take that long? Said you were gone over two weeks," remarked the cop.

"If you could get a look at my girl you would understand. I wasn't in any hurry to get back to work," he answered.

Westburg just as quickly broke his gaze and rose from his chair.

"Keep in touch Jody. We have to get back for a football game so we are out of here. If you get to the city drop by. You are part of our police family after all we have been through. Have to say I'm glad it's over though," said Buzz.

Shaking hands with everyone, he and Sergeant Rush gave Jody a hug and hustled out the door to their car. As Chris watched out the window their taillights disappeared at the end of the street. He let out a frozen breath. *Maybe this will be it.*

*   *   *   *

Westburg kicked the old black unmarked police car up to ninety on the interstate. There was not going to be any love lost with leaving the North Missouri prairie. He would take the city any day. Rush in the passenger seat was a little uneasy so he spoke up.

"What's the hurry?" asked Rush.

"Just enjoying one of the very few perks of police work my friend. Immunity from speeding tickets," he answered smiling.

"Let me ask you something Sergeant. What do you think of that brother of Jody's? Think he could have taken old Braburn. He was close to the right place if you look at a map," said Westburg.

"He has the right demeanor. Comes across as a smart son-of-a-bitch. Think it would take a lot to rile him but when you did you would have a handful. Don't think he is a coldblooded killer though," answered Rush.

241

"Don't know buddy as my mother used to say "still water runs deep". That guy has an eye contact that looks through you, clear to the back of your skull. Enjoys the mental game of it all. Think I will do some digging when we get back. Send me the FBI file on Braburn's killing Monday morning," said Westburg.

As they consumed interstate, Westburg's comment rolled over in Rush's mind. *Sometimes a cop can be too much of a cop. Like my old Granny used to say "don't look a gift horse in the mouth". The world is a better place today. Someone gave it a gift.* As he reviewed the Braburn file contents in his mind he made a mental note to deep six some of the new stuff in that file before turning it over. Particularly, the report of some Indian kid stealing a boat on the river in the mine country of Guyana at the time of Braburn's killing and disappearing out to sea.